Lonely Hearts, Changing Worlds

Robert Wintner

The Permanent Press Sag Harbor, NY 11963

Library of Congress Cataloging-in-Publication Data

Wintner, Robert
Lonely Hearts, Changing Worlds: short stories / by Robert Wintner
p. cm.
ISBN 1-57962-028-0 (alk. Paper)
1. United States –Social life and customs – 20th century –Fiction. 1. Title.

PS3573.I63 L66 2001
813'.54 – dc21

00-064246

THE PERMANENT PRESS
4170 Noyac Road
Sag Harbor, NY 11963

For Flojo,
who comes to me in the night and purrs.

Other Books by Robert Wintner

Whirlaway

The Ice King

Horndog Blue

Hagan's Trial & Other Stories

The Prophet Pasqual

Homunculus

The Modern Outlaws

Contents

Crab Bait for Sale

Dezmun Deyung never set out to build a crab bait business. He only got lazy with his chicken parts, the ones he found in the cavity wrapped in soggy paper—not the gizzards and the livers; he liked to eat those. But the hearts and little odd organs and big fatty globules he trimmed off the haunches and the UCOs (unidentified chicken objects) he cast into the bait bucket. It wasn't a bucket in the technical sense but a stainless steel bowl like they might use for baking down at the jail, if they baked down there and had any interest in coordinating the bakeware with the dinner service. They didn't care about such things, but they wouldn't have called it a bait bowl either, which was marginally disgusting and could denote bait on the menu. Those who weekended in jail would swear it was bait, but it wasn't.

Dezmun knew the jail menu because of his part-time job there, not the county jail but the town jail. The county jail was different, one step shy of hard time. At least the town jail accounted for potential restitution/rehab. It seemed clear to him that a man facing Salisbury steak with mashed potatoes and peas would more likely re-orientate than one looking at non-lubricated sexual trespass. I.e., you can turn more cons on applesauce cake than you can on sandpaper.

He tossed a huge globule to the bucket, wondering if it was a record breaker. How could he measure? Or weigh? And would it matter?

Never mind. Dezmun believed in the efficacy of good eating and would have proven his theory by baking something himself for the boys down at the jail, but the heat stole a man's energy until he could scarcely maintain standards at home much less start baking for the riffraff.

Not that flipping odd parts to the bait bucket made him incontrovertibly lazy. All that stuff in one place was testimonial to tidiness, kind of, once you discounted the flies, which he did, because you can hardly call a mess what you can clean up with the wave of a hand. Dezmun put a plate over the bait bucket. The scent thinned and so did the flies.

A whiff surged now and then, and he wondered how a man too lazy to throw his chicken guts out back could have the gumption to understand the mysteries of life, which he did. Then he smiled at the gifts of clarity and meaning. No—he was not a lazy man; he was industrious. This offal only waited processing in the bait division.

He added the necks to the pile recently, just after Janita Rose down the road told him don't ever eat a chicken's neck. That's where they inject the antibiotics. And if there's a snowball's chance in hell that your own fool doctor hadn't gone and messed you up for good already on too many antibiotics to let anymore be worth a snit, it wouldn't even matter because of the humongous dose you'd get eating a chicken neck. Janita Rose knew about health-related issues because of her herb garden and vitamins, on which she thrived.

If that weren't enough, right in the neck is where they also shoot the hormones that give the chickens heft on nothing but shredded newsprint, but next thing you know you're growing tits on your forehead or hair on your palms or more likely feathers. Janita Rose rubbed her neck and rolled her head, smarting from the horse syringe she could hardly help but imagine stuck there, pumping her full of bad juice. Well, maybe it was only a chicken syringe, but still.

Dezmun's expansive brow bunched deep as Cefus Blodgett's freshly-harrowed turnip patch as if feeling for a stray tit sprouting there, or at least the idea of one, or two. He had room for three but three would be a push and seemed disgusting in a way. You'd likely need to eat several chicken necks a day for a long time to sprout tits on your forehead.

Neither Dezmun nor Janita laughed at the imagery of misplaced breasts or hair or feathers, because ill-bred humor had for years cast aspersion on the native population. The home-towners remaining had had a gullet full. Tales of woeful inbreeding haunted Quenocene since way before the tourist traffic picked up. Innuendo lurked. Dementia loomed. Self-esteem gets undermined before you know it, and nobody yet proved that an extra finger or a forehead vast as a tide flat on a full-moon ebb was in any way correlated to deficient mentality. Just look at Karla Blodgett, graduated with honors from the tech school over in Quinault after having fingers eleven and twelve removed, and you could play checkers on *her* forehead, if she was lying down. Nobody ever questioned Karla's antecedents, except to joke that she was the smartest turnip Cefus Blodgett ever grew. That didn't mean his sister Sissie was Karla's mother or her own sister or both or neither one as well.

Dezmun liked Karla Blodgett well enough to think the best of her and figured she must like him back. He wondered why she went off, but then so many of them did. He doubted she'd be back but then understood the changing world a young person lives in. Pondering odds and potential causation on her return, he picked his chicken clean.

That's a good thing about chicken; once you get the hang of dressing it out you can near do it without thinking, slice it ass to elbow tidy as laying out your Sunday clothes in hardly six moves. The trimming takes more time, but that's personal taste, and Dezmun Deyung, for one, was particular about what he ate. One iota of disgust could foul a whole spread, so he got in there tweezing and cuticle removing to make it look right, because questionable presentation can very well goose your appetite. Karla Blodgett had looked about as good as a woman can look, even though it was only starlight and of that only what leaked through the roof slats. And he only had pictures from magazines as the foundation of a woman's potential look. He'd suspected it could look better than that, and Karla did.

He sighed and wondered why certain moments keep you longing for another go, another chance to engage the senses at their apex. He laughed, digging out that pinch of mushy guts in there on the insides of the thighs; he knew what crowned those special times, no mystery there. It was the fun of the nasty and vice-versa.

That's disgusting, he thought, flicking it into the bait bucket. He thought: tasted like chicken. Of course it didn't, but that's what they say about everything. He wondered if she missed him and figured she did not, since a man needs to be a realist with so many promising young men to choose from and her so smart. Still, you can't really know.

Dezmun dispatched four slices quick and neat, two wings and two hindquarters. He might later part the legs from the thighs but on initial approach he only splayed for whatever direction things would take from there. Multitudinous as points on a compass were the many directions a chicken could take, which was another good thing: versatility. Dezmun Deyung had liked chicken for going on thirty years now, maybe longer.

People compare the taste of it to darn near anything because chicken tastes so different from fried to barbecued to baked, stewed, fricasseed, chopped in a salad or Mexican style with some of that red pepper on it. You name it, and chicken prepared somehow or other will likely taste related to it. He figured chicken just about one of the best things to eat, all told, with its versatility and riboflavin and so forth. He wondered if a long-term love of chicken made him an authority on the subject and figured it did. With crab bait he was practically famous in local circles.

He picked up a wing, his favorite part, all told, though he hated to see those restaurants hawking "buffalo wings." For one thing a buffalo with wings is plain stupid. For another, if a buffalo did have wings, they'd be huge, bigger than turkey wings and bigger still.

No, the wing is your delicacy on your chicken, two to a customer. Experimenting in the realm of scientific understanding he parted the wing into three sections and skinned the middle one, the one with the two bones running nearly parallel for an inch or two. Holding it vertical he closed his eyes, drew it near and thrust his tongue through the meaty center. It was not the same as Karla Blodgett, except for maybe a little bit in texture and feel. He smelled it and set it aside. It wasn't exactly disgusting, but it didn't smell good, but it did smell like fresh chicken.

He smelled it again to remember for comparison the next time Karla came home. Then he flipped it in the bait bucket and imagined that skinned wing converting to a big fat crab. Once you skin a wing it'll never cook up right no matter what. He went ahead and flipped the little end section as well, even though that part will cook up nicely in a stew or a bake—not on a grill, though. Most people set the little end piece aside because they think it's not worth the trouble, or that they might look disgusting sucking out the tidbits from the wing ends. People can miss the best of a thing because they're too lazy or self-conscious. Dezmun believed this about delicacy relative to goodness. He understood the sensitivity of crabs as well.

Most people do not. Most people think that crabs will enjoy a rank chicken most of all. They don't. A crab will pass on rotten chicken as quick as anyone will. Well, maybe not just as quick. A crab might check it out, but then he'll pass. No, a crab likes just the right taint to his chicken. Dezmun figured it for a kind of sexual appetite on the smell part of it. Crabs and people are often curious about what might smell askew, and both are near certain to go in closer, like it'll turn savory with their nose where it shouldn't be. It doesn't, but then the other takes over, which is a sweetness all its own if you have any romantic inclination at all. Dezmun believed this to be the case.

Because romance is perhaps the biggest mystery of nature, because a thing can draw folks on in and then hit them with a noseful of singe, because tawdry has its virtue to a point and then goes to skanky, which is where romance ends. You want to stay right there on the line. And you find it by keeping an open mind to the smaller iota and staying respectful of nature's boundaries.

Like success in the crab bait business. Whoever paid chicken guts half a mind? Folks first thought he was out for easy pickin's. But the business came to him naturally, and folks tend to think the worst when something comes your way and not theirs. They thought poorly of him and Karla Blodgett, easy pickin's, and a prejudice seemed to carry over to where he only put his hand to earn a dollar.

He knew what they said, that he led Karla to the barn for a view of the rafters. But he didn't lead the first time or the last. People might think a man of forty-five knows the wily ways a sight more than a girl of nineteen does. But it was her idea, and she set the pace. He only did what comes natural to a man and was primed to go whole hog, till death do us part, because Karla Blodgett suited him a might differently than any magazine ever had.

She never said she wasn't ready to bog down with a man, but he read her sure enough when she kicked into overdrive and huffed like the preacher chasing demons and made him feel like a service stud. Well, he'd be doing all right if that was the worst he ever felt, so he took the gentlemanly course, obliging a young woman's whim on direction and frequency. She indicated barnwards often enough there for a month or two and then on her odd visits home. Forty-one times ducking into the barn made for seventy-six goes all told; seven times were too late for twice and the first time in was good for three goes and that makes seventy-six, which seems like a bit, but then so does chicken every day. Of course things seem otherwise soon enough.

They were friends, she said, helping each other out. He went along with friendship but couldn't help the shiver in his spine when she took his arm now and then, walking beside him right down the road. People talked. He heard them, denying him what came his way natural as sunlight to the hills. Oh, they loved their commiseration on the bleak future awaiting a man of forty-five hooked up with a girl of nineteen. In another forty-five years he'd be ninety and she'd be seventy-four. So what? They'd all be dead, most of them. So? What would they say then?

No, she'd be sixty-four, even better.

Folks then pointed the same finger and said Dezmun was stuck on easy pickin's, trying to charge good money for some old chicken guts. But anyone taking the time to look could see each bait pack was balanced out with a neck, two or three fat globules, a heart and a butt. That was your basic bait pack. Some people liked to eat the butts. Not Dezmun. Sure, you could be in for some delectable nibbles either side of the tailbone except for one thing: you're eating chicken butt, or would be if you did.

Not Dezmun; he found the idea of munching some chicken's ass disgusting. Why, even a moron wouldn't want to eat something that spent its life a quarter inch from a life-size pile of chicken shit. No, thank you; the butts go to the crabs, who should take to chicken shit no sooner than you should, but then a crab doesn't know about proximity and associative disgust. Maybe that's what makes a man so superior.

Or so much a product of what he's learned. It was plain to Dezmun Deyung that a crave or a cringe likely stems from what you grew up with. Chicken butt; chicken shit; crabs do care if it's fresh. And the feet. Some people don't like the feet and in fact think the feet disgusting, even if your prep person removed that crusty yellow skin that hangs on down there. But people have deep-seeded partialities with no basis in fact. They make another case for not eating chicken feet on account of what was stepped in by the feet for the very same lifetime the butt spent spewing chicken squat. Though parallel, this reasoning is also unfounded and possibly warped.

Because a man who remembers his first timid grasp on a thing and remembers holding it still for eating will love that thing for showing him the means to survival and more, to the enjoyment of life itself. Dezmun loved chicken feet—boiled, baked, you name it. Hot off the grill took him back every time, as if his mother handed him another after all these years and told him to rinse it off if he dropped it. He laughed, as if he wouldn't have known to rinse it off.

Childhood accounted as well for the unlaid eggs found inside if you had the gumption to clean your own chicken. Dezmun had the gumption. What? He should go out and buy a chicken missing a vital cog in his personal economic machinery? I don't think so. He didn't pluck because feathers had no application in the crab bait business. But he was thinking.

Maybe he'd step boldly toward innovation. Pillows seemed a long shot, since a mess of chicken could fall short of filling a pillow. And they stank, the feathers. Maybe the breakthrough would be in fishing lures. He made a mental note to put his mind on feathers later, maybe on the way over to Quinault for some chickens. Maybe step one would be the savings on chicken as yet unplucked.

Because as it was Dezmun Deyung bought his chicken without the feathers, with the guts and without the head. (It just made things so sad.) He could tell you right now that slitting the belly and reaching in for a fistful of chicken guts was no walk in the park, but a man has to do what he doesn't want to do. He could chill the chicken to cut down on the shmush, but chilling reduces viability in the unlaid eggs. Not that these eggs could get laid; they could not. A woman on TV had seven babies at once, then one had eight, so you couldn't confine potential. But that was different.

And the unlaid eggs lost culinary viability if chilled. They could simmer till sundown and not lose flavor or texture. But go chill a pre-cleaned chicken and presto chango, the little yellow balls come out stiff and pliable instead of formless balls of snot, pardon me, which is how they're supposed to be.

Up to the elbow in chicken guts, Dezmun laughed when he hit the mother load, six unlaids and him with nothing but a bait bucket to put them in. One time he reached for a clean cup from the shelf but got chicken twiddle all over the wall and on the dishes in the dish rack and it wasn't worth it. Now he tossed the unlaids to the bait bucket. Big deal; he could sort and rinse later. One time he forgot until Tuesday, four unlaids big as golf balls left in with the bait. But the lid was on for most of that time, and they were fine, or near fine, leastways not stiff like they get from chilling. Truth be told, a man who grows up with unlaid eggs will prefer a few days in a bait bucket to chilling every time.

Truth be told, a man who pays attention to experience will understand the why and wherefore of things and find comfort in his calling. He'll know right from wrong and what side he's on.

Truth be told, nobody was trying to fool anyone. All the chicken guts and necks and butts and UCOs just piled up. Dezmun Deyung never fooled man nor beast in his life but only hated the wastefulness most folks take for granted. So he hung a sign on the fence facing the road.

Crab Bait for Sale

Nobody paid much attention. Nobody stopped in, not for a few weeks, until the weather warmed and the faint, subtle stink of crab bait conveyed the sincerity of the enterprise. Maybe the smell put them in a mind for crabbing. When they saw each bait pack balanced out like it was, with the more decomposable parts held snug in a flow-through square cut from some nylon pantyhose, they understood something too.

You could get your basic crab pack or your bait deLuxe with one foot and one, two or three extra hearts at 35¢ each. Dezmun believed the crabs loved the feet like he did, like the feet walked right out of their youth. And a foot will last all day and into twilight without falling apart no matter how often you pull up your net for a looksee. He topped each pack with two butts or three depending on size and feather nubs. Then he'd throw in some fat and skin. He didn't eat either one, though some people do, and he believed the crabs avoided both as well. But the fat and skin fleshed out the pack, and a savvy operator knows that perceived value is ninety-five percent of the game. Maybe ninety-eight.

The basic bait pack ran a dollar seventy-five at first. Dezmun figured soon enough he could sell the basic till the pigs rolled over and he'd still be screwing the pooch, so he jacked it to three bucks even and went to five-fifty on the deLuxe. Nine out of ten of them wanted the deLuxe with hardly a flinch. Because a body knows he's got only so many chances at crab, and if he's going out there, he might as well up his odds. Dezmun wanted one more price point, but a bait pack beyond deLuxe seemed greedy and crazy. Beyond deLuxe? Yet banging his head on the wall six days straight led again to that which served him best: simplicity. At seven dollars the new top o' the line was called Crabfest and doubled dosage on each item in your basic pack, then went double again on your livers and necks. He threw in a back or two for volume, even though backs are perfectly good eating. The Crabfest sold well enough, not as well as the deLuxe, but that extra dollar and a half was like found money and rounded out the market, securing the mid-range for the primary thrust. This, Dezmun knew, was good, because most people fear extravagance, and the Crabfest let them snuggle in at mid-range.

He felt good in contemplation of economic stability and resignation in life. Clarity re-clarified like a gift re-wrapped over and over again over a relaxing repast that many in the business would have tired of long ago. Not Dezmun. He loved chicken and knew he'd eat some even if the whole world wasn't knocking on his door for what most people throw out.

Maybe he always loved chicken because it meant a greater love tomorrow, which was crab. Of course a man with crab bait inventory can have crab any time he wants it. He had only to bait a trap, throw it out and wait and haul in a feast of crab. That is, if he played the tide right and had some bait a crab wouldn't cringe at. Then again a businessman needs to protect his inventory from personal desire. This and other contemplation went well with legs and thighs, and though a whole chicken in one sitting seemed inordinate for a single man, he felt good about things, resolved for better and worse. He would have the wings, first one, then the other. A jar of cider seemed reasonable too on an evening of such apparent reason. So he ate and drank, savoring the contentment a life can come to if given a chance.

A back isn't much, but he'd save the breasts for tomorrow, for a sandwich, which wouldn't take long to fix, which was good, with bait bagging and an outing for crabs on the schedule.

He wondered again if it would be better bagging fresh bait and letting it ferment or waiting for nature to take its course and then bagging it. He licked his fingers and figured bagging first would spare the bait undue disturbance. Sure, the roil could release the pungent lure, but no; a conservative approach was best here for the sake of stable inventory, shelf life and several other levels of practicality. And he sat in contentment, grateful at reaching that point in life where mere thought can solve a problem.

A problem remained that by preference would remain unnamed if not for the syllables residing on the fringe of his consciousness. He couldn't say what he wouldn't give to have her cross that threshold then and there, knowing full well she'd only wince with a no, no, no on nary a peck on the cheek much less drop her drawers for a bell ringer. Out in the barn would be a horse of a different feather, and he laughed, feeling good tonight, because it was a new time, not a bad time but a time of change and acceptance. These kids today, like it makes a pinch of bait's worth of difference whether you're lying on a bed or in the hay. He wished for the bell ringer all right but wished as hard for a minute or two beforehand to present his view of the thing. Then again, he'd kept his mouth shut and could again if she showed up willing.

He saw her surely as when she stood there, forehead rising, back a bit sway, pretty as a picture and smart as a diplomat explaining the difficulty a girl encounters getting her fill, explaining that Dezmun was different from the boys. He needed no explanation. But she felt free and easy with him, so she went ahead and ventilated her frustration over the boys wanting to feel her up hardly a wink before sticking it any old where while he, Dezmun, was slow as a slug in molasses. It didn't take much more than two directions to make a woman feel good, and he, Dezmun, was good for in and out with a deep respect for both that a girl could appreciate, she said.

She didn't come home now like she did in tech school. Even then it was only holidays and odd weekends, but she always came over to see if Dezmun wanted to drop everything—crab, chicken; she didn't give a care—for a walk down to the barn. Dezmun always nodded, dropping everything and wiping his hands up to the elbows on the way, because a towel is nice to have on certain outings.

Oh, heck, he laughed; a shirttail would do in a pinch. Or a sleeve. Or this bib; he wiped the dribble off his chin and laughed again and finished his cider. Then he sighed and fell asleep in his chair.

Well, a man who doesn't get up from the supper table and go to bed before falling asleep can rightfully worry about things gone wrong. For one, he could be alcoholic, so drunk he'd lost the will to sort things out. A jar of cider didn't seem excessive, so maybe he was aging prematurely, verging on senility. Psychological instability could stem from too much solitude, too much thinking, no dialogue save that between him and a bucket of chicken guts. That made him sweat, never mind the slumber, and before he could say *a l'orange*, he floundered in a tureen of dreamswill, which can be real to a sleeping man.

Nobody needs a nightmare gone to worse yet, with crab guts thrown in and the fat and skin and assorted globules swirling away in a dreamy stink. Dezmun Deyung cringed with a violence he would recall for years to come, reliving that night to the end. For ten hours he moaned like a mourner with an ache in his heart that could not be filled. Opening his eyes on a new day in stiff dishevelment, he felt lost and alone where only the night before resolution had been his.

The pounding in his head gave way to the pneumatic insistence at the door. "We don't open till eight," he called. Even as he spoke he wondered how they would talk about the sound of a man so obviously pained so early in the morning. Who shops for crab bait at sunrise? Well, it could be a body so keen on crab she might know the rarity of spring ebb at first light, which this morning was. This morning was as well scheduled for a pleasant interlude until a night of fitful dreaming turned logical progression to mush. He could still go for crabs and probably should with a bag of deLuxe.

Still and all; six a.m.?

He looked up as the door opened on Karla Blodgett outlined by first light. Wiping his chin from habit or maybe because a man wants to look all right for the woman of his dreams, he tried to speak but could not. He wiped his eyes next and rubbed the crusty goo off his knuckles onto his pants. And he smiled at the balance a bad dream can find. He had only to rise and take her hand and drift dreamily to the barn. Who needs a towel if it's only dream spruzo chilling beneath them? But then a towel might be good since spruzo is the only thing you can bring home from a dream.

So he rose and rubbed his face. He looked down at the wild rooster as if willing it ready for a cockadoodle do. He reached for a towel splotched red but mostly dried, and she said, "Not so fast, Mister Dezmun."

"What?" he asked back, realizing sudden as a goose bump that this was no dream. Karla Blodgett stood at his threshold in the flesh like he'd wished for only awhile ago. What was it he agreed to give for one more go? Oh, heck, who cared? He wished it. Here she was. Let's go! "I... Uh..."

"I know," she said. "I'm done with tech work. It ain't for me. I hear you done good in crab bait. I'll help."

"Hm. Well..."

"You want to go to the barn first?

"Well, I might brush my teeth first."

"Okay. Or we can stay here."

"Here?"

Then she smiled like a sunrise all her own at the cockadoodle do Dezmun Deyung could raise any old time. He'd told her he could and more than once proved it. "Yeah." She said, "Yeah. I said yeah. Again yeah. I read that. In a book."

She would later tell him her arrival at first light was to confirm his solitude, because a woman doesn't want a playboy for a man. She tested true love too, because every man looks ready for a cockadoodle do at sunrise. She made him pee first, to be sure. Distraught but ready to pass muster at sunrise, he went out back for the bracing air available there and aimed to please. He thought she'd be all tucked in when he came back, but she only stood there holding out a wishbone. "Make a wish," she said.

They locked eyes and grasped the little bone at either shank and pressed thumbs on the thumb rest. The sun poured in, and it didn't matter who got the long end to twirl three times overhead for luck, for their wish was the same.

And to think, thought Dezmun Deyung. I thought it couldn't get much better than chicken and crab.

High Rise

Tipsy with Excitement

These fucking people and all their fucking kids, bringing their suburban chaos to my shrine of steam and solitude—my shrine by endowment. I allowed silence there. They destroyed it.

I never talked like that or thought like that before things changed. It wasn't so long ago you had snug harbor at certain places in certain times. You found silence in the woods instead of chain saws and tourists. You could sit in a library and expect silence. You had no bums snoring or children making a racket.

Before things changed, a naughty boy got a spanking, oh, yes, before the days of support and nurturing and therapy to unleash the genius inside. Then the little geniuses arrived in droves, acting out, growing up, actualizing for a better tomorrow. Thoughts and behaviors to the contrary could get you arrested. I was never hostile by nature, not before; I only wanted silence.

"Gramma. I want to go in the cold tub now," said a whiny little villain with brown goo smeared methodically around his mouth hole; this, I suspected, to enhance childish innocence. I found this pug-faced little boy revolting, his puckering grimaces most likely similar from one end to the other. Moreover, this childish display was out of place. Where did anybody expect the effluvia to end up, if not in the filtration? Or on the skin of innocent bystanders who actually paid for this repose? What would the odds makers give you, that the snot-nosed mongrel wouldn't take a whiz in the water? What would you bet?

Yet these people laughed at the juvenile barracuda's unwitting humor—hot tub, cold tub. The old lady on the sun deck was why they were there. She's dead now. She must be. Maybe not. Maybe she's a hundred ten and doesn't get to the library so often. That's where I saw her. I never knew if she came for the reading or to humor me, her quiet neighbor. I need no humor but allowed hers.

Gramma. Her relatives couldn't afford a place like this on their own. You could read their demographic in their big bellies and lard asses. And if you think a place like this is easy on a librarian's salary, try thirty years of service on for size.

I knew Gramma. Not a bad old lady; she kept to herself mostly. She stalked me at the library but never pressed with talk. She only waved and tittered like we were in cahoots, seeing each other in the library like that. I forgave her silly behavior because she understood the value of silence. Even in the building she refrained from cluttering the elevator with chatter. When she couldn't bear the vibration as some people can't, she might comment on the weather. But she wouldn't touch a sex scandal or political corruption or a wickedly twisted insight that might reveal the underbelly of human motivation. No, Gramma viewed the world in simple dichotomy. On the one hand were sugar, spice and everything nice. On the other was pornography, including but not limited to the great, banned literature of the ages. Still, she was better than some of them.

I had a habit of my own in those days, a revolting one, to be sure, and not a habit so much as a technique. By farting out loud on the elevator I could quash the most insipid chatter, or at least affect its ardor. They could pretend it didn't exist or attempt further babble around it. Of course neither option could succeed because it did exist, often with reverberation and sometimes afterglow. I had no bone to pick with Gramma, though I marveled at her ridiculous outlook. I let one rip one morning on a casual descent to the lobby to see how she might field it. I am a master of silence, its many facets and the ripples it absorbs.

Well, she ignored my trumpeter swan impersonation but only for as long as she could hold her breath. Then she said, "I have something for you." We exchanged pleasant smiles and that was that until early that evening when she knocked on my door. She stood there as if her pleasant smile hadn't quivered once all day and handed me a chafing dish of stewed prunes.

The little boy was her grandchild. The baby was a distant niece, both of them peeing in the pool from the first toe dipped. The little boy giggled as it ran down his leg. The baby looked bright-eyed and playful. Or shitting, it was so warm and nice. Gaga goo goo, these people loved to say. They took turns cleaning up the mess, agreeing that it really wasn't bad, so firm and concise with hardly any smell.

The adults were the old lady's children. At least one of them was, among the in-laws and extra kids. The swimming pool was only five feet deep but seemed fathomless compared to the gene pool of this clan, whose idea of terrific fun was a toddler running, jumping, curling into a cannonball and splashing as many people as possible.

What? What? You came to get wet, didn't you? Haw, haw, haw. They allowed further insight to the benefits of global virus. It won't be long now.

The pool was forty feet long by three lanes surrounded by a ten-foot periphery. I hoped a kid would slip and break a leg, allowing these people continued focus somewhere else, in an ambulance perhaps, a nice new one with sirens and lights that would speed them on their way. Or maybe an in-law would get splashed enough to smack the shit out of those kids. I'd have done it, but, Jesus, the price you pay.

I would have complained to management. I would have put my foot down and reclaimed my space, my atmosphere, my peace of mind, my refuge. But it was a weekend and the old lady sat motionless, gazing with a pleasant smile that looked to me like a surgical implant. It moved less than Mona Lisa's. She could have signed on as a statue in a nunnery. I did nothing.

The little boy sputtered nonstop nonsense, getting an early start with his compulsion to share inane visual association. He rounded the pool with a vicious little grin on minced steps designed to look so cute. He squirted everyone in the face with his squirt gun and laughed, exploiting the days of total immunity. He stopped in front of the hot tub and talked to me, though I closed my eyes. But he didn't squirt. I think small children with high-energy who profile as potentially criminally insane and who feed mostly on colas and Ding Dongs can sense an adult who doesn't like them. They can tell if you wouldn't mind them crossing the street without looking either way.

I think I succeeded in conveying my position. He stepped in—children are not allowed in the hot tub—and called to his father, "I'm just taking it easy in the hot tub." The people laughed, he was so cute, so he called again, "I'm just taking it easy in the hot tub." They tittered so he called again, same thing, and again, until his mantra was ignored. He was three or four. "Me and this other guy," he called. Behind closed eyes I could hear no one laughing. I could feel their eyes sorting through the steam for a pervert. "Do you like the hot tub?" the kid asked.

"It depends on the crowd," I said.

"My name is Dickie," he said.

"What kind of name is Dickie?" I asked. "It's a name you'll never grow out of. It's a fake T-shirt."

"It's really Richard," he said. "They call me Dickie because I'm so little and cute."

I showed Dickie what a jaundiced eye looks like. His father got up from a chair at the end of the pool. He watched for a moment, then walked over in case I wanted to brain his kid and then demonstrate a little boy's attempt for a new world record for staying under.

Dickie rambled, "I'm in the hot tub but going to the cold tub. I wish this world, this water, in the whole world. Mr. Steel..." He swung around the stainless steel handrail but lost his momentum and hung from his skinny little arms over a certain dunking. Nobody called out for him to be careful, for all could see that if his little grip failed, he would surely submerge. Caution at that point was too late.

But isn't something to be learned in the very nature of dangling over water? I let him hang. He regained his footing and came back to the vertical and continued, "It'll get better again. That's what he said." He pulled himself up to the top step but then swooned like he was drunk. His father rushed in to catch him. Dickie sensed this, I think, displaying deft skills in making adults hurry or jump or wince. He grabbed the handrail again and stood upright, independent, explaining, "Me and this guy..."

"Are you all right?" his father asked.

"Yes," he said. "I'm all right. What's all right?" The father shook his head and glanced at me.

"He's tipsy with excitement," I said.

"Oh, yeah. He's very excited," the father said, offering his hand, as if we could be friends. "I'm Charles White."

"I've been there myself," I told him. "Not like Dickie, though. Not in quite awhile."

The Bad Seed

The second time Dickie and I engaged socially, he was five or six and thickening, growing stocky from a combination of junk food and bad genes. He caught me staring at his junior gut once. I don't usually stare but I wondered how many frozen pizzas and cupcakes and hot dogs and sugar water had caused him to form like a little fireplug. "Hey. Same to you," he said, but he didn't open fire. I would have beaned him if he had. But perhaps he knew the score by then.

Instead of his old-fashioned, Buck-Rogers-style, single-shot squirt gun, he carried an automatic. It was shaped like an Uzi with a long barrel for range and accuracy. Four D-cell batteries and an internal pump powered his little watering cannon. Its rapid-fire sound-effect enhanced the experience of being splattered soggy by little Dickie, who could deliver a quart from fifty feet with precision and a soundtrack from downtown Beirut. He appeared to feel the power.

Children sometimes complain that some adults don't like them. Usually, they sense their teachers don't like them, but then many children view all adults as teachers. They are assured that these adults don't really dislike them, because grown-ups are inherently wise in the ways of the world and its children, who are all special and cute and lovable and the very stuff of our future. These children are told that adults only want to help them, perhaps by demonstrating alternative behaviors better suited to a word where everyone must fit in.

I think the children who realize early that others might dislike them get too little credit for instinct and intuition. I dislike most children, especially those conforming to their parental paradigm: gain attention, gain access, gain money, gain material goods, have more children. I especially disliked Dickie, in whom the blueprint for trouble seemed indelibly manifest and clearly legible. I freely displayed my dislike for him, but only to him, not to his parents or associate adults. Because we constrain our honesty in this regard, bound by a society that supplements junk food with junk songs and TV specials devoted to the love and care of children. The tired refrain of our future and the future of our world and so on and so forth is strategically relieved by commercial breaks for more junk food. The children crave it, so the parents buy it. And isn't the message sweet, too?

But I couldn't hide my scorn when his parents assured him on each act of destruction and/or animal abuse that "It's not your fault, Dickie. It's not your fault." Dickie generated alarm. He was naturally given to maiming, staining, soiling, bending, breaking, testing, teasing, reaching, poking, seeking that for which the young male of the species hungers. If detected by an adult who didn't haw haw or beam blissfully but instead scowled with disfavor and shaded with stink-eye, Dickie would sob. Slowly at first, he would craftily shorten his little breaths and pump his tear ducts like an innocent little boy, crying.

I observed him from my balcony on the ninth floor. He played on the terrace on the sixth. In unhappy overview of his little world I could see the reflection of that which his parents had wrought. Little Dickie was a perfect microcosm of the world at large, the one bent on destruction. He threw rocks at birds. When he hit one he pulled on its head or plucked its wing feathers. He found a basketball left on the terrace and sliced its equator with a razor blade, maybe to get to the stuff inside, the magic stuff that made it bounce.

Where did he get a razor blade? Well, you don't worry so much about that if you're watching from safe distance as youthful psychosis plays out. You in fact shamelessly hope for a slip to the wrist, for a last, tearful ebb. But alas, the boy could handle a blade.

He chased cats with his squirt gun. He caught one and tried to throw it over the edge of the sixth floor terrace, but it was too big and reached Dickie's face and sunk its claws in for traction, hanging there by only its front paws until it could safely jump back to sure footing. This was fortunate for Dickie and the cat, as well as for me. For I fear rash reaction may have doomed us all. An act of retribution would have surely ensued, one deemed illegal by our society, perhaps one punishable by years of incarceration, even when factoring good behavior.

Meanwhile, Dickie screamed bloody murder and bled like a spigot and got his mother to agree that it was a bad kitty, bad. And evil, and if they could catch it, they would have it "put to sleep."

I went down later and fed the kitty and told it, "Nice work." I followed it to see if it had a home but in the end it followed me home. I named him Rex. He took instantly to my dog Lanny, which is another story entirely, one of three souls adrift and on certain levels alone. Each found friends in the others, friends in whom to confide and trust, with whom to feed, play and rest.

I found little Dickie peeing in a corner of the mail room. I saw him kick a dog whose owner stepped outside. He eyed Lanny with hunger. I saw him scrape a nail on a luxury sedan, which I didn't mind, though I doubted it could ever belong to a member of his family. If it were my car, I would have strangled the little devil, maybe not all the way, because wanton destruction to cars doesn't get me quite so stirred as cruelty to higher, gentler beings. But I'd have put the point across.

Dickie was around more and more as Gramma aged, because his parents came around more. He got his buttons in the wrong holes, so his shirts were crooked. In the winter months he kept two half-melted garden slugs hanging from his nostrils. His eyebrows were nicked as if purposely and his teeth were chipped like he'd tried to bite his way out of a cage. I wondered what madness makes people raise children like this. I found myself staring at Dickie's parents. This was about the time they bought him a new water gun with a three-tank backpack. It had no batteries and no sound track but that was small consolation to a hundred-foot range on a two-gallon payload. Dickie could drench at will. He could leave you soaked head to toe and wondering what hit you as you heard faint laughter in the hundred-foot range. He provided the soundtrack, which, when followed by his unique laughter, was more like a Carnival de Sade than that of conventional warfare.

He stood in my front door one day unarmed with his mother and father, who asked if they might borrow a cup of sugar. I said yes, they could, and I glanced down and wondered how I could fetch the sugar and get rid of them before Dickie trashed my door latch. He tested it for failure, twisting the latch to its limit then pressing to see if he could break it. The parents twitched as if waiting to be invited inside. But neither they nor their delinquent offspring would ever step inside, unless it was over the proverbial dead body of you-know-whom. “I have animals,” I explained, leaving them to factor incongruities of their entrance to my living space. “Wait here.”

I went for the sugar as Dickie turned the deadbolt to the locked position then banged the latch against the jamb. I listened for his parents to scold him or at least stop him. But they only watched, or as their school of discipline called it, they observed him. He soaked up their interest, banging harder, figuring it out. They laughed at me when I came back with a cup of sugar; it was a joke, borrowing a cup of sugar. Get it? Can we borrow a cup of sugar?

Dickie got it; he grinned and banged the door latch again and again, testing something else for failure. Charles smiled. The wife Sharon beamed at little Dickie in this amazing experimental phase of figuring things out, so primitive yet so fundamental to his primary understanding.

I yelled at the little bastard to stop; in fact, “Stop that, you little bastard,” was my precise invocation. The parents were aghast and appeared helpless to respond. Rightfully so, I thought. I further admonished Dickie to step away from the door. “Now sit in the hallway *out*side and be still, hands to yourself. Now, sit! And don’t touch anything!” Little Dickie’s grin became a frown. His eyes welled up and streamed little tears as the parents rushed to assure him it was not his fault.

Charles then mustered a practiced composure and advised me to relax. He sounded like an android on an elevator, rambling over the tedious subject favored by suburban parents, which is their mysterious perception of a mystical connection to life. This view is hidden to those people without children, who can never understand. How could they?

I wanted to invite him to cease his gibberish. I wanted to wish him a painless death. I wanted to fart out loud, so helplessly mute did his propaganda leave me. Charles touched me assuredly, explaining that a small child could not possibly harm a stainless steel bolt. Dickie was only playing, he said. Then he paused for the slow, expansive stretch of the pleasant smile he learned downstairs. And I should specifically relax, he said, over the excellent bottle of wine they would be pouring that evening at Gramma's. Could I come down?

Against core instinct, not to mention better judgment, I allowed chagrin to stick its foot in the door. Worse yet, I assented to breaking bread with these...people.

Later, at dinner, Dickie felt better. He'd been allowed a double ration of cola and four Twinkies to assuage the gods of youthful withdrawal. I wanted to explain to Charles and Sharon and Gramma that their psychopathic progeny was a serial killer looking for a population to decimate, once the sugar failed. I held back because Dickie had convinced me he was on earth to teach his parents a thing or two about life and children, and anything I could add would be incidental. When he thrust his grimy hands into the salad bowl and came up grinning with the contents of said bowl grasped hopelessly in mid-air, ostensibly to serve himself, but moreover to gain a memorable reaction, his parents saw me wince. They chided him softly and talked him down, nurturing him into releasing the greens. Infinitely gently, they incorporated support and hesitation so everyone could see that it clearly wasn't Dickie's fault.

I declined the salad.

Dickie sensed my constraint. He didn't know exactly why I didn't yell or smack him, but he sensed a reason, because adults like me only hold back for a reason. He smiled at me across the table and squeaked that he really liked salad. His parents smiled at that, maybe because they remained oblivious to his natural destructive tendencies. Little Dickie announced again that he really liked thalad, and he dug deep for another handful with his filthy little mitts. The parents giggled, so he made a great show of eating an olive and singing that he really liked olivth. The olive was the single morsel of salad he would eat. I despised him; the salad had looked so good.

The modestly tolerable wine got easier on the second bottle so I drank more to compensate my hunger. I kept one eye on the little beast to see what he might glean from my behavior. Charles and Sharon White took my thirst as a sign of dissipating inhibition, growing warmth and friendship. They shared their excitement over Charles' success in marginally restoring his gum line with his new VibraTonic toothbrush. Sharon said in confidence that even though she was very, very proud of Charles' results, she still wasn't a hundred percent certain she would let Dickie use the VibraTonic, even though it said right on the box that the VibraTonic could brighten the dental future of every child. "But it doesn't say what age children," she vexed.

"I'm theven," Dickie said.

"You're six," Charles said.

"I'm thixth," Dickie said.

"What if... What if they find out it makes your teeth fall out?" she conjectured.

"Mm," I sympathized, wondering what caused the blindness in Sharon and Charles White and what amazing new eye drops might correct it. Dickie's teeth, jagged and vicious as those of a rabid Tasmanian devil, looked like he'd tried to eat a few VibraTonic toothbrushes.

"The VibraTonic toothbrush won't make anybody's teeth fall out," Charles said with authority, adding with a scoff that he paid a hundred thirty dollars for the darn thing. He stopped eating to let extravagance have its moment. He underscored his sanguine purchase by assuring all that a pattern of gum recession that took its toll for years was now reversed. Years.

"I have that too," I said.

"Everyone has it," Charles said, eating again.

"I have new teef," Dickie said, jutting his choppers in a grotesque display of partially chewed olive, meatloaf and residual Twinkie.

Sharon blushed and playfully admonished, "Stop that and eat." Charles wolfed meatloaf; Dickie aped him for two bites. They both drowned it in ketchup. I drank and dabbed at Gramma's potatoes au gratin. Gramma watched me for signs of satisfaction.

I told her, "Mm. Good." She smiled.

Charles expounded on the amazing technologies of modern dentistry and the likelihood of zero-cavity lives for our children; I mean, for the children of today, the future of tomorrow. Charles had pondered dental hygiene since his amazing results with the VibraTonic. Sharon nodded along. I realized that disliking them required a natural dislike for things in general, because Charles and Sharon personified the strange order of suburban America, post-millennium.

I imagined myself only awhile hence, savoring an old movie and a decent sandwich.

Meanwhile, I further loathed these people who claimed a mystical connection for having reared a monster. They squirmed through life in a box and held commerce with the boxed humans on a street of boxes with perfect lawns and aspiring teeth. Change for them came only with remote control.

I disliked them and their ilk naturally. Gramma, I could discount; I would see her in the elevator. I would smile and not fart. She would appear at the library, titter and wave. I would grant her my own rendition of the pleasant smile; she'd earned it.

Charles and Sharon and their satanic offspring made me want away and pronto, but I learned long ago the problem of misanthropy exposed. So I exposed my happy face instead, or at least my pleasantly engaged face.

I listened to Charles' toothbrush rhapsody. Sharon nodded like a fuzzy plastic pooch in a rear window while their vile child slid glop onto his chest and watched it roll to the floor. Gramma winced, too. I was proud of her for that and glad that her pain and my own would soon be eased. We could look forward to a peaceful evening. Charles and Sharon were trapped. I wanted to call them Charry and Sharry but they wouldn't have laughed. My humor is often unfunny to others. It's often humorless to me too.

A moment of silence felt good but Dickie filled it with a question. "Why are you bald?" Charles chuckled; he threatened obesity but had a full head of hair and took superiority where he could find it. Sharon blushed. Then they both gazed moronically as if to measure my game, to see if I would accept the simple reality imposed by innocent youth, or deny it with a shrug.

"Because my hair fell out," I told him. I had no bones about a full-scale engagement, but the evening had used me up.

"Why did your hair fall out?" He pursued as children will, each answer leading to the why of the next question. I knew Dickie wasn't immune to stink-eye because of my past success in making him cry. But with his parents on hand, demonstrably amused and curious, he gained new confidence. Stink-eye only fanned the flames. He asked again why my hair fell out with heightened innocence, seemingly tireless in his stride while I failed to find my second wind.

So I met innocence with truth. "Why did you stop being a cute child? Why did your father gain weight? Why is your mother more nervous since you were born? It's all the same reason, Dickie. Life is hell. Every day of it. And it gets worse. And then one day you're gasping for breath and it's all over. You die, sometimes as ignorant as the day you were born."

"Oh, my," Gramma said.

"You, too, Dick," I said. "It happens to all of us. You, too, will die one day just like my hair fell out. So why does it happen? Whose fault is it?"

Dickie saw my meaning and I hadn't even raised my voice. His little eyes welled up again, not so much for sadness, I think, but for a clear defeat. Tears formed. I smiled, taking the point, and topped off my wine. He filled the next silence effectively as an opportunist seeking advantage, crying his little eyes out, suddenly drenched in the harsh reality of life. His mother drew him near, but she couldn't very well tell him he wasn't to blame, or that it wasn't true that one day he would breathe his last, or that the world would be much happier for it.

I'd set him straight on several levels with a thoroughness I felt he'd earned, a precision I felt he deserved. Dickie was no slouch but existed at advanced levels of development. I merely explained with a lucidity most likely lacking at home that he was fucked anyway he looked at it. I dealt him a round of tit for tat at my own level of development and, frankly, found it most satisfying. And in a gesture I wouldn't have enjoyed nearly as much with someone my own age, I offered him a drink. "Here you go, *Dickie*. You might as well start now. It's what it all gets down to."

Dickie boo hoo hooed, dead certain I was at least as evil as the cat who clawed his face. His mother glared over his sad little head with nearly as much stink-eye as I'd mustered. "Why don't you pick on somebody your own size?" she wanted to know.

I didn't say, Oh, get out of here. I only shrugged sheepishly and said, "He's a formidable little fellow. I think he understands now." He sensed my excellent maneuver and wailed, getting a jump on the veil of tears now hopelessly enshrouding us. Soon beside himself with grief he cried as if for lost love, though I suspect it was only the loss of table dominance he mourned.

They moved as one body, as a family with values loftier than my own and mystical connections I could never share. They rose without discourse, moving inexorably as the changing seasons for their coats, their farewell and the drift for the door. Little Dickie wouldn't bang Gramma's door. I wondered why but didn't ask.

They were leaving before dessert, which was one of Gramma's famous and now rare strawberry pies. Dickie had been lathered for it for hours, maybe days. Departure before three slices running down his neck and all over the floor—before he could even thrust one little fist into it—made him howl.

"Gee, it's a shame you have to go," I called after him. "That strawberry pie looks deeeelicious! Well, more for me. Goodbye!"

My apologies to Gramma were brief but concise. I think she understood.

Dickie and I didn't meet again until he was nine.

Euthanasia

I wanted a trip so badly that the tedious arrangements seemed worthwhile no matter how difficult. How tough could it be to find a babysitter for Lanny and Rex? Lanny was a feisty old bitch but Rex calmed her down, arching his back and rubbing her forelegs. She looked at him like he was nuts, then she licked him. Rex liked that and he loved to play, so maybe one of the neighborhood kids could stay over and care for the animals.

Some of them had met Lanny when she lunged to the end of her leash. They wouldn't stay with her, even though she never really bit anyone. She only did her Hound of the Baskervilles impersonation if you approached incorrectly, at the door or on the street. She bared fang and frothed a bit, but if you talked goo goo and said Lanny, Lanny, Lanny, she stopped. Sometimes she wagged her tail stub and begged forgiveness and something to eat. If you didn't know the goo-goo-Lanny password she still only nipped on the lunge; by the time she reached the meaty part of your forearm, she only lipped and whined and barked some more. What a show, but she never bit anyone.

The neighborhood kids had plans or had to wash their hair or weren't feeling well. It came down to a rational question: What kid doesn't change between the ages of six and nine? It's a fifty-percent age difference, same as twenty to thirty, or forty to sixty. Who doesn't change?

I'd seen Dickie stalking the terrace with his blowgun. I called the resident manager and reported an armed and dangerous delinquent who would be processed internally within two minutes, or I'd call the police. The manager's unit is just off the sixth floor terrace and the deadline was reasonable, so Dickie was given the rules of guns and darts in mere moments. He surfaced again with a paintball gun of apparently high caliber, the kind used by real sportsmen who hunt each other, not exactly for keeps but with a sting and a bruise to go along with the blood splat. Dickie thwacked a few rounds to the side of the building to get a feel for the recoil and torque of the thing. Then he crouched in the position and fired on a sparrow, a pedestrian, a distant window and Rex, who was trying to take a pee on the terrace. I called the resident manager again. "He's back."

But the blowgun and paintball gun confiscation had been more than a year ago, maybe a year and a half. And a notable endearment of Charles and Sharon White's was their propensity to forgive and forget. They said hello in passing, sometimes going out of their way. They seemed so cheerful. I assumed this tolerance stemmed from life in the suburbs. So many people surrounded by so many non-durables and living in such density must tolerate the habits, noise and clutter of their neighbors, lest violence erupt. At least in a high rise you don't have to look at cookie-cutter lawns strewn with hoses, sprinklers, swing sets, American flags and basketball hoops. At least in a high rise you can limit exposure to weather pap on the elevator with now and then a rude intrusion in the spa.

Anyway, as happens with prolonged analysis, I ended up way yonder on a tangent when I ran into Sharon and Charles in the lobby. Sharon asked, "How *are* you?" I didn't exactly look over my shoulder, but then I didn't feel we were old cronies reunited at the mall either. I half expected her to tell me I looked fabulous. So I made it short and sweet; I needed a baby-sitter for the weekend.

Charles was sanguine, confiding that a weekend close to Gramma would be a good thing for them; nobody knew how much longer she could live alone. He urged that we go directly to my place for a run-through, insisting that such a synchronous convergence of needs could only be good for everyone. On the elevator we agreed that the weather may change for the better. Dickie, up close, had hardened into late childhood, his features nearing the definition he would take into maturity. He'd gained weight, not as much as his father but neither had he grown proportionately tall. Sharon read my assessment with a mother's intuition. "I don't know where he gets it," she said. "Dickie's going to be built like his grandfather."

"Then you do know," I said, instantly regretting my glib wit. But wits were just as quickly forgotten once inside, when Dickie spoke. His voice had dropped somewhat from his innocent lilt, but he still lisped.

"Thith cat lookth very thuthpiciouth," he said. "Very, very thuthpiciouth," he grinned, apparently as mindless of mortality and certain death as of having his diaper changed. He, too, bore no grudge. I didn't trust him; call it an outsider's intuition. He said, "I think I met thith cat before." Rex arched his back and rubbed Dickie's legs. Dickie liked that quite a bit and seemed less fiendish, to a degree. I watched him sit on the floor and exchange affections with Rex. I couldn't convince myself that he was now normal, but I felt assured that Charles and Sharon understood my concern. It was only two nights, and I hadn't been away in ages.

Charles confirmed: "Hey, relax. Two nights. We got it covered. Don't worry about a thing. We'll take good care of your pets."

Sharon read me yet again. "It's a new phase," she said. "He's so sensitive to animals. He just loves them to death." I wanted to call it off. What weekend could be worth the welfare of my two best friends? "Just go," she said. "You fuss over them worse than I fuss over mine."

"Do you fuss?"

"Go."

I went in spite of my better knowing. On the way I listened to the gruesome details of an airplane crash with no survivors. Two people had refused to board, because, they said, of a dark premonition. I wondered why some people listen to themselves and some don't. I called Saturday afternoon and was assured Rex was fine, that he and Dickie were fast friends. "And Lanny?"

Well, Dickie was trying to play with her too, but she was so intolerant, they said.

"She's not a pup. She's an adult, an old one," I reminded them. "She requires the same respect any adult requires."

"Well," Sharon said. "She's certainly a strange pet."

"I suppose we often overlook strangeness in our own," I said, again regretting my relentless wit, but believing it integral to clarity and understanding.

I was due home Sunday night but cut it short and got back early in the afternoon to everyone's relief. Lanny had bit Dickie and worse, she'd begun snarling and threatening to attack when he approached or even entered the same room. Sharon came right out and called her a dangerous animal. Charles said, "Dangerous, hell! She's vicious! It's not a pleasant thought but you really should consider putting her to sleep. She bit my son."

"Let me see," I said, displaying calmness admirably. Sharon brought Dickie in from the bedroom, my bedroom. I wanted them out forever. Lanny hid under a chaise lounge on the deck. I stooped to see her, and I called to her, "Hey, Lanny." She whined and wagged her tail the way they do, anxious to share with you what they've been through.

Charles ended our reverie with, "You know it's one thing when something like this happens between friends. We're not going to sue you or anything. But I think she should be quarantined for observation, whatever the rabies time is, ten or fourteen days. Or you make this easier on everyone by finding out tomorrow in the autopsy."

I wanted to smack him around, Charles, the father. He's much bigger than me, but I had the adrenaline advantage. Dickie came in pouting in his nearly tearful posture, the one a nine-year-old can still regress to for maximum sympathy; save the children; bless the children; the children are our future.

Oh, Dickie could work the home crowd. He held his arm like it was broken, like he was one of the winged birds of his youth who would never fly again because of a random act of cruelty. I gently grasped his wrist then yanked the arm to full extension. He whelped. Charles moved in. Dickie had a red area halfway up his forearm that looked liked he'd rubbed profusely. "This is it? The skin isn't broken."

"She bit him," Charles said.

"She's never bit anyone," I said.

"That's not what the neighbors say," he said.

Get out, I wanted to say. Do you know what the neighbors say about this mongrel child? Are you blind to psychosis? What in the world keeps you from helping little Dickie out with the forty thousand volts he needs? These and other indictments and rational questions were what I wanted to pursue. But I left it with lukewarm rhetoric, asking, "What if children came in litters and the unwanted and unfit were gassed humanely?" This, on my way to the door, where I stood holding it open.

As they gathered their things with indignation and the silence thickened, Dickie went into the kitchen and helped himself to twelve dog biscuits. He carried them to the deck, where he sat down and lured Lanny out from under. "I love Lanny," he said. He patted her tenderly, then forcefully, then as if her head was a bongo drum. He barked at her. She winced. She shrank. She snarled.

"Dickie!" I yelled. "Never touch my dog or cat again! If you do..." Dickie stopped short and turned to hear my threat, perhaps too startled to cry. "If you do, I'll whip you to within an inch of your life." I thought clarity best here too for all parties, though here too I understood the liability attendant to the truth.

"Then I will sue," Charles said.

"So? Sue! Now if you don't mind, I'd like to put my place back in order."

They left. On the way out, Sharon said, "I'm sorry."

Charles said, "We're only suggesting what's best for everyone, including Lanny."

"If you offered to put your son to sleep," I said, fully aware that all stops were pulled, "It would be a bad trade off. She's so much more noble, more caring, more sensitive and compassionate. Take the blinders off, Charles. Lanny is a close personal friend of mine, no danger to anyone unless they harm her."

They left. Lanny and Rex came to me. Rex arched and rubbed. Lanny whined and cried her tale of woe. She nipped at me when I stroked her hindquarters, where I found two staples in her butt. The brown spots on Rex's ass were cigarette burns. I took pictures of both, Exhibit A, your Honor, then plucked the staples and dressed the wounds. I spent a quiet Sunday night at home with my friends. We retired to the sofa where we snacked and watched TV to our hearts content. Yet we wondered when the imbalance in nature would be corrected.

The Wonder Years

Nearly everyone who lives in a high rise has binoculars or a telescope. I remember seeing Gramma's on one of her shelves and wondering what kind of birds she watched from the seventh floor. She kept them on a high shelf, and when I asked to see them she put a finger to her lips, lifting them down gently as a mouse lifting cheese from a trap. She knew.

Gramma finally moved out or at least got moved out. What does a ninety-two year old woman want with fifteen hundred square feet? The question circulated among those helping with the move, along with assorted statements of fact, like: She can't keep up with it. The cleaning is too much. She's all alone. She needs company. The market isn't strong enough right now. We'll wait until it improves. We're only moving in temporarily. Oh, yes, we found a wonderful school for him.

A wonderful school for the gifted criminally insane, I thought. Even with modern standards, armed guards and security stations, Dickie White wouldn't make it past recess without an arrest record in public school. No, the little fellow needed help, like trainers with whips and chairs and maybe pistols.

Before too long we shared an elevator, Dickie and I. He wore the little blue Fauntleroy suit favored by parochial schools. He must have been twelve, judging by the puffing and redness on the volcanic surface of his face. He'd continued filling in, filling out, not fat like his father but thick like a Big Ten fullback just out of a hot drier.

We glanced at each other. He seemed painfully shy now. He seemed to suffer further imbalance physically than I'd assessed in him mentally. He appeared to have shaved. Little stubble splotches grew unevenly, threatening torment when the little moguls culminated in eruption. He blushed with an awkward purpling, yellowing smile.

Hey, he was only a kid. "You're not Catholic," I said. He knew that I knew.

He shrugged. "They took me. I'm a problem." Just like that he fessed up. He knew, as I suspected he'd always known, but hearing his confession felt better than a cry of uncle in submission to a head lock. He didn't exactly endear himself, but he became more, well, human, for what that's worth. I realized then that even reptiles and rodents share moments of communion with their offspring or owners. I still didn't trust him. But I realized as well that I didn't need to trust him, and I didn't need to hate him either, that sharing a few words on the elevator couldn't hurt, that maybe he would grow out of himself.

I was on my way down to the garage. Dickie got off at the lobby. He blushed again and offered a weak wave of his hand and said, "Bye."

"Goodbye, Dick," I heard myself say. He walked out with the dejected slouch of a child bound for school, of a young man bound for difficulty in life. He seemed to sense it now as keenly as I had over the years; he slouched under the burden of his thick, impenetrable self.

In his back pocket he carried a stainless steel sling shot, the professional Wrist Rocket model with a leather ammo sling, surgical tubing for maximum launch torque, a wrist brace for accuracy and, arcing over the hot spot through which the projectile would blaze, chromium cross hairs encircled. Now Dickie could fire a quarter ounce ball bearing with deadeye accuracy at the intake of a modern jet engine for instant implosion, a lovable mushroom cloud, some impressive statistics and really neat replays. I gave quiet thanks that I, too, was not Catholic or in education.

"Bye Leonard," he said, waving and shuffling past the doorman.

Work, for me, was unchanged. Not that I ever thought it would change. What changes in a library? The lunchtime reading series had begun by then with moderate success, especially on rainy days. It gives the local authors a chance to read their work in public as well as providing some higher contact for the street bums, now called the homeless. Far more summer programs were in service than when I started, and indexing was computerized.

I never considered mid-life crisis or its meaning but thought it mostly affected wealthy men, men of material comfort who doubted their lasting worth.

I'm not wealthy and don't doubt my contribution to a segment of society that contents itself with sitting quietly, reading. But I remember starting out three decades ago with rapture at the prospect of a career in books. It's the whole world close at hand, really. I thought a condo in such a good building assured my happiness.

But I found myself asking, is this it? I still surged with small triumphs like organizational strategies and reader incentives. But the blush went away, then the vigor. I never thought all was lost but couldn't say why it wasn't. The stacks gathered dust in reassuring accretion until I felt like part of the whole, dustable.

Maybe patterns in life are timed mercilessly to make you so sad that you become depressed. I felt fatigue with the smallest tasks and soon understood the blessing of death. No worries then. I understood it for myself but it took new meaning when Lanny died. I wanted to curl up beside her and go along with her, so empty was the space she left. Sure, Rex was a comfort. He compelled me to live if for no other reason than to pour another bowl of crunchies. He rubbed my leg as if pleading for her return and for solace.

Well, you know going in that a dog will die on you. You can damn near predict your age when it will happen. Rex stayed near after that, maybe hoping I would grow as a playmate. I knew another cat wasn't the answer. And another dog seemed, well, not quite right.

School days seemed surprisingly uneventful for Dickie and his family. He discovered fireworks and for weeks entertained himself with firecrackers and bottle rockets. I suspected the heavy artillery would roll any day, but I suspected as well that he'd learned about low profile. We shared the elevator from time to time in the awkward company of a truancy official or a priest obviously frustrated by life's relentless challenge. Dickie looked forlorn then. I smiled, not ruefully but in the spirit of amusement. Dickie was a sociological phenomenon seeking meaning and a place to fit in. He was our future, arrived.

In one volatile suspension and escort home, the yelling, accusation and denial filled the lobby and floated down the street. Dickie had been accused of the old prank of flushing cherry bombs down the toilet. Nobody haw hawed; the ancient plumbing was severely compromised, and a nun was nearly killed. Dickie denied everything, unsuccessfully. Two days later we met on the elevator.

It was the week Lanny died. I had carried her out and appreciated the condolences but really wanted privacy on the subject. I needed to reconcile my innate dislike for humans to the loss of my truest friend. I needed to sort things out and contemplate my future or lack thereof.

It was this relentless void that engaged me most of the time those days. Descending from nine to seven I wondered how a man could go so wrong, when the door opened and Dickie got on. I suppose it was all around the building by then; Lanny had been so visible, and I was so long in the face. At any rate, Dickie stood there mute and still. We remained silent until the doors closed and he said, "You might not believe me. But I loved Lanny. She wanted to take care of things."

Well, he took me aback. He left me speechless unlike he had in the past. He conveyed the most effective condolence to date on Lanny's passing. I struggled with composure from seven down to one and finally managed, "Thank you."

Dickie half-smiled and said, "Hang in there." He carried three red sticks in his hand, each with a six-ounce skyrocket on the end.

Escalation came as no surprise; where the boy of ten had opened fire with his pellet rifle on the street lights across the alley because they "kept everybody up at night," the adolescent went ground to air on the Live Five Weather Cam Helicopter, just because. He shrugged with no defense other than, "They fly right by our balcony."

I wondered if the same police officers answered this call as the last. They seemed older, weary and resigned. Dickie was fourteen and incorrigible. What could they do? Take him downtown? All three cops cast their eyes down, most likely hoping one of the other two would take initiative. Finally, one cop looked up and repeated the defense as if for credulity, "They fly right by your balcony?"

"Yeah. Guys looking in the windows, sneaking peeks at my mom getting out of the shower and stuff. Disturbing the peace. Using up fossil fuels. You know, look up, man, the sun is shining. Here comes these guys—Whop whop whop whop whop!... Right in our apartment. I just wanted to, you know, scare 'em back some."

The cops shook their heads in disbelief like wise men amazed. We stood in the lobby where they'd waited while Dickie and Sharon came down. I was on my way up but also waited, pretending to check my mail, fiddling with my key and the lock and the junk coupons, to see how law enforcement would handle the realized potential of little Dickie White. It was a rare moment, when the variables of life aligned just right for a soft *I told you so*, for a sweet vindication on the blind parent, who is the cause of the world's troubles today. But one look at Sharon White told you that she too, like Dickie and I, had always known.

Yet I knew as well that one good turn deserves another. I have no use for warm and fuzzy shibboleth, particularly where human behavior is concerned; let them do each other in and spare the world for nature. But I found myself speaking up. "He's right. I would have told you it was crazy to fire rockets on the Live Five Weather Cam Helicopter a few months ago. But not anymore. They don't need to come within twenty feet. Dickie keeps them on their toes. I've complained a dozen times. You can check their files. But what have they done? Nothing. And now here you are, because a twelve-year-old boy pulls a prank and it's effective."

Dickie twitched with a brief smile before looking down and saying, "I'm fourteen."

It was rhubarb, rhubarb, mumbo jumbo after that, the cops agreeing to agree on something and agreeing to see about something. Maybe they would write something up or write something down or go hide in an alley with a bag of donuts, fresh, hot, gooey goobers that would slide right down with some cheap, burned coffee. They left.

Sharon White said nothing, possibly suffering acute dejection on realizing that her cute little boy was prime candidate for *Tower-Sniper Magazine*'s Juvenile of the Year. She went up. I went back to sorting my mail, certain that if not for junk mail I'd get no mail at all. Dickie stood still as a post, waiting for me. When I came back to ride up, he got in with me and said he couldn't drive yet. But if I wanted to go for a really neat ride we could head out to Boom City where they have the best stuff.

I laughed to myself. A really neat ride? Dickie and me? Boom City? I'd pressed nine but he'd pressed nothing. He would follow me. So I pressed seven and he stepped halfway off, straddling the ledge between the seventh floor and the elevator, apparently comfortable to let the door bang him in the back, recede and bang him again and again. So I said, "Boom City?"

"Yeah. That's what they call it. It's an Indian reservation. They're the only ones allowed to sell the neat stuff. They got the little stuff too, but they got freaking dynamite sticks and mortar rounds!"

I wanted to say no thanks. I wanted to know what you could do with mortar rounds without a mortar, or dynamite without blasting caps. But you don't just pick up a rattler and shove him back in his box. You respect his potential; oh, yes, Dickie reached a milestone that day. He grew up to be the man I always knew he could be. "Let me think about it, okay?"

He shrugged. "Sure." He stepped sideways. The door closed, almost, until he thrust his fingers fearlessly into the last inch of opening. When it opened he said, "Thanks for...you know." I nodded.

It passed. I spent the next days and weeks anticipating Dickie at my door, wanting to know if I was ready to go, intimating what might happen if I refused. He'd never threatened verbally, but the boy was growing in leaps and bounds, figuratively speaking. Sharon was stiff and polite in passing. Charles grimaced and shook his head, as if confiding cognizance of the problem. Dickie came and went, looking down, once saying it was okay; he knew I didn't want to go with him. Then he just said hi.

The following September Dickie transferred to a public school for streetwise students. He still looked wider than he was tall but not exactly fat because of his immense barrel chest. He must have weighed two hundred pounds but was considered too short for football. This, I learned from Charles with a dash of regret; Dickie could have been an All Star. Yes, I wanted to tell him, and Ghengis Khan could have been a ballerina.

But he fit in, as far as I could tell, until he got on the elevator one day looking as bright and proud as the day I first saw him grab a fistful of salad. "You look like the cat who swallowed the canary," I said, he so rarely showed emotion. Maybe he reminded me of myself in that regard, however obliquely. He took it for an accusation. "It's a figure of speech, Dick. It means you look happy."

"Hm," he said, an expression I felt certain he'd used successfully at school. I didn't ask why he was happy but he beamed again and finally he said, "I got a pager." He twisted his tree stump of a body so I could see his pager in its holster on his belt.

I couldn't help myself. "Are you that difficult to reach? Or that much in demand?"

He shrugged, "You never know."

Armageddon

You never know. I thought of my tenure at the library as over thirty years but realized I was pushing thirty-seven. I'd rounded the clubhouse bend to forty. Most people can't imagine forty years in a library, but to me it played like one long day in study hall. I loved study hall.

Maybe life patterns itself as well to assuage the bitter knowing. This, for me, was it. But I didn't mind. With the world heading south on the express, the library remained an oasis, its cool air tingling with information rendering the world as the world should be.

Maybe life had eased into the stretch. I eased as well, perhaps allowing a glint to the jaundiced eye. I backed up to the kitchen wall to mark my height with a pencil and wrote my name and the date to measure my shrinkage. It wasn't so bad. Down a half-inch in a year. Who cared?

Soon I would be eye to eye with Dickie White. Sixteen now; God help us, he could drive. It seemed a milestone in the world's devolution to me, that such a one so thoroughly known as armed and dangerous would not be held responsible but would be licensed for a deadly weapon, which was his father's Oldsmobile. Maybe life's pattern is a mosaic of comedies and tragedies to make you laugh to keep from crying. Diminishing stature, danger on the roads and a shuffling gate. Who cared?

The latter resulted from chronic sciatica, from nearly forty years of service on my feet. Pain was not my friend but by then was a constant boarder. I'd read that muggers are like all predators; they seek the weak and wounded, the dead and dying. They avoid the counter strike. You become aware of these things but still feel secure in your own garage with two security controls for parking level access. Still, so many luxury sedans and fancy roadsters lure them through the net like fresh chum.

So? It happens, I thought. Give them the wallet, its replaceable cards and the measly few bucks. Give the watch and the ring, because sentiment too, is a frail, human attachment. So why would they kick me in the ass? Truth be told, I think they eased the sciatica past its difficult inch toward resolution. I did not ask that they do that again, for they and I were taken just then by an odd plaint from the shadowy corner. "Daddy? Oh, Daddy, no!" Dickie struggled into the light with his eyes puffed. He drooled and gasped and carried on like a wounded duck with mild retardation.

The two muggers were about his age, and I knew, forgive me, that he was one of them. Yet we know so little of the truth in its evolution. One boy pulled me up and then hooked my arm and from behind grabbed my chin and jerked me into an arch. He made me whimper with a sound painfully similar to that of an old man going under. The other boy wielded an odd-shaped knife with a large, hooked blade. He slashed it at eye level at Dickie, who hung his head and sobbed, shuffling near with a hobble resembling my own, into slash radius until looking up, voicing a high-pitched, "Beep! Beep! Beep! Beep! Beep!"

They thought him demented and maybe marginally dangerous but hardly a threat. Woe unto them. For Dickie perked up, announcing, "It's my pager! Somebody called me up!" Unhinging the device at this belt, he flipped it up as if to read the dial. Tweaking a tiny control he held it out—"Here. You take a look!" The mugger with the knife glanced down. Dickie ducked and thrust like a swordsman as if to poke him with the pager, a move so meager that the mugger chortled; what a nut—until Dickie paged him with the same forty thousand volts I once prescribed for an incorrigibly evil little boy.

Stun gun. The mugger twitched with short circuitry and went horizontal to the garage floor.

Dickie gasped honestly now with the fulsome blush of a hunter taking game. The accomplice turned to go, but a hooked arm becomes an arm hooked. I held him while Dickie moved in deftly for the two-bagger. Good thing, as I approached respiratory failure.

Dickie put a foot on the big one's chest and beat his own chest, beaming insanely. The only thing better could be three.

Who cared? I shuffled to the nearest wall, leaned back as if for a baseline from which to measure shrinkage, and I shrank, as it were, surrendering to the vicissitudes of old age and a mugging. Dickie frisked the bad boys casually. "Kubuona renegade knife. Big deal. These guys. Boy." He retrieved my things and a few things for himself, like the knife and some brass knuckles he identified as a Beijing paperweight, the real item; now that was a score. He came over and sat beside me to inventory the spoils.

"That was fun." I would have argued but could not. "I wasn't following you. I hang out down here sometimes." I doubted him, couldn't help it. "I could still go either way, you know. But you're my friend. You took up for me. Remember?"

I nodded. I remembered. I examined his stun gun. "Dickie? This thing says three hundred thousand volts."

"Yeah. If you want to kill. I find forty thou leaves you with enough ammo for the next guy, and really, they twitch better on low voltage."

"You find?"

"Yeah," he laughed on reflection, catching my amazement at a teenage boy researching the effects of voltage. "How else you gonna know?"

Dickie and Me

They don't exactly put you out to pasture from the library, but they cut your hours way back. I have more time now. Dickie lost his driver's license. He didn't misplace it but had it revoked after a high-speed chase, after tailgating a patrol car until it flashed its light and signaled a pull over. That's when Dickie pulled out and fled. He laughed in the retelling, pointing out that it's okay for them to tailgate you, but you try it on them and see what happens.

I don't exactly drive him around now. But we cruised to Boom City last week. We also visited a place called The Supply Depot that specializes in modern military hardware. Dickie gets very excited over ordnance and weaponry. His birthday is coming up. He claims eighteen and calls it old. I laugh. He says I would buy wine for him anyway, so who in their right mind would want to be eighteen? It's a harsh birthday that marks a man as nothing but eligible to be tried as an adult these days. Then again, he says, they're televising prosecution on the frigging fourteen-year-olds. So what's the diff?

I can only sympathize for a world of growing demands. I got him books for his birthday, because a young man who reads will better understand the world. They weren't my idea; he left the catalogue open with his choices circled. He wanted *Home Workshop Silencers*, *The Anarchist Handbook* and my favorite, *Improvised Home-Built Recoilless Launchers*. These kids.

We're friends now, Dickie and me. He's excited about finishing school and making his mark. I don't press for specifics, but then no one second-guessed Attilla the

Hun, either. I enjoy our friendship, for Dickie in his way empowers me. I am only a man who spent his prime in the library and chanced upon an arsenal. He's a regular sidewinder with stealth capacity, a nuclear warhead with tomahawk inclination and tomcat dexterity, and he's practically mine to aim and squeeze the trigger.

I took him to a place where a radical environmental group screens prospective members. How did I find such a place? At the library, of course.

Dickie passed muster and met a girl. She wears earrings in her nose and her ears and, he tells me, on one of her nipples. She tells me the earrings are cold in winter, but she likes them, especially the one in her nipple. It reminds her that she's a woman. All the girls in the group call themselves women and love the reminders. Dolores, Dickie's woman, asked if I'd like to be "fixed up." She says sex with someone twenty years older or younger is a rage, and since men under five are usually disgusted by the notion, men like me are a find. I told her I was overqualified. She said wow. I'm keeping an open mind. I had a woman once.

Dolores is stocky like Dickie but feminine in her way, if you look past the body-piercing, tattoos and axillary hair. She's affectionate by nature, like Dickie, with the same passive aggressiveness. I think they're a match. They don't go steady the way we used to do, but he says they'll be tight for awhile.

Dickie and Dolores and I worked through his animal abuse. It was unfortunate, an evil component of modern boyhood, but now he sees. He's fond of the radicals; they do so much "neat stuff," like processing personal problems together and disabling heavy equipment, sabotaging dams, taking out high-power stanchions, moving survey markers, spiking trees, defacing billboards and much, much more. He has a sense of belonging now, not to mention purpose.

I no longer sense sanity at any level, public or private, but I adapt every day. Call it a mystical connection reserved for the lucky few who grow old.

I'm on the research committee. We visit the forests frequently to feel what we strive for. I find snug harbor there in the quiet, rain or shine. I can read or sketch a tree while looking out, while Dickie plays with his friends. They gave me a whistle to blow. They say I'm perfect. I don't feel perfect but like to hear them say it. These kids today; they do know how to make an old man feel good.

Between 8s & 9s

Not in their dreams had Lillian or Pauline planned on a career in catering. With five children between them, nine grandchildren and eight great-grands, they had no plan at all. Career shmareer; who needs plans to relax and wonder what in the world a body might want for lunch?

If you live long enough life goes as it's meant to be, and they agreed: it was high time to relax after what they'd endured, with the divorces and nasty lawyers and one thing and another. "Don't get me started," Lillian said.

"Please. Don't start," Pauline complied. "But you know what I still can't believe?"

Well Lillian knew what Pauline couldn't believe. Whether the heartlessness of husband number one, the dullness of number two or the unfathomable gall of number three, Lillian knew of Pauline's disbelief, down to dialogue and historical coordinates. "You know what he said to me?" Pauline often asked. Lillian knew chapter and verse who said what to whom and the dire fallout of those unfortunate syllables. But Lillian waited patiently to hear again what he said. That's what friends are for, to a point, at which she seized the baton, because a relay takes more than one runner.

"You think that's something?" Lillian grabbed it and tucked it away just as Pauline paused to sigh and reflect. Something? What? What something? But she was off, Lillian, with, "Do you know what Helen Ginsberg had the nerve to tell me at Rose Paulson's funeral? No, no, not Rose Paulson. Ha! She's not gone yet. Rose Scheffler. Rose *Scheffler's* funeral. Do you know what she had the nerve to say to me?"

And so it was Pauline's turn to wait and listen, sharing momentum to mid-morning.

They talked on the telephone or face to face, since they lived only two doors apart, twenty paces down the posh hallway. It was carpeted and climate-controlled, third floor, which was the top floor, which was how it should be, finally, after what they'd been through. Still, the phone was best for convenience, and it allowed each to choose the channel on her own TV and watch from the kitchen table with no argument over the news, the stock market report or *Talk Back Flora.*

Flora also endured as the morning rage for senior women, but the market report could not be missed. Besides, where did Flora get off with her saccharine sweetness and dumb comments? Flora could not and should not eat fruit straight from the icebox because it hurt her teeth. "Who the hell cares?" Pauline wanted to know.

"Nobody," Lillian assured her.

If not the market report, the news was best for drama and real life, what Pauline and Lillian knew about best. If a crash, flood, fire, earthquake, tidal wave, disease, despair, general agony, sexual scandal or special bulletin would interrupt this program, Lillian would say, "I'll call you right back. Channel 5." They would hang up. Pauline would tune into Channel 5, and minutes later they would commiserate over tragedy and anguish, remembering when and assessing guilt, make-up and color coordination of the TV women.

Pauline might ask, "Do you have Montel Tech?" Lillian had three thousand shares of Montel. Pauline knew this. So why the question? Because it was up 3¾ in the last two hours, which made Lillian ten thousand dollars more secure before sunrise. Not that ten grand went too far with the cost of geriatric care these days, which (say a little prayer) neither needed yet, but you never knew.

Lillian changed the subject and hoped Pauline understood that lunch would still be Dutch, because what goes easily up can sink to the bottom of the ocean just as quickly. She moved adroitly to Edgar Ferman, gone four years now, who counseled Montel Tech not thirty days before passing on. Edgar Ferman had known the score; it was a racket. The commissions could kill you. You could lose it all in your sleep. But what could you do with interest at five percent?

By ten they discussed lunch and at ten thirty met in the garage. They took turns driving.

Both Pauline and Lillian could still drive during the day. They had their mobility and each other. And they understood the rarity of friendship at any age, much less the prospects at their age. Pauline said, "When they go, they're gone. And I mean gone." Lillian laughed short. Pauline nodded.

The problem was, many places don't open until eleven thirty, which is too late if you're up since four. The early morning hours are the best of the day, they agreed, though both wanted to sleep longer. They could not. It happens when you age. So? What can you do? You get up and make the best of it. Besides, Louis Rukeyser was replayed at five from the night before. Pauline said, "He is a doll." She served decaf and chocolate chip cookies fresh from the oven.

"And so smart," Lillian agreed. They agreed that he would not be kicked out of bed, but the real catch would be

Merlon Melborne, former crooner, current promo man for the all new Chrysler Mendoza. "He's a doll," Lillian said.

"Oh, yes," Pauline concurred. This, as Pauline's son, Harold the lawyer, stopped by on his way in, to see his mother and pick up some chocolate chip cookies. He should eat them in good health, never mind the fat; fat shmat, he would ride his bicycle a little farther.

Harold said, "Merlon Melborne? He's older than you are."

"Not so old," Pauline said. "Just you wait."

"That's right," Lillian said. "You get to be our age, ten years is nothing." Harold said ten years was nothing at his age. "You wait," Lillian said.

Pauline said to finish the cookies and return the tin for more. Harold explained on his way out that if cookies weren't rationed at his age his suits would shrink. And he left. "I swear," Lillian said. "These kids. In and out."

Pauline nodded. "Not ten minutes for his mother. Well, he's busy."

"What kind of a lawyer is Harold now?" Lillian asked.

Pauline shrugged. "How should I know? Criminals, I guess." She scrubbed the last pan. "I tell him: as long as they pay."

Lillian picked up the remote and thrust it toward the TV as she pushed the little button to restore the sound. Pauline shook her head, so many times had Lillian been told that the remote control need not be thrust at the TV. Some things Lillian simply could not accept.

Never mind; Flora proceeded to make a perfect fool of herself in a chiffon dress, calling out, "Hell-oh-oh…" Can you imagine? Chiffon? It was too much, especially with her matching chiffon manners. It was plain to see that Flora would shrink to a big fat zero if she hadn't been seen leaving the Brentwood home of Hollywood Producer

Lawrence Sniffen at *seven a.m.!* The scandal occurred three days ago. Flora denied everything with the simply transparent statement, “We’re friends.”

“Yeah,” Lillian said, “Friends who like a little schtupping.”

“What does anyone see in her?” Pauline said.

“He’s ten years younger,” Lillian said.

“Lawrence Sniffen? Who’s he?”

“Some Hollywood bigshot. A nobody is who.”

“Do you think she did?”

“What’s she got to lose?”

“Not a damn thing. Look at her. What a mess. Between eights and nines. And at her age.”

“Ridiculous. And they put it on TV. That’s what I can’t see.”

“Who needs it?”

And so it went with difficulty, an hour ahead of schedule so the cookies would be ready for Harold’s arrival. So Lillian went back to her place for awhile. Pauline went to the sofa to read for awhile, maybe to doze for awhile. It was only seven thirty; the lunch places wouldn’t open for another four hours. And let’s face it, you still couldn’t get anywhere near as good as you got at home. Then again, who wants to stay home all the time? No, it’s good to get out.

* * *

Well, things were going every bit as well as either Pauline or Lillian could hope for, but every now and then, maybe once a day, time weighed heavily. How much TV can you watch? How many books can you read? It wasn’t so bad. If you get up at four, a little mid-morning snooze can’t hurt you. And before you know it, something comes up to fill the time. Like Stephanie’s graduation party. She would have a few friends over for cocktails. "So grown up," Pauline said.

"These kids," Lillian said, tucking the baton under her arm for a canter down the road of amazing greatness. She touched on Stephanie's nearly perfect grades, her emergent beauty and darling figure, her success with boys and her brilliant future, and Stephanie didn't forget her grandmother. "I can't stand to see her like this," Lillian said. Pauline understood. "To the last minute she waits to ask for help with her party. Between eights and nines."

"She's a sweet girl," Pauline said, snatching the baton so they could proceed. Chocolate chip cookies were obvious. Lillian thought it best to ask, since the emphasis was on cocktails. "Just you wait," Pauline said, confident that a platter of chocolate chip cookies would vanish quicker than a piglet in piranhas. Lillian arched her eyebrows in exasperation. She simply couldn't argue with Pauline. She, Lillian, would make her famous mints.

Pauline suggested little gefilte fish balls but Lillian laughed and said, "Are you kidding?" Pauline laughed too. What a joke; gefilte fish for kids. They were good, the fish balls. But still. Pauline suggested meatballs. Lillian concurred. They were on track. It was Thursday. Stephanie called last night. The party would be tomorrow night.

They shook their heads; these kids, as if you could wave a magic wand and have a party planned and prepared just like that. What did they think, that the shopping and baking and the back and the forth happened automatically? Well, of course they did, and it did with two women from the front ranks of the doers. And what a party it would be. Pauline said it could be better yet if the cards were shuffled right. Lillian asked what, from cards? But she knew. Pauline itched for knishes, for kreplach with meat or spinach or cottage cheese, for blintzes with ricotta. Hold the sour cream if you must, but don't forget the noodle kugel with raisins and cinnamon, the herring, the lox spread and yes, gefilte fish balls with cold, sliced carrots and horseradish. Sheer flavor filled the pall. They knew; neither man nor kid can live by cookies, meatballs and mints alone.

"And oy," Lillian drifted. "The pastrami, just a taste, unless you don't mind ruining your dinner. You know I can't eat that stuff every day. But every once in awhile..."

"Come on," Pauline said. "We have to hurry." Lillian understood, and they were off, flush with purpose, and it was only six a.m. Plontken's Delicatessen opened at six, Flotzle's Bakery opened at seven and Schultz's Supermarket opened at eight. "It couldn't be more perfect," Pauline said. Lillian agreed; lunch shmunch. Who needs it?

A little fresh air, a drive down the road, perfect timing with just enough pressure to hurry things along, and next thing you know ideas are sprouting like spore growth on a rotting log. Well, why not pastrami? These kids most likely never even tasted it. So why not? So they would. They would prepare little hot pastrami club sandwiches in keeping with the theme of the event, so grown up.

The knishes could possibly be finessed as crepes but maybe not, but who would care once they took a taste? And how much more grown up can you get than the best flavor to survive these last five thousand seven hundred sixty-one years? Lillian said knishes must have been developed in that very first year, they were so simple. Oh, but the work, but what else do you have to do? And the kreplach, they agreed, could pass for dumplings if pressed—the issue, not the kreplach. Let them eat one bite. Then they could ask.

As for baked goods, who had time to do it right? They had no choice but to buy, so they indulged in loaves of tiny pumpernickel and rye and miniature bagels with poppy seeds and onion.

Forget the paradise coffeecake, Pauline said. It would only go stale, trying to compete with her cookies. Lillian picked up a couple anyway, because some of them, the kids, couldn't eat chocolate.

"Can't eat chocolate?" Pauline asked. Whoever heard of such a thing? But Lillian was on to the fresh produce, so she couldn't hear, giving the bone of contention a decent burial.

The next night everyone agreed; you wanted to simply stare at it. In fact, you could cringe at the thought of disturbing such a delectable landscape. Lillian nearly swatted the grubby fellow who snatched a gefilte fish ball with his hands, which, if you asked her, *he didn't even wash(!)*. Too late; the ragamuffin gobbled it with no more reflection on the labor of love than if he gorged on donut holes. Then he had the nerve to ask, "What was that?" As if *that* wasn't the best thing he ever tasted. Well, at least the kids didn't stand on ceremony once the ice was broken. Chowing down, instructing each other on correct pronunciations of things they never heard of, they mumbled awesome, yum and gnarly.

Pauline and Lillian watched. Stephanie's friends ate and praised her grandmother's cooking. "And her grandmother's friend," Lillian corrected. "This is Pauline."

And Pauline, the graduates agreed. The afterglow held for a week, and so did the talk, especially between Pauline and Lillian, who reviewed dishes, arrangement and reaction over and over again.

Rehash ended on two rings; Terry Kotzwinkle's mother called to say that Terry was still praising the buffet at Stephanie's party. Lillian blushed; Pauline watched with concern. Terry Kotzwinkle's mother Myrna didn't want to impose, she said, but could Stephanie's grandmother and her friend Pauline cater a small event for Terry's younger brother Mark, a bar mitzvah only three weeks away?

Lillian shook her head. "Oh, I don't… I don't…"

"It's a small reception," Myrna Kotzwinkle said. "About thirty people. Stephanie had twenty-two. Plontken's wants eighteen dollars a head, which I don't mind, but now they can't take me, after they promised! I'm in a fix and I'd rather spend the money with you anyway. Because, frankly, I think they're, well, you know."

"Mm. Yes. We know." She wrote *18 x 30?* on a piece of scratch paper. Pauline did the math while Lillian said she just didn't know, because she and her friend Pauline never really considered a catering *bus*iness.

"Well, you should," Myrna Kotzwinkle said, insisting on no pressure, giving her phone number and asking for a call back—"this afternoon if that's okay."

"Five hundred and forty dollars," Pauline said when Lillian hung up and repeated her exchange with Myrna Kotzwinkle, and over another cup of decaf, Lillian said the decision was not theirs to make. Pauline agreed, as if it was God's choice. What else could they do? What else could Terry Kotzwinkle's mother do?

Well, one thing led, as they say, to another. The Kotzwinkle bar mitzvah reception was still a week away when Betty Messler called in a dither; how in the world could she have known that Bill's mother would get so sick two weeks before Leslie's engagement party? She never in her life needed a caterer, but she did now, please, because it would hardly be more than fifty people. Betty Messler assumed that catering services were available and said she knew perfectly well that Myrna Kotzwinkle was paying eighteen dollars a person, but frankly she, Betty, thought that was too high. Was there any way the price could come down, considering the bigger crowd?

Lillian said, “Hold the wire, please.” She cupped the phone and debriefed for Pauline, who smiled and took the phone and asked Betty Messler,

“You want us to shop *and* prepare?”

“Well, of course. I don’t have time to… Bill’s mother is running a hundred and one!”

“It’s eighteen dollars a head. I’m sorry. The only way we can lower the price is if someone else does the shopping, which includes the parking, the schlepping, the here and the there if something doesn’t look so good. You know. Then it’s sixteen dollars a head, and hey, it’s like found money. A hundred dollars in your case.”

“No. You do the shopping,” Betty Messler said. “I’m sure it’ll be fine.” Pauline wrote down the date and phone number and said she would call to review the menu once the deposit was received. Three hundred ought to do it.

Lillian beamed, to think her partner was such an operator. Pauline said, “It’s a pain in the neck for someone who doesn’t love it. But getting paid? Us?” They laughed.

“Isn’t that the way it goes?” Lillian said and suggested they take a few minutes to write down their schedule of services so a woman could determine what level of service she might need. That way they could avoid the quibbling. Yet each knew that you never avoid the quibbling. Well, that was all right too, if you knew how to quibble.

Two weeks after the Kotzwinkle bar mitzvah and a week after the Messler engagement party, Lillian and Pauline were booked solid for the following month. A baby shower, two more bar mitzvahs, a general entertainment in the home of a very important man, another engagement and an actual wedding.

Word got around. Pauline said it made her dizzy, not really, but you know. It reminded her of those movies where the washed-up prize fighter starts knocking men out, or the swayback nag starts winning races, or the underdogs start winning games, or the aging alcoholic starts pitching no-hitters or hitting home runs.

"We're not washed up," Lillian said. "Or swayback or alcoholic or any of those things."

"That's not what I meant," Pauline laughed. "It's like when they show the newspapers rolling off the presses with glorious headlines."

"What?" Lillian asked. "Old Girls Cater Big Time?"

"Yes," Pauline said. "That'll do."

But idle fantasy would have to wait, and though the two friends agreed to take regular days off, both rose to accelerating demand because they couldn't help it. One such "afternoon off" provided time to refine their identity and their services. They had evolved by circumstance as a short-notice catering service for spur-of-the-moment gatherings, or for events befallen unexpectedly by need.

Lillian felt strongly that they needed a mission statement. Pauline felt uncomfortable with that word, mission. Lillian conceded that a mission statement might indeed give the appearance of converting suburban natives in order to gain access to their resources. "Okay," Lillian said. "No mission statement. But we do need a name."

"Name shname," Pauline said. "I only know we're wasting time. We have to hurry."

Lillian assured her that a few minutes here would save hours in the long run. "A company must have a name."

"We're not a company. We're simply *famisht*, putting things together. Between eights and nines."

"That's it," Lillian said, writing it down.

"Wha? *Simply Famisht*?"

"No. *Between 8s & 9s.*"

They further reviewed inventory requirements for the short term and the long term. Services should be quantified,

Lillian felt. Clientele should be able to order a level of grandeur from the marginal Schnapps 'n Herring to the moderate So Maybe it's a Little Soup You Want on up to The Whole Megillah. Top drawer catering would include something you simply cannot get, unless someone makes it for you, like, well, like any of those things you actually can get but everyone knows they're shlock. Like matzo ball soup or borscht or schav. Who ever heard of getting the real item from a jar?

The phone rang. Lillian answered, "8s & 9s. Can I help you?" Sure enough, one Rose Kretchmer was leaving town with her husband for a vacation and needed to entertain a small group immediately on her return a week from Tuesday. Just like that, nearly eight hundred dollars.

It rang again. Pauline picked it up. It was her phone, after all, not that she minded Lillian answering, but she wanted to feel the big money roll in for herself. Alas, Alan Plontken on the line expressed his appreciation for their patronage all these years. Moreover, he was elated to hear of the new catering venture's success and wanted to wish Pauline and Lillian all the luck in the world. But he wasn't knocking himself out by spending tens of thousands of dollars to keep his operation in health department compliance for nothing. Because commercial catering means playing by the rules. That means zoning, inspections and, oy, commercial equipment.

Pauline knew from having a son like Harold the lawyer to say, "Thank you very much." Then she hung up and with trembling hands dialed her son, Harold the lawyer. Lillian joined the tremble, listening to Pauline spell it out.

Harold counseled no worries. He would research things a bit, but in the meantime, say nothing to anyone.

"To whom am I going to say something?" Pauline asked, but Harold was already off the line. Well, nothing changed, except that intangible, dreamy air of success, that giddy excitement that anticipates perfection at last. You want to give in to your heart's desire, that time in the sun has come. Hey, life was plenty sunny before. Pauline and Lillian were loved as mothers and grandmothers and great grandmothers. But here suddenly and with equal merit, they ascended as angels of service and salvation; we deliver.

Rarely in the collective experience of all the condominia and adjacent suburbs for miles around had anyone met two better harbingers of redemption. Nicknames abounded, like *P and L* or *Team Delicious* or *The Last Best Hope*. Pauline and Lillian had acquired a taste for the sporting glory.

Yet they stared and stewed. "One bad apple," Lillian said. Pauline nodded. Imperfection cast a shadow. Alan Plontken was so affectionate and well-wishing and miserly and petty that you had to wonder what made his clock tick. "The miserable sonofabitch," Lillian said.

Pauline nodded. "As if he could have taken the jobs at all, much less delivered the goods. He has a heart condition you know."

"No."

"Yes. And *she's* one step from you-know-where. They should be grateful."

"Hmm."

"Mm hm." And there was nothing more to be said, for considerable crowds waited in the near future with growing appetite and expectation. "We have to hurry," Pauline said. But of course Lillian knew that.

* * *

Much later that day Harold called. "So quick," Lillian said. "Your son the lawyer it pays to have in the family."

"Psh," Pauline said, "Ten hours already. His own mother he treats like another client."

But Harold was thorough, concise and confident. He advised changing nothing. Leave the burden of initiative on Alan Plontken or whoever wanted to quash fair competition. 8s & 9s was not preparing food for sale but was merely repackaging and delivering as a service.

Pauline corrected him; the gefilte fish was cooked. "Do you think you can call it homemade and charge these kinds of prices for taking it out of a jar and putting it in a bowl? Phooey. It's all cooked, Alan. What do you think…"

"Pauline," Alan intoned smoothly as a successful lawyer who might one day provide analysis on TV. "You are possibly one of the best cooks in the world." That shut her up. "Leave this recipe to me. Alan Plontken will spend fifty thousand dollars proving me wrong. By that time he'll have other distractions, and you'll be so big you'll *need* the room at the old library that's already plumbed and wired as a commercial kitchen and is managed by someone who owes me a very big favor. This room may be available at just the right time for seventy cents a foot! Case dismissed, your Honor. Oh, justice be not proud."

"My son the lawyer. Seventy cents for each foot?"

"Pauline. It's a steal."

"How many feet?"

"Just enough."

"Well. If you say so…"

"I say so. Here's my fee: I need a huge favor."

"For the fellow with the room?"

"No. For a fellow in a position to back me up on a… Well, on a very important case. He did a pro bono defense for a woman and lost. He's very capable, but losing pro bono carries the stigma of, you know, inadequate effort. But he tried. Now his client, the woman who lost, has a request that I normally wouldn't ask you to do, but in this particular situation…"

"What? You want me to cook for her? For one woman?"

"Her last meal."

"Last? Who knows what meal will be her last?"

"She does. She's on a tight schedule."

"Vayizmere!"

"What?" Lillian could wait no more. "What?"

"He wants us to cook for a…a… a woman."

"So? We'll cook." Lillian pulled out the calendar to check for openings.

"She's heard of you," Harold said. "I'm telling you, I thought you were great. I thought you were celebrities. But in the state penitentiary? On death row? Pauline. You're a major motion picture. October tenth. Ninish. She wants the full buffet, the one with the gefilte fish and little pastrami sandwiches. Can you believe it?"

Pauline could not believe it, not that she was a celebrity or that her name had been spoken on death row or that she was wanted there, or that she would cook for a…a… a what? A murderer?

Alan Plontken shrank instantly to proper size in the greater scheme of things. Reverie changed complexion as a mosquito buzzing in your ear might suddenly transform to a California condor. Lillian spoke first. "You know, it's not so easy cooking for one person."

"No. And what are you going to do with the leftovers? Bring them home?"

"Well, I'm sure the others…" Lillian stopped short, realizing the others would be murderers, rapists and the worst kind of con men, or women.

"Mm!" Pauline understood.

"What if they…don't like it?"

"Don't even think such a thing."

"They'll be in their cages, won't they?"

"How should I know?" Pauline asked, and they stared at the grim prospect of The Whole Megillah being sampled by women of violence, women who would ask, *What is this?,* women in striped suits who knew about revenge.

* * *

The condemned woman, Ruby Marlette, didn't seem in the least like a bad person to Pauline. Open and warm, she said she understood how "creepy" it must be to cater a meal on death row, but the girls there had so little to look forward to that a festive occasion with good things to eat might help balance out the other.

The word from the warden on a social gathering of all the girls was a big fat no. "We're not running a tea party here," he said, but Ruby was optimistic the girls would be allowed the leftovers. Ruby then said she had some money and didn't want to check out as a charity case. She had nothing to save it for and no one to leave it to, so, if it was all the same to Miss Pauline and her friend, Miss Lillian, she'd like to pay.

Pauline said it would be good to have the event paid for, but the money ought to go to a charity, maybe the charity of Ruby's choice. Ruby said that was a good idea, except that she'd received no charity in her life. Maybe that's why she ended up here. And though she'd found the Lord, ("Oy.") she wasn't motivated to give to a society that gave her so little. Truly, she realized that her few dollars could well represent the turning point for a person such as herself, but if you believe that a few dollars could turn anything in this world you might as well spend them on lottery tickets. "And that's the way it falls," Ruby said. "I can't help how I feel."

"Well," Pauline said. "There's always the Humane Society."

Ruby brightened. "You're a smart woman, Miss Pauline. And a good Christian besides. There's really so few of them, you know."

"Well, I'm not, actually. I'm…"

"Oh, yes you are. Don'chou go argue with me now. I know what I see when I'm looking right at it."

In fact, arguing with Ruby Marlette was near the top of Pauline's list of things to avoid, so she smiled in the spirit of good Christianity. She agreed as well to charge Ruby every last cent, so the lost dogs would get the money instead of the bastards who ran the prison.

"And the cats, too," Ruby reflected. "Yeah. I like them. The little ones and the grown-up ones, too."

Pauline nodded and proceeded with the menu, touching ever so delicately on the vicissitudes of taste, texture and possible difficulty with those items on the menu a girl like Ruby may not have grown up with.

"Oh, no. Don'chou worry about that. I don't have much more time for growing up, and I'll have less even then. I mean, look, Miss Pauline. What would taste right at a time like that? I think something you and your friend Miss Lillian are famous for—something I might never in my life would have tried otherwise will be perfect."

Later that afternoon, Pauline related to Lillian that Ruby Marlette was so disarming and engaging, that you forgot where you were and what she'd done. Lillian couldn't go because she simply could not. Ruby Marlette had first killed her third husband and understood why she was where she was and the consequence of returning to Albuquerque to track down and kill her second husband, who hadn't beat her like the third one, but he'd pushed her around. "He was a sniveling, no-count bastard," as well, she said. "He deserved it."

"But," Pauline queried. "You married him."

"Yeah. He was a unbelievable screw—" Ruby touched Pauline's arm. "I hope you don't mind. That's the way I talk. I feel like we're friends already. That's important to me, so I'd just as soon not be on my good behavior, if you know what I mean."

"It's all right," Pauline said. "You're not the first girl to make a foolish mistake."

"Oh, I know that. But the thing of it is, Pauline. I mostly hate not making it over to Miami to get that other bastard. The first one. He never beat me up or pushed me around. But he was the worst screw you ever had, and he was so damn… Oh, hell, you know what I mean?"

"I think I do," Pauline said, wondering what makes some women wish their husbands would die, and some don't hesitate to help things along. But this Ruby Marlette had a screw loose herself, to say the least. Already rid of the husbands, she went back! Pauline had fantasized as well, but actually killing the bastards? "You know, I had three myself," Pauline said.

Ruby smiled. "I know you didn't kill 'em. Did you?"

Pauline shook her head. "Divorced two. Outlived one."

Ruby nodded, "Bastards. I just hope Jesus forgives me for hating them like I do. 'Course now I'm easier on the hate. Two of 'em's dead. Ain't so bad when they're dead."

Pauline wagged her head as if to say it could still be bad after they were dead. Then she said she really had to go. She said she'd enjoyed their meeting, and unless she heard otherwise, it would be dinner at nine on the tenth for fourteen women at eighteen dollars a head.

"I got twelve hundred dollars," Ruby said. "Whatever that makes it. Figure it out. And pull out the stops for the girls. They deserve it, no matter what anyone says."

Pauline assured her the stops would be pulled. She drove home assuring herself that nobody gets too old to view dimensions undreamed of. She assured Lillian that the show would go on, and that she, Lillian, would participate.

Lillian promised to try. She sounded shaky, maybe queasy, but Pauline pressed onward. Sharing down the middle was their agreement, tacit and otherwise.

It was time to go, and go they must. And just as a seasick woman sets the bilious symptoms aside for a critical task, so Lillian performed.

The warden would not allow all fourteen women on death row to convene for dinner, not for a sit-down or an informal buffet. He relented in the end, agreeing to distribute the leftover edibles to the other inmates and to those guards designated by Ruby Marlette.

In the following days and weeks, Lillian and Pauline would condone the warden's political expedience, avoiding commotion and keeping the media dogs at bay with this ounce of flexibility. They would further agree on Ruby's astute inclusion of certain guards to minimize scrutiny and stirring of the delectable dishes. The chosen guards and other inmates attempted good cheer and casual atmosphere, even levity over them gofilter fish who gave their balls for the occasion.

Not everyone was joking; some slid the little spheres back to hind molars for the slow crush and savor.

Ruby Marlette alone was allowed wine, and she mostly drank, watching her inmates in destiny enjoy a brief reprieve. She tasted everything, some things quickly and some things slowly. She winced at the herring in cream sauce but called the pastrami dee-licious and sorely wished she'd known about it before now. The others laughed and asked for more pastrami. Lillian apologized for its being cold, but the Sterno warmers weren't allowed past the first cage door—"I mean cell door."

The others laughed again and told her she got it right the first time. Pauline followed up with two kinds of mustard, sweet and hot 'n spicy. Both got dolloped in equal measure with comments on sweetness, heat and spice. A pall ensued when all the women ate their pastrami clubs—clubs much thicker than usual because Pauline piled it on to compensate the grim reality. They weren't clubs at all when she was done but were the most memorable sandwiches she'd prepared, so fat they practically required unhinged jaws. Ruby watched, drank her wine and smiled sadly.

"You know, you really shouldn't eat this stuff too often," Pauline said. "But every once in a while..." Ruby laughed and assured Pauline that the girls would wait a long time before their next pastrami sandwiches.

"That ain't true," called a woman down the row, explaining that she was next, only four months away, and pastrami was already on the menu.

Lillian looked troubled. Pauline said, "Oh, who cares? It makes you feel good."

And so the buffet dwindled. In awhile Ruby Marlette asked Pauline if she would mind hanging around for, well, you know. Pauline blushed but couldn't refuse. She hung around; it was only another hour or so. Lillian had to go.

* * *

Pauline said later that she felt terrible for having nothing to say, nothing at all of comfort or consolation. Ruby allowed a clergyman in, but only for the Lord's prayer before telling him, "You can go now, please."

Then she touched Pauline on the arm and said, "I can tell this makes you uncomfortable, Miss Pauline. But you don't have to say a word. Just you being here makes this a whole sight easier for me. It's not just that you're old and maybe lived the life I never will. It's like I told you the first time I met you. I see what you got in you. I want some of that by my side, if you don't mind. I'm sorry you're uncomfortable, but honey, I am uncomfortable too. I don't know what happens after, but I swear I'll look after you if I can."

Pauline laughed nervously and said that Ruby really shouldn't worry about her, because her son, Harold the lawyer, looked after her, and she hadn't done too badly looking after herself. Ruby insisted it would be no worry. "For one thing, dead people don't have no worries. For another, if you don't mind, I might enjoy, you know, taking care of someone for a change. Shoot, we all got to die. I know that. Someone like you knows that. I might, you know, ease you along in your sleep or something."

Pauline couldn't help looking worried then and nearly said she had to go. But she stayed. She couldn't watch, even though it was only a lethal injection.

* * *

"But she really was a nice girl. Once you got to know her." Lillian agreed politely, assuring Pauline that 8s and 9s were one thing and death row was quite another. She, Lillian, would not return, no matter how critical the request. She simply could not. Pauline understood. In a minute Lillian conceded a strange gratification derived from the experience, her utter fear notwithstanding. "They seemed...cheerful. On death row. I guess they have to be that way."

"We're all on death row," Pauline said.

"We're not on death row," Lillian said. "We can come and go and do as we please."

"I know," Pauline said. "They just reminded me of, well, you know."

"I don't know anything of the kind and I don't want to talk about it anymore." Lillian sat erect; so there. Then she eased back into casual comfort. "Pauline, it was a wonderful thing you did, just being there for someone like Ruby Marlette." Pauline expressed her sense of helplessness but Lillian poo pooed.

They stared and sipped another cup of decaf, inured to the mounting pressures of success. A thriving business awaited, and there they sat. Even the TV was off. In a minute Lillian asked if the Christian thing wasn't a bother. Pauline said, "Well, after all, she was entitled to that. It didn't bother me. You know, there's a time and place for everything."

And soon it was time to shop; though today, they agreed, they would stop for lunch. Pauline wasn't wild about Chinese but agreed to go along, because Lillian had heard that the new Szechwan place would leave out those red hot peppers if you asked them to, and she had missed the Chinese.

And besides, if they arrived and Pauline still didn't like it, they could go elsewhere. They had the time. What's the rush?

I, Rufus

Uh...

You might think dogs are dumb. I'm not so dumb. I know who put Edna Mumph in the oneway box.

I got Chicken Pox. Now that's dumb, calling a cat Chicken Pox on account of its spots. And for kind of a joke, I think. Chicken Pox Mumph. That's not funny. She's not a chicken. I'm not so dumb.

I got Chicken Pox when they brought her down here after Edna went oneway. I didn't go after Chicken Pox. She jumped onto a chair and turned around. So? I sniffed it for her. She turned back and scratched my nose. That hurts. I didn't eat her. They wouldn't let me.

My name is Tuza. My long name is Tuza Showers but they call me Tuza unless they want me to fetch or roll over or come home or heel or not pee somewhere or leave a cat alone or stop humping a leg or something and I don't do it. They usually yell when they call me Tuza Showers. Most of the time they call me Tuza.

My real name is Rufus but they changed it. Maybe they forgot I already had a name.

They forgot to feed me twice already. They forget to fill my waterbowl sometimes.

Harry went to the oneway box. He was my man so I got sent down here. Then they started calling me Tuza Showers.

They used to call all the dogs Tuza Showers. Well, uh, Billy Bohne did every time he stood at the end of the kennels. He'd click his heels and stick his hand out like a pointer, and then he'd whine and strain and squeeze his eyes shut and point out there toward the oneway box and yell at all the dogs: "Tuza Showers!" He got redder in the face than Fifi's rosette and just as scrunched up too. He was funny, Billy Bohne. Everybody knew he wasn't really mad at us. He got fired, I don't know why.

Everybody knows dogs take baths, not showers. Maybe that's why they fired him. Harry took showers. Harry was funny, all wet.

After Billy went away, a woman came who looked like she ate three times a day. She went down the line with a clipboard, banging cage doors, dragging out the dogs for the oneway box. Sometimes she was in a hurry. Sometimes she snapped at the dogs who didn't want to go. "Come on, you," she said. "You've taken up space too long." I think it must be more crowded in the oneway box than it used to get on Harry's couch. Most dogs were afraid of her. Her name is Hortense Puetzle. Hortense is in a big kennel now. I heard them say she might get the chair. I'd much rather have the couch, even if it was crowded.

Hortense used to carry a bag of needles and oneway juice with her all the time. She said they were for emergencies. I don't get it. Why would a dog need to take a nap in an emergency? Most of the dogs were afraid of Hortense. Not me. I'd go to the bushes on the other side when I saw her, but I wasn't afraid. I'd give her the old ten-hole kiss on the calf if she got near me with her bag, but I wasn't afraid. I wasn't.

I went to the bushes on the other side when Billy Bohne called us up to the oneway box. But I wasn't afraid. I had to pee. I missed my turn for the box. Billy didn't mind. He said I'd get my chance, just wait and see. He said it was like paradise in the box, as good as Madagascar. What's Madagascar? Billy was funny. On the day he took all the dogs to the oneway box and I got left out, I barked because it was just him and me and the whole afternoon to play in. But he said, "Too late, Tutor. But don't vorry. Ze next train leaves mit der sundown."

Oh, brother, I thought. Now my name is Tutor. Billy marched up to me and yelled, "Veh iss your papahs? You must haff your papahs." Billy was funny.

He got fired for bad behavior.

What's a Nazi?

They kept me around. They call me a survivor or a mascot or a shelter dog. Sometimes they get together and talk about me all at once. They think I did something great. It was easy. I really had to pee.

They call me old. I'm not so old. I'm eight. Or five. I forget. I know I'm not one. But I was. I was two, too. But not anymore.

Hortense yelled at Billy. He didn't care. She fired him. Meezul said she couldn't do that. Hortense yelled at Meezul. Nobody ever yelled at Meezul.

Meezul is executive director. He would be tall, but he can't stand up straight. He's submissive, with puffy cheeks like a chipmunk. He doesn't have a tail, but you can still see it between his legs. He looks down with short grins and lets you know you can smell first if you want to. I've seen dogs like that. Maybe he got beat as a pup. I don't know. Edna got him the job. I remember when he first looked at Hortense to see if she was receptive. Hortense laughed. She called him Meezul the Weasel.

What's a weasel?

Hortense said Billy only got the job because Meezul used to schtup Billy's mother in New York, and she's the one who first got Edna on the board. So now we had a Hitler Yüngen running the crematorium like a death camp, and no board of directors in the world would allow that. I think schtup means mate.

Meezul said any board of directors could plainly see that traffic to the box varied directly with the approach of Hortense's menstrual cycle. He said he had graphs to prove it.

I think the crematorium is that white powder they put in their coffee.

I don't know what a menstrual cycle is. Harry had a Vespa.

Hortense said Meezul had no more business directing an animal shelter than she had in a nunnery.

What's a nunnery?

What's business?

I never saw Billy's mother.

Hortense said Meezul was only a nuisance on his very best days. She said he'd worked his way into Edna Mumph's will like a heartworm.

I know what a nuisance is.

I'm heartworm negative, and I have good days.

She said he hated animals and only kept the job so he could weasel into Edna's pockets, because she had millions, because she never had children like a normal woman, so a parasite like Meezul could move in for the kill.

Why does a normal woman need to have children? I had parasites once.

Meezul looked pretty worried there for a minute. Hortense said Billy Bohne was in violation of veterinary-care regulations so she could fire him, which is exactly what she had done, and fired he would remain.

Meezul got so mad he yelled at Hortense. Nobody ever yelled at Hortense. And Meezul never yelled at anybody. He yelled, "You're pleasure bent!" He yelled that she was preoccupied with the mating act, because she'd never been loved, because she was so unlovable, and now she took it out on the dogs and cats.

What's preoccupied?

I don't love Hortense. I humped Zazu while Hortense watched. Hortense sent Zazu to the box.

Hortense yelled back that Meezul knew as much about love as he knew about managing an organization. She said he was scared of his own shadow. She said he was a coward. She said he avoided every opportunity to improve the place the same way he avoided people. She asked how many people he'd spoken to in person today.

Meezul cringed. He's submissive.

Hortense is dominant. She said he spent two thousand dollars installing a surveillance camera so he could sit in his office all day watching the footage from the night before. He said he had some pretty good footage of her. She said she'd punch him in the nose. He said she was fired. She told him he couldn't do that.

He said she was in violation of executive rule, and that yes he *could* fire her. Yes he *had* fired her. And yes, *fired* she would remain. Everyone scurried for a few days then, looking both ways and whispering. It was fun, like everyone peed on the rug and didn't want to get caught.

Then Edna Mumph got the oneway ticket.

I didn't mind that Edna went oneway. Edna Mumph was never funny. I didn't know her forever but a dog can tell. She liked cats. I know some people who like them. That's okay. That doesn't mean they're not funny. I don't like cats. It's always, Hey, wanna smell my asshole? Every cat you see pops the question and gives you the bird's eye. I tried it with Chicken Pox. It smelled like cat dukey. Duh. I didn't like it. Then she cut me three slices on the nose. I let her have it. I got in trouble.

I saw a dog eat cat dukey.

I puked a rat.

To tell you the truth Mildred Puetzle isn't funny either. Mildred is Hortense's mother. Mildred looks much older than Hortense and only eats twice a day. She doesn't like cats so much, but she goes goo goo over them if people are watching. She likes dogs. But she isn't funny. I let Mildred pet my head sometimes. She won't do it unless other people are around. Sometimes if a crowd of people is around she scratches under my neck and around my ears. She's really good at it when people are around. She kissed me once and told everyone that she loved me so much. She never told me that when people weren't watching. I'm not so dumb. And she whacks me too hard on the flank. What? Does she think I like that? Sometimes I roll over and she rubs my belly. I like that. Sometimes I get ready to mate. She gets upset but she never says, "Tuza Showers!" She just stops and walks away. I try not to get ready to mate, but I can't help it. She rubs my belly so good.

I like to lick my balls after a belly rub. Then she yells at me, "Tuza Showers!"

What? She won't do it. So what?

Mildred Puetzle and Edna Mumph postured tooth and nail all the time but never really had a good go at it. They just prissed around trying to see who could out snooty who. That's what happens if you hang around cats. I wanted them to go at it. They wouldn't do it.

To tell you the truth there wasn't much difference between the two, Edna and Mildred, if you only looked at them. A couple old alpha bitch has-beens, if you want my opinion. I would have guessed littermates myself, blue-haired ridgebacks bred for snooping around. Some big differences showed up once you got to know them, but that was more from where they'd been rather than their breeding lines. Like I said, littermates, scrambling for hind tit. Mildred is old. Edna's way past that. Mildred mostly mumbled about Edna, mostly asking, "What's that awful woman up to now?" She asked me that all the time. How was I supposed to know?

Edna mostly mumbled about Jesus and how much she loved him. I don't know Jesus. Maybe he was a dog she used to have who went to the oneway box and so she missed him. Then again, knowing Edna, Jesus was probably a cat. Jesus. Who would ever name a cat Jesus? Edna mumbled about Jesus and stroked her i.d. tag with both hands. She got upset and mumbled things like, "Thank you, Jesus," and "Oh, Jesus, take me when it's my time." Pretty strange stuff to be mumbling about some old dead cat if you ask me. Sometimes Edna stroked her i.d. when she talked to other humans. You can always tell that soon after the stroking started she'd remember Jesus. "Jesus will prevail," she'd say.

One time Hortense told Edna that having sex with a man was the most unbelievable thing in the world.

I don't know what sex is. I think it's like mating.

Edna turned red. So did Hortense. Hortense said, "Having him way up in you like that. You wouldn't want to try it sometime?"

Edna stroked her i.d. tag and nearly pulled it off of her collar. She said, "You wouldn't feel like that if you had Jesus in your life."

I don't know. Maybe Jesus wasn't a cat.

I didn't go to the bushes on the other side when Edna came around, but I didn't go get a pet on the head either. I didn't think she'd hurt me, but I thought of her and those cats. I didn't trust her. A dog can tell.

Edna wanted to mate with Meezul even though she was too old to be in heat, and sometimes she bragged that she'd never mated in her life. She bragged to Hortense. Hortense bragged back about all her mating and having it way up in her. Hortense won the bragging competition.

Hortense was mean. She was meaner than Billy Bohne. I really didn't like her.

She sent everyone to the oneway box and scared them, like it was a bad place. She was never funny. The smart ones figured out that you had to go to the bushes on the other side when Hortense panted and twitched. She hurt Edna's feelings. I felt sorry for Edna then.

Edna never mated, not that anyone needs another litter. Just look around this place, all of them crying and peeing on themselves and loading up the box like that.

I really like to mate. I like to mate all the time.

I like to pee, too.

And eat.

Not Edna. Scrawny, mumbly Edna didn't like to mate or eat. I never saw her pee. But I think she wanted to mate with Meezul. I don't know, maybe she only wanted the company. Meezul wasn't around much during the day, on account of all the people. He came in late in the afternoon when everyone was leaving. Sometimes Edna came around with some papers for review. They sat together in Meezul's office. She brought wine and glasses. He popped the cork. He poured. She said, "Thank you, gallant sir." He said the pleasure was all his. She said the evening was certainly lovely. He said it was all the more charming with her presence. She smiled, much less stern than she was back in the alpha days. She drank. He did too. He poured some more. He said he felt the shelter was on solid ground now, with much firmer footings and a sure course and a bright future. He said she was a guiding light and he looked forward to years of success and happy landings. He said all's well that ends well and tomorrow is only a day away. He said he was grateful for her leadership.

She drank her wine. He poured more. She said he was a very special man indeed. He said she was the one who made him special, and he looked forward to knowing her for as long as he lived. They soaked it up.

She said he would certainly outlive her. Why, she was nearly twice his age. He said spirits could dance beyond physical constraint. She said, oh my, that is a beautiful thought. She said she had a surprise for him, but she wouldn't be the one to present it. She said she could divulge no more, but one day when he might feel sad, something would at least be there to cheer him up. She said you don't have to love dogs to help them.

He said he knew that. She said it was far more effective to be a good manager. He said she was the one. She looked up at him just like me when I know there's a bone somewhere. She was the one, he said again, the one who had taught him a thing or two.

* * *

Hortense said Edna didn't have millions, but she had a few hundred thou.

What's divulge?

Edna was as scared of Hortense as anybody was, but she never went to the bushes on the other side. People seem afraid of the bushes, but I'm not afraid. They come in pretty handy. Edna didn't like Mildred either. She said so. One time she told Mildred, "I'm so sick of you!"

Mildred said, "I'm sick of you, too, but I never said you were a bad president."

Mildred and Edna were presidents. That means alpha, kind of, but it changes back and forth and doesn't make sense. They bare fang, but then they yak yak yak. I don't get it. First Mildred was president for a long time. Then Edna was president for a long time. Now Mildred again. Edna hated that. She said Mildred would ruin the place. She wanted to know why any board of directors would want Mildred Puetzle as an emissary to the Mayor and the County Clerk. Mildred said her hands were tied since Edna made such a shambles of the books. Mildred's hands weren't tied. Anyone could see that. And the books are on the shelf all in a row. Mildred's funny.

After Hortense fired Billy Bohne and Meezul fired Hortense and Hortense spilled the beans on Meezul getting into Edna's will, the directors split into two packs. One followed Edna and agreed that Billy Bohne wasn't a Nazi and Meezul was doing a great job.

The other pack didn't exactly follow Mildred but they all insisted that a boy who clicked his heals and shot a salute from the chest and yelled, "Tuza Showers!" to the dogs on their way to the oneway box was a Nazi. They agreed that Meezul was a weasel who only hired Billy and then kept him in place because he used to schtup Billy's mother.

It came down to who had to go, Hortense or Meezul, and who had the votes.

* * *

Hortense was in heat. She was always in heat, always receptive. She only let them mount at night though. She would lie on the table in the oneway box. I think she has a strong scent for a human because the ringer is usually for her. "Hortense. It's for you," they yell. Hortense changes her voice when she talks to the ringer. She sounds receptive. I've never seen her mate with the ringer though. That would be funny.

Meezul watched one time. He hid behind a cabinet and was very still. Hortense came in with a man. They mated on the table in the oneway box. Meezul and I watched. I nudged Meezul and said, "Mmph." It was funny.

Meezul said, "Sh."

Hortense said, "What was that."

The man said, "Mm! Oh... Oh... Oh..."

Hortense said, "I heard something."

The man said, "Oh... Oh... Oh..."

I said, "Woof!"

Hortense said, "Oh. Oh! Oh! Not so fast! You're hurting me!"

The man said, "Numph! Mmph. Oh. Yes."

Meezul tiptoed away quiet as a cat. I think he has a litter box, too. I stayed. It wasn't funny anymore. I felt sorry for Hortense. The man left. She mumbled like her mother and Edna. She mumbled that she hated that man. She asked me why she did that.

How was I supposed to know? But I told her, "Mmph," because she needed someone to tell her something.

She said, "Yeah, yeah. Anymore lip out of you, I got a needle in the bag with your name on it." I went to the bushes on the other side. Hortense is very unfunny sometimes. One night she lay on the table in the oneway box by herself and said, "Oh... Oh... Oh..." It was funny, but I've watched better.

Meezul told the ringer what Hortense had done. He said the man was a director. But I knew the directors and that man wasn't a director. Meezul likes to tell the ringer all kinds of things that aren't true.

That's okay. I like to pee.

He said he dreaded having to relate such foul activity to one so graceful, so poised, so charming.

I had some bad cheese on my stomach then so I went ahead and puked.

* * *

One day we went to a picnic. That's when you take the food and the bowls with you out into a field and eat and play. But the people got tired like they do and wanted to sit around and talk. It was all the directors and kennel attendants and animal control officers and me and Mildred and Hortense and Edna and Meezul and Felix. He's a cat. He's not so bad. Sometimes he's funny. I can't figure that one out.

Everyone was smiling and petting my head so Mildred gave me a big hug and kissed me on the lips. I didn't like it. Why do they do that? It was disgusting. She won't lick my balls. She scratched my neck and around my ears and I couldn't help it; I rolled over so she could scratch my belly. She did. I closed my eyes and thought about cats. It worked. I didn't get ready to mate. Mildred was telling everyone how much she loved me. She told a story about how she saved me from Billy Bohne. I never heard it before. It was funny. She said nobody knew what kind of shenanigans Billy pulled around there, but she was uncovering plenty every day.

What are shenanigans?

Why would they be buried?

She was rubbing me good and telling everybody that I, Rufus, represented everything the Humane Society ever stood for. She called me Rufus. She was the only one who did. I liked that. I really wanted her to lick my balls, they get so dry.

Sometimes the fleas get up in there and itch. I think she was ready. But then I got ready to mate and Walter said, "Tuza Showers!" He's a director. He's black. I am too. I'm a setter mix, but Billy always said I wasn't nearly as dumb as a setter.

Mildred stopped rubbing.

Edna said that Billy Bohne was a harmless boy who read too many comic books and had a warped sense of humor. Edna said he was this year's scapegoat for those people who needed distraction from their own failures. She said nobody needed a rhetorical lecture on the mission statement of the shelter, not when other issues of such dire consequence were before the board. Edna talked like that often, not really funny, but then not really not funny.

Everyone looked at Mildred. It was her turn.

Mildred said she only wanted to fulfill her duties as president by reminding the directors of their mandate and by allowing dissension from the floor, unlike presidents of the recent past. Mildred said that a neo-Nazi kennel attendant is a dire consequence in itself.

Everyone looked at Edna.

Edna said no president of the recent past was guilty of nepotism. Clark asked who was engaged in nepotism now? Edna said Mildred hired her own daughter Hortense to be the shelter vet. Clark said that the board of directors hired Hortense, not Mildred, and so that wasn't nepotism.

I knew that.

Mildred said the shelter was insolvent because no one had managed the books for two years.

Edna wanted to say something but couldn't. She got red and started coughing and sputtering.

Clark said, "Could be the big one." He said it very low. He's a director. Hortense laughed. It was funny. Clark looked at Hortense. She was receptive. I was going to move on Hortense if he didn't.

But Edna got redder and redder so Meezul jumped up and poured some water into a glass and took it to her and patted her on the back and helped pour it down her gullet.

She breathed easy after a minute. Just a hairball. Would have been better if she coughed it up, but you can't always do that. Nobody put Vaseline on her nose. I think Meezul would have. I think Meezul would have done anything for Edna.

I went over to lick Edna's nose.

They'd been giving me hot dogs, my favorite, but they made me eat the buns. I hate the buns. They make my mouth gummy.

If I licked Edna's nose she might be able to get her hairball up. Edna was mumbling to her old cat Jesus, but that didn't seem like a problem, so I went on in for the greasing. She pushed me away and said, "You get out of here!"

Everyone looked at Edna.

Hortense sat next to her. Hortense grabbed me and gave me a hug. She never did that before. It was scary. I liked it. I looked at Hortense to see if she was receptive. Hortense talked goo goo. I was ready to mate so I started on her leg. She said, "No, Tuza. No." I heard her say that before at night on the table in the oneway box. Not no, Tuza, but no, Jack, or no, Tom, or no, Dick. Those guys kept going. So I did too. She pushed me away. I don't get it. You try to help out. You try to give back. Sometimes they just push you away.

Edna got up. She said, "If you'll excuse me, I'll be back in a few minutes. Please confine the meeting to old business until I return." She had picked up her purse, but just as she spoke she reached into Hortense's purse and snatched Hortense's bag with the needles and oneway juice. She was sneaky as a cat, that Edna. She said, "I love this dog as much as anyone. And I know our mission as well as anyone. I couldn't breathe. That's all. Come with me, dog."

I guess Edna had to pee and wanted me to come and watch or pee with her. But I'm not so dumb. Edna hates dogs. She had the oneway bag. She called me. What could I do? Everyone watched me follow Edna into the trees. We walked for a long time for her. Maybe she wanted to find a spot with no scent. I like to do that sometimes.

When we stopped, she sat down on a log and stared and breathed hard. I wanted her to pee so we could get back and play some more. Edna didn't want to play. I knew that. She shook her head and said something about the sun not setting on her wrath and the forgiveness of

Jesus for those who would throw off the yoke of oppression. She talked funny, but we were wasting time.

She opened Hortense's bag and pulled out a needle and fastened it onto a little thing and pulled out the juice and stuck the needle in the juice and said, "You're old, dog. You've had enough life. Let that little slut explain this one away." She held the oneway needle up in front of her face and squeezed a few drops of oneway juice out, then a few more. "We don't want you to die right away. Do we? We need a little while. Come here. Sit."

I'm not so dumb. I know how to step up and sit down.

"Now. Shake."

I can do that. It's dumb, but I'm not.

She squeezed my leg and got a vein to come up and held it with her fingers. Hortense always says you're not supposed to do it that way.

I know why. I nudged Edna with my nose. Not in the crotch. She never liked that. Besides, she was sitting down. And anyway. She stuck herself. She froze.

I nudged her again.

She looked very unfunny. She said, "Oh, sweet, sweet Jesus. My time has come..." She laid down. She went to sleep.

I went back to the picnic. I didn't like Edna. She was the most unfunny person I ever met. She wasn't scary like Hortense, but she hated dogs. What was I supposed to do? I came out from the trees just as Hortense was running up to where the trail started, complaining that someone, most likely that bitch Edna, had run off with her emergency bag. She ran down the trail. I didn't follow. I wanted some hot dogs. Maybe the people were rested and someone would want to throw a ball or wrestle with a towel or dig a hole or go exploring. I really like picnics.

But that one had to stop because Edna couldn't get up from her nap. But she was always tired anyway. I can't figure that one out either.

* * *

Somebody said we won't ever get to have another picnic, not since Edna went oneway on the last one. Somebody else asked why the hell not. Someone said yeah, she was just an old bag looking for a life at the expense of the animals. I heard Clark ask Walter if he ever got to mate with Hortense. Walter said that Clark was crude. Clark asked, "You mean like Tuza Showers?" He petted my head and said, "You're crude aren't you, Boy?" He scratched around my neck and my ears and hung on in for the rollover. He said he didn't know why but something about that Hortense just made him want to mate. And now he'd never get the chance, not for twenty years to life anyway.

What's twenty years to life?

Clark says the place is much different now with all the loony bitches gone. He says it's much better.

What's a loony?

I like bitches.

Clark is a lawyer. He says a loony is a person who can really jam up the works. He says Meezul won't get into Edna's estate now any sooner than he, Clark, will get into Hortense's knickers.

What's knickers?

Clark says he might take me home with him. He says I'm quite a dog. He calls me Rufus most of the time. I like Clark. He's funny. He's president now too, since he bared fang with Walter, and Walter shoved him, and he slammed Walter up against the wall and said, “You voted wrong long enough old man.” Walter voted for Edna for a long time. Then he ran for president. Then he lost. Then he resigned.

The place does feel different with nobody to scare you into the bushes on the other side, except when they come out with the clipboard and round up a few for the box. Even now with Hortense gone that box has a creepy smell. I don’t like it. I dream about it sometimes and twitch so hard it wakes me up.

I wish Clark would take me home. He’s funny. I think I could do all right at home. I like Clark. You don’t have to be so smart to know a good one when you see one.

A dog can tell.

The Deal

Manny Binder loved deals. His father-in-law recognized Manny's instinct for a fair advantage and called Manny the kid, in the spirit of a young prizefighter, an up-and-comer. Manny liked the recognition, until a more manly esteem seemed appropriate. Even a kid could see that Irving Lieberman could bog you down on a nickname, unless you became your own man.

He was simply compelled, Irving, to goose the boy's potential. A son-in-law is not a son, not blood or the same as blood. But the grandchildren are and nobody lives forever. So? What can you do but seek maximum return?

So Irving told Manny, "Go. Don't go looking, but something comes up, let me know, we'll take a look, see how you do." Irving wondered if Manny knew the meaning of this test, but he didn't wonder long.

Manny asked with less emotion than that of a constrictor engorging on a rat, "What's the order of magnitude we're dealing with here?"

"Magnitude? What's the order of magnitude?" Irving, a known master of the loquacious back-quote, had riled many men over the years, because a man riled is open to foolish, impassioned disclosure. From there, a man often plays himself out, while a skilled operator like Irving Lieberman allows no slack and reels him in. But those were lesser men than the kid, who sensed the game and remained calm. You could process Irving's guile if you let him stare and wait for you to be a smart aleck. The kid only nodded. Irving took note and said, "Mm. Say ten. Or fifty. Don't go over a hundred."

Manny didn't smile but nodded again, calmly as a man hearing twenty-five cents. He set to work, putting the word out that he would look at whatever came across his desk. And he wasn't even thirty.

A few operators with considerable experience in the field came to eye him up and down as if to ask, *What? Money? You? From money? What?* It was common knowledge in the field that Manny Binder had married into the mother lode. So those who knew the front-line trenches and incendiary bickering sniggered. *Ah! He'd still be washing dishes if not for such and such or blah blah blah.* Yet they knew the score and the ablest among them knew as well that it doesn't matter where your money comes from; you have it, or you don't. If people know you're next to money they stop assessing and small-talking and start asking.

Oh, the deals came in, deals the banks wouldn't touch, like second and third mortgages on properties in "transition" neighborhoods, where no one but Manny would roll the bones. Manny reminded the other players of his pivotal position when they forgot. His father-in-law saw. Manny could go two-fifty by the time he was thirty-five. This, when two-fifty was some real money. From there, the numbers only got bigger.

"You listen to me, Harry," Manny advised. "Seventeen years I been in this business. A hundred times I've seen people like you, got nothing, come to people like me and want it for free. Sweat equity is what you call it. That's what you *wish* you could call it. You take that sweat and wipe it on your tuchas. You hear! It doesn't exist." Manny Binder called everyone Harry when emphasizing a point. On this point he spoke to Ted Millman, who wanted to build a four-plex but had no commercial construction track record and struck out at the bank. Manny would make the loan, but only with serious consideration for the many facets of risk involved and the return to cover those risks. He said, "seventeen years" with a weariness so thorough it would serve him another forty. Then he could say "fifty-seven years" as if one syllable at a time was how they passed.

But he was only thirty-nine at the time of Ted Millman, only in business since marrying Bonita Lieberman when he was twenty-two. Bonita was twenty-three then. Her arms wobbled like Jell-O already, but he went along. Parents on both sides advised: "She's healthy. You'll have a family. You'll learn to love her." They agreed, the parents, that love is learned, once practicalities are processed.

Bonita was the only child of Silvia and Irving, who'd done terribly well in commercial cleaning solvents. The standard joke in the Lieberman household was that Irving had cleaned up. Or he was plenty solvent. It was no secret the Liebermans were loaded; they drove a new Cadillac every year. Manny had no use for that kind of show. But he did like comfort and security, so he went along. What? He should waste his prime on building some decent operating capital? With *his* perseverance and natural skills? Or should he make the smart move and jump way ahead of the game? Who wants to go big time at twenty-two? Are you kidding? And he could learn to love her.

Like his in-laws before him Manny also did terribly well, and with none of the pesky skin irritation attendant to cleaning solvents. And he did learn to love his wife. She went two-fifty at thirty-six, which was the same year Manny went two-twenty, but hey, he liked to joke, she's a year older. I'll catch up. It was the same year Manny went two-fifty on his front-end magnitude, as if her poundage equaled his potential or vice versa. It would have been another great joke and a lucky number, two-fifty, but it was left unspoken. Dollars measured wealth, and Bonita's weight was quietly accepted as a measure of something else. Call the pounds a measure of what Bonita had to give as a wife.

Life was good, Manny said. First off, what a cook she was. And what a terrific mother. Manny loved his three daughters and knew that they too would make three fellows very happy at dinnertime. Their arms also wobbled like Jell-O. They were learning. Nobody knew what exactly got into Manny when he rounded the clubhouse turn to forty and bought fancy new running shoes and started running. He was a good provider, so nobody begrudged him an eccentricity. Still, they talked, because a man so apparently on his way to visible wealth is the kind of man warranting talk. *What? Not tennis shoes but running shoes? Running; tennis; it's a hundred dollars is what. For tennis shoes?*

Well, Manny Binder wasn't the first fat baldy huffing and puffing around the block. Hardly a runner, more of a bouncing ball, he nonetheless circled the block much as the tiger chased its tail, until the butter melted down. For a year Manny said, "Thirty pounds. Thirty *pounds!*" Everyone was proud, even Bonita, because a full-figured gal doesn't mind one bit if the trim fellow beside her is her hubby. Manny's weight was the first number to decrease in the Binder household since the beginning. Not that he was exactly trim that year, but he was down from two-twenty to one-ninety. And trim was where he headed, around the block and then around the track at the club. Manny focused down to one-seventy, one-sixty, and so on to one-forty, long since ceasing his announcements of lost poundage. Asked for his secret he would wag a finger and instruct, "Never go back for seconds! No matter what!" At one-thirty his friends told him to stop. Others suspected a vile disease.

Manny knew who was which, loving the concern of his friends, disproving his critics with sheer vitality. He stood in the locker room in front of the mirror practically admiring his rib cage, standing next to Max Wallman. "God! I hate that!" Manny bellowed when Max stretched the ten-inch strands on the side of his head and then folded them over the naked top. "Just cut it short!" Manny buffed his own chrome dome with the palm of his hand, demonstrating easy maintenance and sublime contentment.

"You know what I hate?" Max asked. "A reformed fat ass. Go. Shave your head. Eat seeds." It was true, and Manny grinned so the other fellows could see his pleasure. He loved the recognition that he, fat ass no more, was down to fighting weight, lean and mean, making money and proving that life was good.

Manny also loved his four-bedroom house on a short bluff on a prime corner in a select subdivision hardly a stone's throw from town. The lot wasn't a bluff when he bought it. But a man of instinct understands the long-term value of a measly few grand in dirt. View enhancement and a little altitude justified the investment.

Not that a man of means needs justification. Never mind; it was money in the bank, and Manny loved pulling in after a long day at the office. You couldn't see his house from the road without looking up, which seemed poetic, much less justified.

* * *

Manny had no business talking to Russel Fox. He didn't even know where Russel Fox lived. He knew Russel drove a beat-up car and never had a job to speak of but often as not hustled one thing or another. Manny was as amazed as the next guy that Russel could even find a woman to talk to, much less a looker. But hey, some women love men who stink. So? Go figure.

Not that Russel stank. He didn't stink. It was only a figure of speech for the sake of making a point, because saying a man stinks can be a better politic in the locker room than saying he can't rub two nickels together. Russel didn't mind. And who cared about Russel's so-called girlfriends or where they came from? What a laugh; Manny could pat Russel on the back with the rest of the fellows at the club. It was a gesture, something like rubbing a boy's head. Russel was kind of a mascot that way. Sometimes one of the guys would ask Russel about the dish he was out with last night, and Russel would slough it off and say something casual about friendship and good looks and real women. In fact, Russel absorbed all the jokes and comments good-naturedly, because all the guys at the club were friends.

Russel was a regular member more or less. He paid full dues, because nobody got a break on dues without a dispensation voted by the membership. It hadn't come up, not for Russel or anyone, nor would it as long as Manny was on the executive committee. Because busy men should not be distracted by charity cases like Russel when they want to relax with camaraderie and maybe some exercise. Manny couldn't see where some people got off. Well, let it go; Russel Fox hadn't asked for a dispensation, though Manny felt certain he wanted one, and more than one regular member had wondered aloud where a guy like Russel came up with the eighty bucks a month.

Manny supposed a few of the fellows had helped Russel out now and then with petty cash loans and odd jobs, but that was none of his, Manny's, business. It wasn't even business but the endless need of an idle man. And to think, they were nearly the same age.

Now it was fish.

Russel said he saw the light while watching his fish; that is, while playing with his fish bowl. A grown man playing with a fish bowl? So rose the muttering and laughter here and there and the jokes about grabbing the grouper and sniffing the tuna.

It was only Russel spewing again in the steam room, then the locker room, bouncing around the basketball court and then huffing and puffing in the weight room. Russel, insensitive to low-level analysis, shared his sudden illumination. He suddenly *knew* the reason he wasn't yet rich "like the rest of you guys." All heads turned. "Well, like some of you guys, anyway." A few of the guys looked down. The rest looked around. Russel said it was because the one thing he'd known about all these years was fish, and he hadn't even known it.

"I mean I knew about it but didn't know I knew... I mean... You know what I mean." Bumbling explanations were a standing joke; it was Russel's habit, practically a tradition. Russel's bumbling led to group exasperation until *some*one in earshot was compelled to explain what Russel could not.

Manny Binder put it concisely, "Fish bowls?" Now all heads turned to Manny, which Manny rather enjoyed. Because making fun of the foibles of the other fellows was expected at the club. Manny understood the critical need for low profile, but hey, this was the club. And what's a mascot for if not some good-natured fun? At the club a man could be himself and take his knocks. Like Manny; recognized nearly every afternoon for his uncanny power in the marketplace. Hey, it was all good-natured fun. A man like Russel could fantasize wealth in fish bowls, and a man like Manny could respond. This was social democracy in action and, frankly, Manny liked the action.

Russel perked as well. Manny had money. Everyone knew it. And he wasn't a bad guy, Manny, and could help out. Russel smiled and said, "No. It's like if you..."

"I'll tell you what, Mr. Russel. You come down to my office tomorrow." It was a first, Manny offering a lead *in the club*, where no business took place, by unspoken rule. But this was Russel, not really business, and it was nearly dues time again, and what a goof if not a laugh, so why not? It was only a gesture of help and made Manny look good and feel good, and after all, he was known for giving in the right places. Wasn't he? "No, wait," Manny said as if changing his mind. He hadn't changed; he only let Russel hover before saying, "I can't tomorrow. Come down Wednesday. Wednesday morning. I'll take a look at these fish bowls you want to charge people money to see." Manny embellished his receptivity and charity.

"Tanks," Russel said.

"Don't mention it," Manny said.

"No. It's tanks. Not bowls."

"Hey. See you Wednesday," Manny said, as a disquieting majority chuckled and shook their heads.

*　　*　　*

Russel called midmorning on Wednesday to see what time he should come in. Manny pictured Russel in a payphone, casually wiping a finger through the coin return in case this might be a lucky day or a lucky phone or a lucky call or something. Manny briefly wondered if Russel had just called one of his floozies, one of the incredibly stacked numbers in one of those shamelessly tight and ridiculous skirts. And those plunging necklines that left *nothing* to the imagination. "What?" Manny asked. "Oh, yeah. Fish bowls." He arched an eyebrow for his father-in-law who stood in the door watching another deal germinate.

Hey, the kid (Manny) didn't do anything special; that's what made him a natural. Like now, listening to a deal, a good deal for all we know, and schpieling it right back into the phone in simple, non-dynamic terms. Because a deal is nothing more than someone selling and someone buying. And since the guys with the money usually do the buying, what could be better than a simple rendition of the deal as one more cockamamie idea? Because the best dealmakers in the world have two questions ready at all times, which are 1) You want what? And 2) For this piece o' shit? Well, that was a joke, for sure, but still.

"Wait a minute. What is it you want to do?" Manny sounded incredulous that some nincompoop could even conceive of coming into the office of a kingpin dealmaker and actually using up *time* much less thinking anyone could rub two nickels together on such a crazy scheme as this one and come up with twelve cents. He winked at Irving in the doorway and delivered the buyer's version: "You want to set up some big fish bowls and charge people money to see the fish in them?" Manny flipped on the speakerphone so Irving could enjoy the volley. Irving nodded, shuffled in, sat down and took another chew on his unlit cigar stub. Irving had been warned by his doctor against lighting up.

"Hey, Manny," Russel said. "This wasn't..."

"Russel. Hold on." Manny pressed the mute button to A) take the psychological upper hand by interrupting and putting the deal on hold and B) fill Irving in with a profile. "Russel Fox," Manny whispered, even though his thumb pressed the mute. "A real schmendrik. Not a stupid fellow but not stupid like a fox either. He's talking up this fish bowl idea down at the club. I told him give me a ring. Hey, I think maybe he's got something."

Manny quickly snugged the phone between his ear and shoulder, held up one finger for silence, released the muting thumb and punched the speaker button off for the clear, concise closing. "Yeah, Russel. Sorry about the interruption. We got more deals here than a dog has fleas."

"Hey, Manny..."

"Yeah, look, Russ. Today's not so good. Maybe this afternoon. After the regular hours. You know. We'll get a beer." Manny paused so Russel could finish speaking. Then he said, "Okay, you want to meet at Fern's. What? Six-thirty? Yeah, whatever."

Russel said "Sure. Six-thirty's cool. Whatever you need." Manny had never been to Fern's but he'd driven by. He'd looked inside and seen social intercourse many times. He'd seen Russel in the window, gesticulating, animated, most likely making a fool of himself with the floozies there. Manny was curious about the place and what went on there. Hey, who knew? Maybe there was money waiting to be made in the bar business. He hung up and shook his head. "Bastard wants to strike it rich in fish bowls. I'll take a look."

* * *

Manny left early in the afternoon to allow time for shopping. He bought a pair of blue jeans, his first in what, thirty years? Well, twenty-five anyway, because blue jeans were for kids and he'd worked like six men these last twenty years. But what was so wrong with being a kid again, in blue jeans even? He got a good deal at fourteen dollars because he was still an old-fashioned kid who came up the hard way having to make do. And he was still one of the smarter kids who would no sooner spend good money on jeans that were already washed, much less a pair that was already beat up, than the man in the moon. Besides, how different could jeans be? These were fine and they'd break-in in no time. In the meantime, so? They were stiff and shiny as roofing shingles, and he had to roll up the cuffs. So? The kids do that now. Don't they? But he did wish his bargain jeans wouldn't pop out like a squeeze bottle every time he took a step.

Oh, well, when in Rome, he thought, ambling into Fern's. The place was dead, empty except for Russel at the bar and a heavy-set woman at a corner table who wasn't even a floozy. Manny was two steps in when Russel turned to the sound of chafing denim. Russel didn't laugh or say something in mockery like, hey, nice pants. He only said, "Hey, Manny."

"Hey," Manny said. "What's this? I thought this place was jumping?"

Russel explained, "It is. I mean, it's not now. It's Wednesday."

"So? Why a pox on Wednesdays?"

"Because it's lady's night at Grogan's. Free drinks for the women. You know, Manny. The women go for the drinks, and the guys go where the women go."

Manny wanted to ask what in the hell they were doing at Fern's if Grogan's was the place. But he didn't ask. He only looked around again, like maybe a floozie or two might seep from the woodwork.

"What are you looking for?" Russel asked.

"Nothing. I just thought this place was jumping."

"It is. It's just not jumping right now."

"Yeah, yeah." Manny slid coolly onto a stool then slid off to rearrange his unit where the cheap denim rubbed it wrong. Then he slid back on but kept his eyes on the door. Then he figured out that the mirror on the back bar facing the door had the action covered. "Okay, what you got?"

Russel plowed in, pulling a crushed roll of papers from his hip pocket and spreading them across the bar. One sheet showed a detailed list of tanks, filters, pumps, stands, lids, lighting and all the minutiae of the modern aquarium enthusiast. Russel was most excited over the news that pre-fab tanks of three hundred gallons were now available. The manufacturer was hardly two hundred miles away, and they cost barely over five hundred dollars each, *complete*, which included the filters, pumps, stands, lids, lighting, tubing and minutiae.

Furthermore, Russel's friend happened to be a skilled draftsperson and had drawn up this rough layout. Twenty tanks would line an arched pathway that would be dark, like the bottom of the ocean, except for the tanks. Russel was all over the bar with blueprints and enthusiasm.

Manny listened idly, nodding, glancing, watching the mirror and the door.

Russel wrapped it up with the kind of summary he knew he'd been short on all these years. He reviewed projections for ticket sales and the traffic generated by a busy mall nearby that had already agreed to share its parking lot. The availability of the location had been confirmed, and he felt the project would gross two-fifty a year with total costs of sixty and a start-up budget of... Russel faltered here, couldn't help it, because the start-up budget was cold, hard cash. He cleared his throat and said, "Fifty thousand dollars."

Manny laughed short and wondered who in the hell this guy thought he was, but he didn't ask it. He thought maybe it could make a few bucks, but you couldn't tell how many. The location made perfect sense, and the schlemiel who owned it would be just dumb enough to rent it for too little, but the schlemiel undoubtedly figured the place worthless without parking, which Russel had already weaseled out of the shopping mall.

Russel hadn't factored a salary for himself, but Manny didn't question that either. He only asked what Russel intended to give the money man, who, after all, was the only man who could make this thing happen.

Russel shrugged, "Fifty-fifty."

"What? You want fifty thousand dollars and you put up what? The work? A little sweat and a sandwich in a bag? You put up zilch, and you want to call that even?

You listen to me, Harry. Nineteen years I been in this business. Hell, twenty. A hundred times I've seen people like you, two hundred times, got nothing, come to people like me, and then want it for free. Sweat equity. It doesn't exist."

"You make it sound unfair, but it's not," Russel said. "I put up the idea and the work. And the expertise." Manny laughed; expertise with fish bowls. "If it works, it makes much more than your fifty thousand in the first year. What's wrong with that? What are you going to do with a measly fifty grand anyway? Put it in the bank? What are you gonna get there? Interest?"

Manny had a good mind to tell this schmegeggy a thing or two about risk, which was the only thing rewarded in our mixed free-enterprise system. Manny was set to illuminate the night on who would take the risk, all the risk and nothing but the risk. And if these fish bowls and minutiae fail, who would eat the loss? The same guy who stood to reap the reward is who. Oh, Manny had it on the tip of his tongue so his primitive friend could see. But then it happened.

Two floozies walked in. Not just any old floozies; these were floozies extraordinaíre. These were floozies the likes of which a man like Manny Binder could only dream of, could only see on the street and ridicule to his wife, with whom he shared something substantial, something palpable with lasting value, something that would survive him. "Oh. Jeez-us," he said.

"Hey, Carol," Russel mellifluously intoned.

"Mm," Carol replied, drifting smoothly as fog on a marsh, enveloping Russel with her long, perfect arms. "Russel." She smooched him on the neck so deliberately and for such a long time that Manny knew it was meant to be a joke. So he smiled.

Russel asked, "Who's your friend?" Carol came up for air and said, "This is Marcy."

"Hi, Marcy."

"Hi, Russel."

"Hey, this is my friend, Manny."

"Hi, there," Manny said, amazed at how things fell into place so casually in the world of footloose singles. Hey, there's nothing better than a lovely home and family, but you could have some real fun out there with the drinks and the floozies and the who-knew-where an evening would lead to. Manny wondered if they had any idea what he represented or if that sort of thing mattered to women like this. He felt cool and properly dressed, so he played it cool, which was the right thing to do.

Carol, the leggy one, was obviously hot for Russel, leaving Marcy, the—uh hum!—busty one, ripe for the Mannymeister. And oh, did her eyes ever sparkle? You bet they did, just before she looked away and blushed. Now this was a side of life a businessman should not forget. This, Manny knew, playing it cool with a cool smile and a cool disposition as Carol said they had to "powder their noses." They'd be right back.

Manny found himself leaning out from the bar to better watch their derrières. He watched their luscious movement down the length of the bar and knew the night was meant for him. He chided himself for not stopping ahead of time to pick up some rubbers. But, hey, who knew? Russel had some rubbers. He had to. But hey, what was a man like Manny Binder supposed to do, put his life on the line betting that a guy like Russel Fox would have some rubbers? Not a chance. Forget it. Well, don't forget it. They sell rubbers in the men's room for occasions such as this. Don't they? Well, if they didn't, everyone was adult and a two-minute stop for rubbers was only reasonable.

"So?" Russel asked. "What do you think?"

"What's to think," Manny said. "Hubba hubba hubba? I think I've never hung out with you like this. I think it's a good idea. I think a man my age owes it to himself to have a little fun."

Russel laughed briefly. "No. I mean, what do you think about the aquarium."

"Aquarium? You mean the fish?"

"Aquarium. Seaquarium. I'm not sure what to call it yet, because Seaquarium usually means you have marine mammals, which I don't want. I think it's depressing, seeing those guys in there." Russel drank his beer reflectively, wondering how a fish felt about confinement. "It's kind of like doing time when they didn't do the crime. I don't know. It seems different with fish." But Manny focused on the women's bathroom door, hungry for these extraordinary beasts of pleasure. It was time. He was ready. "Manny?"

"Yeah. Hey, you know what? Why don't you come by the office tomorrow, uh, Russel. It's so much easier to talk business, you know what I mean, in that kind of atmosphere." He slid the lists and plans and sketches toward Russel for folding and stuffing back into a pocket, so they could be ready to entertain their dates.

Russel looked concerned. "To tell you the truth, Manny, I ran this by Bob Goldman..."

"Bob Goldman Homes? That Bob Goldman?"

Russel nodded. "He said he didn't want to move in on you, but he was good for half if you didn't want to do it."

Manny stared at the little hustler beside him, because that's what it came down to, even though Russel stared back with the overview at six-one next to Manny's five-seven. Focused now on getting this nonsense out of the way, he put it plain and simple. "Half doesn't work Russel. You need complete capitalization, or you got zilch. Bob Goldman. Did I ever tell you the story about the scorpion and the turtle? Okay, this turtle and this scorpion are on this island. Middle of this river..."

"Manny. You remember about a year ago I was selling advertising?" Manny neither remembered nor appreciated the interruption. "Well, Norman Stuhrs, the guy I worked for, said he'd go the other half." Russel finished his pint, turned and said. "Especially if Bob Goldman is in on it. He liked that."

So where does a guy get off? Manny said, "You got zilch, Russ. These guys, what? They promised the money. So where's the money?"

Russel smiled. "I felt like I owed you first shot, Manny. You offered to help before anyone else did."

"That's right. So what's different now, except that you got a couple of you-know-whats doing you up. Hey. Take their money. I don't need this."

Manny sipped his beer wondering how people can drink the stuff, in pints no less. Russel shrugged. "Okay." He folded all the papers and rolled the pile and mashed it kind of flat and stuffed it into his back pocket. "Didn't mean to get you upset."

"Russel. Come see me tomorrow."

"What for?"

Manny drank up. "You want to do a deal or not?"

Russel looked puzzled as Carol and Marcy emerged. Manny was peeved at Russel, distracting things with such a good time at hand—the good time he never had on account of the sacrifices required to get to where he was, so the money would be available for guys like Russel Fox and their cockamamie deals. But boy, an eyeful of USDA Prime Floozy was a distraction to his distraction. This was like running but better, with the heart pumping, the sweats coming on and some oo la la just over the rainbow. On impulse—one reflecting generosity and discretionary income—Manny called, "Bartender. Can we have some service, please." Drinks would be on him.

"Nah!" Russel protested. "We gotta go."

Stuck briefly on the inclusion issue, Manny recovered nicely with a simple question, "Go? Go where?"

Russel shrugged. "We don't know yet." Carol nestled in, taking his arm.

"So? Have a drink. Decisions can be made here."

To his disappointment, Marcy snuggled on Russel's other side. Manny felt the slow ache of desire inch across his chest as she practically wedged his arm between her impressive floozy breasts. "Nah," Russel said, sliding off his stool and easing out. "This place is dead."

Manny nodded slowly, no longer stuck but waiting for word on the inclusion issue. Russel dispatched the verdict casually. "Hey, man. See you down at the club." And just like that he drifted into space and the Promised Land. Then they were gone.

"Yes, sir," the bartender said. Manny nodded, accepting what he'd known all along, given a split second to think about it. Oil and water don't mix, and a man of means, a man of responsibility with a lovely home and a family can't very well mix with bums and floozies. Because that was exactly what they were. The bartender served the fresh pint, so cloudy it looked like an old urine sample. "That's four dollars." Manny peeled off a five. Four bucks for a beer when you can drink perfectly good beer at home for what, fifty, sixty cents? And a lovely home at that, on a bluff. On a corner lot. Then the bartender gave him back a dollar bill. Like what, he was supposed to leave the whole thing for a tip?

Jeez-us, he thought, tasting the foamy brew. Who drinks this stuff? He took another taste, admitting that it wasn't as bad as some beer he'd tried, not by a long shot. He swigged half of it so he could get rid of it and get the heck out of there. It wasn't so bad after the first of it, but he would never, ever acquire a taste for it. That's what they said about beer, that you had to acquire a taste. They didn't know about Manny Binder's perseverance. He drank it down to the last two inches and weighed cost/benefit on leaving what was left.

Then, to his surprise, a floozy walked in, hardly extraordinary but not so bad. He watched her in the mirror, preserving his cool. She slid onto a stool, opened her purse for a smoke and lit up. The bartender didn't say hello or ask what she wanted.

"You don't care about lady's night at Gogan's?" Manny asked by way of a smooth, casual ice-breaker.

"It's Grogan's," she said. "Gag me Grogan's. And hell no I don't care about it. Scratch that. I do care. That's why I'm here." She took a hard pull on her cigarette. She smoked the extra long variety. She corrected her posture as Manny took her in, late-thirties, chunky in the middle but not bad. Too much make-up but not bad. Some saddle spread but not too bad. And who minds frizzy hair in the dark?

"So?" Manny said. "So what?" She exhaled. "So what are you drinking?"

"Gimme a sunrise, Harry," she said. Turning to Manny she agreed, "Gimme me some privacy any night."

Manny nodded and factored cost/benefit on one more cloudy beer. And what could be the harm of another little while on a night like tonight for a man out on the town? Time was free. Well, maybe not free, but things were picking up, factoring nicely and looking good.

Everything You Need to Know

A woman surviving her forties with a svelte figure has earned her place in the sun. Anyone thinking otherwise should give it a go; kids, no kids, it doesn't matter. A man can look good at seventy with less effort than a woman who still turns heads at fifty. And if you don't think twenty years hard labor is a sentence, then you're still squeezing into your britches.

Breasts are easy enough. You wear a bra—wear it to bed if they're big enough and always wear it jogging if you can stand jogging.

Barbara North could not stand jogging, not with all that bouncing, jamming and soreness. Sure, it provides the sense of well-being we all seek in endorphin-releasing exercise, but it's still her least favorite of the pneumatic pursuits. Bicycling is a far better ticket to quick and easy calorie burning with none of the pounding. You should sit proud on a bicycle to preserve spinal integrity, and a couple hundred sit-ups are an excellent warm-up. They compensate as well for the tummy sag occurring so easily on a bicycle. Barbara rides every day, weather permitting.

Thighs and buttocks can be more problematic than tummy and breasts, but like most aspects of fitness, this one, too, comes down to diet. Lay off the fats and sugars.

That's all there is to it. Liposuction is a viable alternative, depending on your standards; a woman who has worked her way into the sun can tell the difference between what's been earned and what's been bought. The tone is different, and even though they claim less scarring these days, a woman knows.

Barbara North loves swimming as much as bicycling, but water and chlorine dry the skin so badly that swimming is strictly a foul-weather pursuit. She lived in McCreary County six months, through spring and summer, before finding the public pool one rainy day in late September. In a nylon one-piece so skimpy and clingy that many women half her age couldn't wear it successfully, she took the plunge.

She thought it was chance that Ian Davidson sat in the lifeguard stand that day as she dipped her toe in the water and adjusted her goggles. She looked up with a friendly smile. He looked down with the same. He too wore a nylon one-piece with no overhang or stretch, only the sleek silhouette of young manhood.

Yet slouched on the lifeguard seat as if the apex of youth and energy were lost on this gig, Ian Davidson pulled in his stomach and sat up straight. He wondered: How much beer is in a beer belly? Surely more than the few he had on the weekend. And though a young man leaning hard on eighteen knows that things are changing, they don't change that fast. The physical man outpaces the boy inside, who can only hurry and wait to catch up. He smiled and stretched, twisting his body and arms to maximum advantage in an unbridled display of fitness, abdominal ripple and triceps development.

He didn't need to do that, she thought. That's one of the problems with young men; they just don't accept the obvious. They have no faith in the intelligence and subtlety of those around them. A male and female, no matter what ages, trading friendly smiles and friendly eyefuls in their nylon one-pieces generate a spark. It cannot be otherwise with muscle tone at such a high level and combined body fat so low. Besides that, she thought, many boys fantasize a classy woman. Barbara North is classy, even with her long silky hair tied back in a bun. She smiled again to herself, glad that she'd buffed her nails last night instead of waiting—toenails too. Men love a woman with pretty feet, she thought.

He smiled again too. Wow, he thought.

She was cool, slipping in with hardly a ripple, her reach and pull as graceful as that of a once-great swimmer. He's watching, she thought, but he can't see me smile now. I love swimming. It feels so good and keeps a woman so trim. She made a mental note to hold her own stomach in when she got out, which wouldn't be cheating if you factored the years she was giving away, and besides, she's a woman. At least she could still hold her stomach in. She planned twenty laps but agreed with herself to cut it short if she got sloppy or too much stuff started coming out her nose.

With only two children in a private lesson on the far side, Ian Davidson's attention was hardly divided. Pushing eighteen is old enough for a guy to get around. It was mostly hand jobs in junior high, but since senior year started with working the pool, sexual experience accumulated on a regular basis. He'd felt his fair share of breasts in the last month. And once, when Lori Boatright was the other lifeguard, and it was only the two of them cleaning up, closing up, warming up and feeling up, she got so excited rubbing him, she took it out of his Speedos and stared at it. He shifted position in the lifeguard stand just as he had shifted in the hands of Lori Boatright, as if his vocal chords were stuck. Wiggling like a worm on a hook he strove to encourage her to take the bait, or rub the bait, or do something with it.

Lori Boatright practically thought they were going steady after that. Ian thought her strange, getting so enamored after simply staring at it. Not that he wouldn't want to stare at hers, but his would have stood at attention for nearly any of the girls staring at it. Lori must have thought it really appreciated her stare. He wondered if he should have slid her suit down, and though he regretted the missed opportunity, he thought his conservatism best. With her swimsuit down around her knees, she could hardly have run if someone walked in.

He had asked Lori Boatright if she would, you know, want to get a Coke or something. Uncertain where to go to see what came next, he thought forward motion best, because one thing just might lead to another. He hadn't thought of Lori Boatright in a sexual way but, like everyone else did, he considered her generous. She was full of school spirit, which Ian thought corny but had to admit, he loved it when they cheered for him. He really wanted to score the big one, because it was time, and Lori Boatright seemed fine for a try.

Then again, maybe she was only bucking for a more public relationship. He would be a starter this year on the varsity waterpolo team, and he had excellent triceps and a heft in his Speedos. Why wouldn't she want to get a Coke? She would. Then they could see what happened. One thing was certain; she liked looking at it.

He wondered if Lorry B would do it with her mouth. That would be generous. He thought she would if they were going steady—really steady, seriously. He wondered if you could go seriously steady for a few days and then, you know, just be friends again. He wondered if the old lady fox swimming laps ever did it with her mouth. He bet she had.

*   *   *

Eighteen. That's enough, she thought, even though she was still looking good and hardly any stuff was coming out her nose. She coasted into the shallows, stood up, removed her goggles and hair band and shook out her hair. At the ladder she pulled her tummy in and pulled herself up. She gathered her things and headed out, passing closely to the lifeguard stand. "Is the pool open every day?" she asked.

"Yes, Ma'm" he said. "Lap swim every day, two to five." He stared at her nipples. She covered her chest with her towel. He turned beet red; caught.

"Thanks." She left.

She swam daily after that. They caught each other looking, but dialogue remained sparse. They wouldn't meet by chance in town, because she didn't go out, except to her job or with certain select men. And even if she did go out alone, where would a woman her age run into a teenage boy? Besides, she stayed in to paint. Painting fulfilled her. Still, they considered each other and suspected as much of the other. Sometimes they spoke to each other in their fantasies. But nothing would come of it, she thought, if he didn't have the brains required to connect with a woman. So she asked one day what happens after lap swim.

He looked puzzled. "What happens?"

"Does the pool close?"

He shrugged, "Yeah."

"Thanks."

She arrived late that day and went only ten laps when she noticed the clock at 5:05. She hesitated and looked up to Ian for guidance. He told her to take her time, he still had to put things away and clean up. "Thanks," she burbled, easing back into her long, graceful stroke, wondering if she could swim longer than it would take him to clean up.

Ian found himself contemplating assistance in clean up. Lori Boatright was already assisting and that would have been fine, but two prospects seemed like a crowd, and he frankly itched for something more than a stare. He favored the old one, she seemed so much more likely to know what to do after staring at it. At 5:12, Lori beamed that she had to go, but she would, like, check him later. Okay? Sure, he shrugged, wondering if this was what a run of luck felt like and if he should just ask the old lady fox if she wanted to see it. He laughed; what a fool.

Barbara North gave up when her stroke shortened and grace failed about 5:17. How freaking clean does the place have to be? But then he was done.

"Whenever you're ready," he said.

"I'm ready." She got out and hit the showers. They could hear each other's showers and imagine each other soaping up. But she would never soap; it was so drying. She wondered if he had a car and promised herself not to offer him a ride if he didn't. Availability was one thing; cold pursuit was something else.

He wondered what kind of line Vegas would put on the evening's prospect. He'd heard about women that old. He knew she was at least thirty-five. Maybe thirty-eight. That's old, but that's okay because they know they don't have much time left, and all you need is the first affirmative to take it all the way. He'd even heard that they not only do things the young ones won't do but that they like it, some of them, some of it. So what could he ask? You want to go to your place?

It isn't hard for a woman to take longer dressing than a man or a boy. He waited for her at the door. He looked side to side. He looked outside. He looked down. He looked away, opening the door.

"Thanks," she said, slipping out.

He gritted his teeth. "Want to get a beer?"

"Sure," she said. He breathed short with a gasp of relief and amazement. She stopped and turned. "How old do you have to be around here?"

He dropped his voice a notch and said, "I'm old enough." She laughed. He didn't have to do that.

He laughed too, to fit in. My mother is forty-two, he thought.

"Is your car okay?" she asked, thinking way ahead.

"Sure," he shrugged. So she followed him to a pub in the mall. It was the only place he felt sure of.

Dumb as a kid ever was, she thought, sipping her beer, wondering if he would find two syllables.

"I like this place," he said, making a commitment to measured good taste. Low-lit with bumpy-glass candleholders and dirty, dark, hofbrau decor, the place closed in with its imposing scent and overbearing familiarity.

"Seems strange to me," she said. "A hofbrau pub in a mall?"

"What's so strange about that?"

She shrugged, remembering when a roadhouse was on the road, remembering the olden days, before the mall era. "I don't know," she said. "It's so dark. And stuffy."

"Yeah," he said. "It's too stuffy." He nodded, looking down at the napkin he slowly twisted. "I like the beer though."

The beer was sour, most likely because the tap hadn't been cleaned this year. She drank a light beer that tasted like light kerosene. She glanced over then turned and took him in. The great thing about boys is their shyness, she thought. It gives you a chance to look them over; you can scrutinize down to the fuzz on their ears. She liked that. He was a cutie, his cheeks still half-blushed from something he thought he said wrong or maybe from some naked thought. She wondered if he got kinky with his fantasies. A man once asked her what she fantasized, no holds barred, and next thing you know—well, before sunrise anyway—there she was, seeking the dream with this guy she hardly knew. What a jerk, too, once the sun came up.

But this was different. This kid was no jerk, not yet. He could be fun but boy, did he need help.

She looked away, her hand brushing his. Were those heat ripples? She looked back to catch the beautiful blush. A boy's wildest dream isn't rocket science. He looked down to focus on his twisting.

Any psychic could read her appetite, could see her assessment. He was so young, so sweet, so physically prime, so brimful of shelf-life. Here he was on the threshold of sexual adventure—psychic hell; Bugs Bunny could read this picture. But not him. He sat here assuming the pose of intellectual brooding, cool as a cucumber—a big, ripe thumper. Plans for college? She didn't ask. Who cares? Live at home? School going well? Got a girlfriend? Been swimming long? Parents divorced? Who cares? Who cares? Who cares?

"Got a curfew?" she asked.

He nodded slowly and kind of side to side, meaning that rules were made to be broken, especially if you're already practically eighteen. "They get, like, jumpy if I don't call."

"Got a girlfriend?"

"No."

She looked into her drink. "You know, the thing about women is they want to think certain things."

"I know."

"What do you know?"

"They want to think you like them. And maybe you'll, you know, maybe not exactly go steady, but maybe, you know, maybe you will."

She laughed, regretting that she found him laughable. So she took his hand and shook her head. "I don't want to go steady," she said. "But I'll tell you something. I think you're not so dumb." She laughed again. "Sorry. I'll let you in on a little secret. It's a mental thing."

"I know."

"Shut up, Mr. Smarty Pants. You don't know. Most women don't care if you split tomorrow. Never seen or heard from again. Deep down inside, they get over it sooner or later. They want to think it's their call."

"Like a control thing."

"Not exactly. I don't need to control anyone. I only want to think I can get in line for seconds if I want to."

"You mean, like, tonight?"

Her turn to blush. "Any time."

"Why couldn't you? I mean, you're beautiful."

She blushed harder. Eighteen years old and taking her through the turns. She turned away. When she turned back, he glanced at her neck where it creased above her collarbone. She brought her torso square to flatten the wrinkles and covered her collarbone with her hand to be sure. She had great hands with smooth skin and long nails, her own. What was it she was going to say? It was right on the tip of her tongue. He said she was beautiful... Oh, yeah: "Want to come over some time?"

"Yes," he said with a fidget but also with restraint, because he knew that women, even real women, need to go very slowly.

"Well. First I need to tell you something." He was all ears with a dash of disappointment. He slouched into what could be a long wait, anticipating the hard news; six children with extreme needs, an insanely jealous husband or two, a potentially contagious disease or, worst of all, a week's delay for no reason at all. He glanced around. He could buy a new condom in the bathroom and they could just go somewhere in the back of her car and do it. Well, they could use his car, but hers seemed more—"Pay attention, please."

"I am." He settled in; real women don't do it in the back of a car; he knew that. Well, if it was set up right, you know, like with everyone laughing and maybe a few beers to go...

"I have views on sex that most people don't share. But they should." He waited for her views on sex. "I think it's completely natural. I think it's what people do all the time. They love it. They like hearing about it and seeing it on TV. They especially like hearing about politicians doing it, but I doubt politicians do it with any more imagination than they display with politics. I mean, it's no big deal." She took another sip of her beer and remembered its sour taste. She set it down with disgust.

He smiled with an air of finality; he could handle her unique worldview and was ready to go. She sat back and sighed. He followed suit. It seemed settled.

She reached into her purse for a few bucks, slid out and stood up and asked, "Ready?"

"That's it?"

"That's it," she said, hooking his arm with her own.

That feels weird, he thought walking out with her on his arm. It was so clingy and made them look like they were going steady already, when she was so...old. He glanced her way to see her up close, wondering if she would change.

Out from under the hofbrau shadow they hit the deluge of mall lighting and a thousand eyes suddenly focused on the old lady and the kid. What is that? He felt a hot flash from his core, this one non-hormonal, but rather embarrassing. Forget it, he told himself, rising to the occasion, standing taller, taking her hand with his free hand; guys take their aunts for a beer all the time, or their mothers. With this in mind he sent another smile her way, one of family warmth, rated G. His eyes settled on the gossamer wrinkles veiling her complexion.

Oh, man, he thought, but gave in to momentum when his eyes rolled down her blouse and stayed there way past cool. He felt uncertain but knew he was doing the right thing.

What a pup, she thought. "Could you blink if you had to?"

"What?"

"Stop looking down my blouse."

"Sorry."

"You don't have to be sorry. Just don't do it." He felt glum, blowing it so badly so soon. "Not here."

Man oh man, he thought; she said 'not here,' meaning it would be okay somewhere else.

"There's something else," she said in the parking lot. She wondered why she couldn't just take the kid home and enjoy herself without gumming things up.

"What?"

"Women are different than men."

"I know."

"They get attached very fast."

"I know."

"Will you shut up."

"Yes."

"I don't get attached. Maybe that's why I'm not married. But I sometimes feel a bond after, you know. It scares me." He knew what she meant; that she might just stare at it, or maybe she'd want to go ahead and do it with her mouth, or maybe they'd just do the big score, but any way it played out would be cool. They could still go for a Coke, I mean beer, and just be friends. And that's the way he wanted it, too.

"I mean, I'm not a masochist," she said. He knew what masochist meant as well. He knew he did. It was... It had something to do with getting beat up. "Nobody wants to suffer."

He knew that, too, but he only shrugged and nodded. She laughed. Smart boy. Then they parted for the long drive to her place. She asked herself what she was doing and why. And she laughed, knowing what and why and wherefore art thou my tender fountain of youth. He wondered briefly if his luck would hold and tried to help it along by thinking, *Come on, come on, come on!*

She lived in somebody's garage. Not a garage, really, it was all fixed up like Snow White's place. He wondered how many other dwarfs she brought home. She set her purse down, stepped up to him and put her hands on his shoulders. She stared at him for a long time, then kissed him softly on the lips. She slid her hands down to his hips and drew him near for the Morse code that spelled eighteen-year-old male. Well, nearly eighteen.

There's really nothing like it, she thought. She wondered if she would rather undress him or drive him wild undressing herself. She decided on a mixed plate and began slowly with her buttons. He stood and stared, until she pushed him to the edge of the bed where he sat and stared. He wondered if she always wore a lace bra that you could actually see through and actually see her nipples. He thought she most likely did and knew that he would too if he was her. Besides, she was that classy. She unhooked her bra in the center and stepped up to him.

He went as slow as he could, which was down to about sixty miles an hour with a slight tremble, peeling off the bra to get to the breasts. They were proud and a source of pride as well. These breasts had been cared for, nurtured, protected from the ravages of gravity, suction and impact. These breasts were in excellent shape, their presentation dramatically enhanced by a racy tan line. This, a woman knows. A woman contemplates return on effort in the act of honing her body. She felt confident and thought: *Wait till he sees my tummy.*

But the kid was far from done with the breasts. He felt them carefully, nearly scientifically, gathering data in the laboratory that is everyboy's brain. He wanted to lick them but didn't want to offend her or make her think he was a sex maniac. No, far better to take the thoughtful approach for now. It's what a man of the world would do, a man for whom terrific breasts were a casual, common occurrence. "It's like..." Going again to intellectual assessment, he paused to order his thoughts before speaking them. Contemplation was pleasant distraction as well for the license his fingertips took, right on the nubs. "It's like, you won't look like you could be in Playboy forever. And then we'll, you know, have to...you know...just be friends."

"Jesus," she said, slumping as her bubble burst, wondering how long you have to live before you stop finding yourself in ridiculous situations. "You're such a fool."

He dropped his hands and tensed. He'd been bad but wasn't certain how. If only he'd learn some day to keep his big mouth shut.

She pulled him to the front of the full-length dressing mirror and removed his shirt, pulled down his trousers, knelt and pulled down his drawers. She didn't exactly stare at it but didn't lose sight of it either as she spoke around it. She explained that modern times call for certain measures. "You mean condoms," he said.

She said, "Yes." He reached into his back pocket for the crumpled, shriveled, emergency packet he'd carried around since summer before last, soon after learning about condoms in health class. She said, "I have a fresh one. But don't worry about that now."

He shrugged and said, "Okay, but..." But next thing you know she was doing what he imagined Lori Boatright would do some day but this was much better—not better than Lori Boatright could do; who knew? But it was better than he'd imagined; he could hardly believe his eyes or the unfathomable feeling between his legs.

Yet telling himself it was true, all true, he remembered Coach Griffith's warning in health class, the session where the boys learned about condoms. Coach admonished to always wear one, even for fellatio, or fellation. "Oh, heck. You guys know what blowjobs are." Well, of course the boys knew but hearing Coach Griffith admit that he knew that they knew was enough to bust a gasket, which it did, especially when smart-guy Roger Rimsley asked if you had to wear a rubber if your wife was giving you a blowjob. Coach Griffith wanted to give Roger a few demerits for that one, but he couldn't, because Roger had him. Everyone knew you didn't need to wear a rubber if your wife was giving you a blowjob. But nobody was married except for Coach, who took a second or two and finally said, "We didn't even know you were engaged, Roger. Who's the lucky girl?" That let everyone laugh all over Roger, who loved being the center of attention. Coach brought everyone back to the severity of the moment with assurance that even a blowjob can transmit disease, including the dreaded disease.

"Uh, the...thing of it...is..." Ian said, but heck, she looked like she knew as much about it as Coach, and anyway, what was he supposed to do, go up Niagara Falls in a barrel? Then he blushed with embarrassment and love, gushing from the heart.

Well, she thought, catching her breath and sorting things out. The good thing about boys is they don't keep you waiting. She led him back to the bed, sat him on the edge and said, "Look, I think, first, we should talk about love."

His brief laugh rose above his spiritual fatigue. She was life itself letting him know why he lived, and she echoed from the abyss between boyish fantasy and a blowjob that would haunt his dreams for years. "First?"

She touched his cheek. "That's what I meant," she said. "People get so excited about a blowjob. That's all it was. A blowjob."

"Yeah, well, maybe, but...you..."

"I like you. It doesn't happen that often."

How often? He wanted to know but dare not ask, dabbling at last in the skills of worldliness. "Do you?... Do you want me to...you know?"

She smiled. "That would be nice, if you want to." He glanced down but wouldn't look squarely at it, maybe for fear of upsetting the apple cart again, or maybe just from fear. "Maybe later," she said. "It'll give us something to look forward to."

"Well..."

"Forget it. Let's talk about something."

He lay back. "Okay."

She was ready to do him again, he thought, even though he hadn't rubbed her or anything, and she'd hardly even stared at it. He nodded his head, thinking he could have asked her to do it with her mouth right off the bat, but maybe not, and anyway this was kind of right off the bat, but still, if he'd known then what he knew now.

"What?" she asked.

He shrugged. "Just thinking."

"About what?"

"About you. And...you know."

"Did you like it?"

"Yeah."

She eased on down beside him, resting a hand on his thigh. They lay there, her hand easing inward, touching and feeling the relentless pulse of youth, until she finally said, "Okay. I'm ready."

Ready for what would have been a stupid question; even Ian Davidson knew that. And he wasn't afraid, not truly. But he'd never even looked at one before, much less stared at it, much less gotten in as close as he wanted and, well, touched it. With his tongue? These things he now did, filling Barbara North with a sense of guilt; she so loved the awkward fiddling of a teenage boy, and he would most likely think he'd done it right. He didn't do so badly, except for sniffing it first and then tasting it like it was cinnamon dill or chocolate Parmesan or something of frightening consequence. She finally told him he could stick his tongue in there and move it around, or they both had better things to do. So he advanced a half-inch of tongue and moved it around, making her sympathetic to the teachers of today. But sympathies turned academic when she held his head in there for the last little bit.

He came up gasping. He'd held his breath. What a pooch, but that's what messing around with boys will get you. The gaffs are all theirs, but then so is the durability. Game as a pogo stick, once he wiped his face, Ian Davidson was up and in quicker than a b-ball with two seconds before the buzzer. Not that this go was necessary, but capping things off properly seemed best for all parties. And a woman likes to know she can still inspire rapid recovery.

They relaxed for awhile afterward in pleasant dialogue on school, dating, water polo, his parents and what kind of car he would have some day. And then, so naturally he didn't even wonder why she had them around, they played a few video games while munching Cheez-its and enjoying a few Miller Lites. She allowed him one more go front and center, because the boys are all gushers. He hardly spoke during, until she suggested that he wear one of her flimsy negligees some time. He looked worried and asked why. She said because. He said oh. Oh. Oh. Oh.

Then he had to go. He didn't want to go, so she took his hand and said, "Come with me," and she led him to the door. She leaned back on it and said goodbye, but he lingered, still amazed at the free license to pull her sweater open, see and touch her breasts.

"They're different when you're standing up," he said. What a pooch, she thought. He wanted to stay, just for a minute or two, so she could see him off by doing him again with her mouth. And though experience builds confidence in a young man, he could muster only a longing twitch, a beggar's body language, as if polite formality was the grown-up thing to do.

A woman knows what a man wants, even a junior man. Incredible, she thought, ready in ten minutes. But she too felt practical constraints; no sooner would she compliment or relieve him than the certain arrogance would go straight to his head, so to speak. Not that she disliked his stamina. But one of them had to understand the benefits of moderation. Besides, she had to get ready.

So she explained that some things were meant to be reserved for special occasions, that she only showed him something before. Exploitation isn't nice and would lead to stale relations. Ian Davidson nodded comprehension on the intellectual plane but still twitched on the subterranean as if to say, *pulleeeze!*

Finally, whining like a pup who got no chow, he was eased out the door. "Now you can go," she said.

She leaned on the jamb, thinking. There is simply nothing like them, the boys. She regretted the loss of a comfortable format for swimming, but that's the way it goes; it's selection or convenience, quality or price, comfort or speed, security or adventure. This one was pure fun, up to snuff and sure to be back, but with any luck not until tomorrow after lunch.

He drove home dazed. He would confess to drug experimentation when his parents detected euphoria. Surely they would. What else could he say? That he'd had his horn honked good and plenty by an old lady fox? Older than Mom? Well, maybe not older than Mom, but still, they'd go through the roof. Mom would anyway. Dad might understand but wouldn't admit it, not in front of Mom. He half-wondered if Mom and Dad, like, you know, but he squelched the image quick because it was disgusting. He savored instead this incredible new feeling. In coming years he would call it fresh-fucked, but for now he thought it only something different from all that came before. He contemplated dinner. Then he would outline a term paper he shouldn't have put off. Then he would savor a hard night's sleep.

Barbara North contemplated dinner as well, either French or Italian. She hadn't decided yet but had to hurry, because fixing your face and changing modes from playful to classic in forty-five minutes is no walk in the park. Well, maybe she had an hour, which was a good and bad thing about Sylvan Weidermeyer of Weidermeyer Industries; the guy was always late.

But jovial, with a generous warmth commensurate to his fortunes, Sylvan could have his pick of the girls. It was no small gratification to a woman like Barbara North that he'd picked her. He wasn't the same kind of fun as a boy like Ian, but then Ian didn't own the world and everything in it like Sylvan. Barbara freshened her blush and redefined her liner and thought, hey, some men have two cars, so why shouldn't I?

Not that Sylvan Weidermeyer was a stuffy sedan. He enjoyed a plush ride as well as the next man, usually once per evening, an evening or two per week. And even if he rolled over and snored, he didn't snore loudly; in fact, he most often snored gently. His gentle snore endeared him, if indeed a snore can endear a man struggling through his slumbers. Sylvan also appreciated special favors, but not like a boy who trembles from his very core. Now that was fun, and where else could they get it, the boys? From the pom pom girls? No, that kind of skill doesn't turn up overnight; not over one night anyway.

But where the boys seemed overwrought with faulty wiring, practically arcing with voltage overload, a man like Sylvan Weidermeyer could allow for friendship. The money allowed for comfort. Barbara North did not fear the aging process and knew it drew nigh when she thought of him as a dear, sweet man. She'd considered men in these terms before but never a man with whom she engaged in sexual relations. She wondered why sexual relations had become a focal point for her, and if frictional pursuit would remain a preoccupation. She felt confident she could adapt as necessary but saw no change on the horizon. She knew some men would be jealous, but what could a teenage boy be jealous of? That she had a real life? And what could Sylvan mind, not that he wouldn't, but still, Ian was a boy, a kid. Nothing but a fling, a little fun to make her feel, as the song said, how she used to feel. Besides, she would never reach the summit with Ian; this, she knew. He wouldn't find himself for years.

These and other assessments accompanied the quick change of an aerobically fit woman with excellent tone who could still lure the lifeguard home, to the elegant companion of a man of means, a man of consequence, a man, as another song said, of wealth and taste. Barbara North needed very little highlight but loved the shadow over her eyes and the blue green accent below. Applying her artistry she wondered how many songs there were with phrases describing the men she could please—well, no, please is the wrong word; any woman can please any man. Better would be the kind of men I could suit.

It didn't matter. She capped the liner and eyed herself once over, slamming the hood and cranking it up, as it were. Boys and men were all she needed. Why carry things any further? Then came a knock on the door.

"Oh, Sylvan." She expected him, but her little show of surprise served their common amusement. He was a pleasant surprise in the context of her life, of which this evening would be one more pleasant interlude. She was the prize he'd worked toward.

For the briefest moment the landscape out the front door shone with power and drama as lightning forked its billion volts. As if serendipitously, the flash back-lit the seasoned man who'd come calling, lighting as well the lovely spirit that spanned her years.

As a woman of intrinsic femininity, a woman innately womanly, she never worried about the years. She would tell her age no more freely than a ten-penny nail lets go of a plank without a crowbar. Yet it was only a meaningless number, as long as physical failure was held at bay. Fear of aging isn't gender-based but is normal for everyone. Who wants to fall apart?

She'd proven that forty is hardly different from late youth, and fifty isn't nearly as old from the hind side. Millions of men want a w-o-m-a-n, sixty be damned, and so it would go, life on earth as we know it, with the lovely hormones, their incessant itching and scratching. Twenty years or twenty-five; it isn't so long ago if you were only pushing thirty. She felt no different. She felt better in some ways, more relaxed. She moved out of the thrilling flash of knowing with a slow writhe.

He liked that. She still had it, every bit of it, especially in the afterglow, where romance plays best.

No, she wasn't worried about making the cut for Playboy—what a little pooch. She would miss the boys when they ceased going gaga. Until then the years ahead would be rife with fun.

Sylvan Weidermeyer stepped up to embrace the body that still had it. As they snuggled she wondered if in fifteen years she would snuggle like this to a genteel man named Ian Davidson. She'd only be...

Well, she'd still have it.

Yet a specter loomed like smoke after the lightning strike. All women look like Norman Bates's mother sooner or later, and the day would come for spiritual preparation. That's the last time you'd want men around. It made her shiver, these unwelcome thoughts of aging. In her trembling, a frightened laugh escaped, like that of a child holding down the lid on the pressure cooker.

"Chilled?" Sylvan asked. She made a contented moan. He rubbed his beefy hands up and down her arms and said, "You look good in goose bumps."

She tittered. He leaned in and sniffed her neck, which put her on the swinging bridge over the canyon, the one with the rotten shreds between here and eternity. Oh, God, she thought.

"Mm," he said. "It's you. I'd know it blindfolded."

"Mm," she concurred.

"Mm, yes, lovely," he pursued, pulling her in and bridging the canyon anew with a propitiously available log. His own scent was that of middle-aged man and aftershave. She felt his stubble round her mouth. He wanted her. It was all right but really shouldn't occur until later, after dinner and drinks and a reasonable respite from that sort of thing. Besides, a woman begins to feel used when a sensitive, companionable man comes on too soon, too strongly.

"Sylvan," she said.

"I know," he said. "I wonder if you could humor me this once. I don't know what's got into me, except you. I had a strange day. Things went well. It was uncanny, left me fresh, if you understand."

"I understand. I just, well, a girl hardly...you know."

"I know, and I won't insist. It was just an idea. A lovely one, I thought."

He left it there for musing, which is the thing you have to love about a mature man, a man who can let a woman choose between the early amorous and the elegant repast. Still, he was man, fiddling with the buttons in back of her dress, reaching in to unhook her bra, peeling all from her shoulders delicately as grape skin until she stood in the open door half-naked and chilled, grasping his obtrusive self, because reciprocity is the bedrock of companionship.

But then he asked, "What the?..." when Ian pulled up, lighting the meadows of life anew.

A man like Sylvan Weidermeyer is not easily ruffled. With casual aplomb he tucked himself in as his date stepped back to rearrange herself. When Ian was up the walkway, Sylvan asked, "Yes?"

Well, of course poor Ian could not wait until tomorrow after lunch. He surprised everyone, himself included, and all those present regretted that a young man of such apparent ability and confidence should here appear so lost and alone. "I uh... I forgot uh... I forgot my notebook."

Oh, you could feel the wheels turn in a mind like Sylvan Weidermeyer's, a mind that knew the sum of two plus two but ground down to bare metal trying to sum up two plus oranges. "Your notebook?"

"Yeah, I left it, you know, inside."

Sylvan turned slowly to the shadow behind the door. "I'll get it," she said, scurrying off to find a notebook she knew was never there but could be if she could find a notebook. Stepping into the living room, since that's where a notebook would be left, she froze. She shuffled the old magazines and books on her coffee table and came up with a loose volume of the Time Life Series on Remodeling Your Bathroom Yourself. Resigning herself to another difficult truth, *I'll never get to it*, she perked and said, "Ah, there it is." She took a minute for realignment and was back out front in a jiff.

"I found it," she said, turning into the stretch. Sylvan and Ian were having a nice chat, in which Ian explained the highlights of his senior year, including water polo and life guarding and the trouble he was having in, uh, uh...

"If x equals y, and y equals z, then x equals z. That's everything you need to know for the first phase," she laughed good-naturedly, thinking there is a god in heaven and a reason to take algebra in high school. Or was that geometry? Swinging the volume deftly from her blind side up to Ian's side, she snugged it under his arm so he wouldn't lose it again. *Well, good night Ian* was on the tip of her tongue when Ian showed the tip of his own, and joined her in unison,

"Well, good night." She and Sylvan smiled good-naturedly. Then Ian smiled good-naturedly and waited, as if there was some way he could, you know, for a few minutes... But he turned and left, foolishly repeating, "Good night."

They watched him down the walkway, Sylvan easing her back to the shadow before Ian was out of sight. The door eased as well and clicked securely. "Where were we?" he asked.

"Mm," she said, sensing the jig was up; for no man lets another man pass like that without knowing what was up. But what can a girl do? Play it out is what. Apparently aroused now for a wallow before dinner, he left little choice, and she soon stood naked. He remained clothed. Isn't that the way it goes? She smiled on the outside but cringed within; *fucking pigs; sometimes I've had enough.* But she said, "Mm," and led him to the boudoir to get this over with. At least he disrobed.

"My God you're a beauty," he said, compensating the crude pressure with what a woman wants to hear. But praise was brief before he launched himself like a lumberjack on a bowl of beans. She stroked his head in resignation; she knew he knew, and she had to love the older men for their acceptance of what life comes down to. He came up with a sigh. "I hope you make the boys wear their rubbers."

"I make them wear all kinds of things," she said, playfully ignoring the sordid truth. This answer seemed acceptable. He resumed. She feigned the summit but was in fact fatigued. She shrugged at the boy in the window but soon looked anywhere but the window, because Sylvan was up, wiping his chin and saying, "Your turn, dearest. Clean your plate, young lady. Peas and carrots too or no desert."

Well, a girl in a pinch can only make the best of a ticklish situation. She wondered how a boy would accept things as she knelt to the task. Sylvan went pneumatic, holding her head in place and delivering the mature version of the mother lode. He too shrugged for the boy in the window but with a grimace and a grin.

He made a great show of the dam bursting.

Pulling away gently, sitting on the bed and looking for his underpants he said, "It doesn't matter. You'd never remodel your bathroom anyway." Sylvan could cut to the quick like that. That was his intrigue and most likely counted for his success in industry; he knew things all along. "I'm starved," he said. "How about you?"

Befuddled again in the dark with a queasy yen for a cola and a determination to pace herself anew, Barbara North said, "Sure. Starving."

Sylvan knew things and could keep you guessing. You had to appreciate the older men for the experience and repartee they had to offer, like when he said, "Take the kid if you want. Seems like a nice enough boy."

The Monk

I have the background and the training. I'm not the athlete I was twenty-five years ago, but the spirit lingers like sipping whiskey. It smoothes out with fermentation and loses its recoil. An older man is more efficient with less effort where a younger man can only scramble.

The recipe for an aging athlete is simple: take what's left of agility, season liberally with resilience, flavor with gamesmanship to taste. Oh, I can take a punch with high style. I never planned to enter the ring myself, but how much of life ever follows your plan?

I'm way too small for starters and too old to boot. But I've been around the block and know what there is to lose. It's nothing, any way you go. So I don't mind going where most guys wouldn't last ten minutes. I don't care about tough stuff; I know the ropes. And if you don't go in alone and mix it up, how can you know? So you take a few kicks in the head. So?

I know the moves and follow easy as the next guy. The throws are planned and the punches are pulled—except for a few that miss. A fake Smash to the Jaw is easy as pie if the smasher pulls the fake. But a beefy forearm a half-inch over ain't cotton candy. And a humongous tub o' goo jumping off the top rope to pound your face with his big, fat gam feels better than a French kiss from a freight train, but not by much. Smothering in an avalanche of hairy, sweaty beef is no walk in the park, and I can't take the misses like before, when I could. I need a protégé, a wrestler I can train. But then by the time he could move like a shadow and float like a feather, he'd be as old as me.

I been watching since before these guys were born, watching since you could get a plate of spaghetti at a table ringside at the Chase and five bouts of championship action for two dollars. That was a few years ago, back when it was pure and clean, simple and honest, and two dollars was fair tariff. They pulled the punches and choreographed then too, in those days of bleached blond hair and blood ampoules under the putty. We didn't need this Halloween stuff you see now. We had the Red Devil, who was never unmasked, though most people fairly knew he was Duke Snyder, same build, similar moves and all. And Phantom Phil was meaner than any man needs to be, so people hated him, until he got unmasked and turned out to be Bobby Rice, good guy. He cried like a baby, promising to be good again, but he never was. Now it's jewelry, make-up, costumes and props—you name it.

That stuff would be okay if any of them could develop into something, but none last longer than the time it takes some monkey to out-gimmick the last monkey. It's more colorful now with the sumo guy (talk about a tub o' goo), the commie with his stupid sickle and hammer, the Nazi and the farmers and werewolves. Now you got road bums bulked up and greased up and talking like trailer trash with their simpleton smirks and dirty faces.

But they can't come near the monumental moment of six-hundred-five pounds of low-end traction in bib overalls, which was Haystack Calhoun. They only sully the spirit of the canvas with the imitation punk in face paint or the muscle boy or the vampire or the flaming sexual-preference alternate. They all come from the same make-up department, which makes them look right out of the same comic book. And they all use the same voice: gruff, hostile and looking for violence. But do they let her rip? All talk. No character to speak of, if you ask me. Mixed metaphors in drag.

I don't see a speck of pride in the lot of them, all shameless knock-offs of the old greats, as if slapping each other silly will amount to something. It won't. They can only reach, these new guys, drifting from the lost realm of real talent. I remember Johnny Valentine, Rip Hawk, Dick the Bruiser, Cowboy Bob Ellis, Lou Thesz, Haystack Calhoun and the rest, back when some of the blood squirted from under the putty, and some didn't.

It's mostly fake shouting now, and anyone can see that the prize isn't the championship but the market share. That kills me; that motivates me. I don't need the money, and I sure don't need the beating. But you reach a point in life where ask yourself what you might give back. Because a man needs a legacy, even in this crazy world where nature takes the count daily to make room for airwaves and the deluge of convenience. Maybe I need the action. Maybe I want to see my message play.

I know going in that I might get my socks lowered. So I read the magazines and watch the pay-per-views and the videos for only $19.95. It's all gone to hell on merchandising, but I call the 900 numbers too at $4.95 for the first minute and $2.87 for each additional minute, must be 18 years of age my ass, because good research is complete research. Some goofball comes on the line breathing heavy right at fifty cents a breath and asks which superstar you want to talk to. Then they stretch it worse than a phone slut playing pussy cat asking why you like that bum and what you'd ask if they could get the bum on the line; two and half minutes and counting. Then the goofball puts you on hold for a buck and half and comes back with a fake voice, like you're supposed to believe this is the bum you want to talk to. Shameless.

All these knock-offs without an original thought in their head. So now you got Yokozuna Mr. Fuji. Yokozuna is a Japanese sumo ranking and Fuji is a mountain. You got the Yellow Peril, which came from WW2, and Kiko Man—that's soy sauce. Razor Ramon could still be Mr. Bill if Razor Ruddock the boxer hadn't come along with a name to steal. Some clown calls himself Vader, as if Darth didn't think of it first. The Snake is hoping none of his teenage market-share watched the Oakland Raiders when Ken Stabler was QB. Now *he was* the Snake. You got your Gorilla, your Monsoon, your Diesel, but all these one-word disaster guys come across like their namesake movies with one-word ratings: stinko. Hash slingers every one. And how about Brett Hart? Maybe it's coincidental that he has the same name as the realist author of the last century who wrote about Br'er Rabbit and Br'er Fox and Br'er Bear. But maybe not.

So much for name recognition and wholesale theft. You got more people now and more airwaves to feed them. Nobody claims the whole pie, not like they did back when Fritz Von Erich put the Iron Claw on Bobo Brazil. Fritz squeezed more blood from the big coconut than was ever squeezed from a grapefruit, and it looked like curtains for Bobo. All bets were off on the gentle giant, until he came out of nowhere with a Forearm Smash and the move that made him champ, the Koko Head Butt. You want to talk superstars? That's what Fritz saw—super stars, the Nazi bastard. So? Who didn't see it? Who didn't know?

You got a world so thick with evil these days the new guys can't even be honest about their homes but come up with silly places like Bitters, Arkansas or Mud Lick, Kentucky or Lizard, Texas. Give me a break. If you knew big time wrestling before, you felt proud that Owensville, Indiana turned out a Verne Dodney, or that Nick Garcia came from Terre Haute.

They worked a circuit of fixed venues, but what was wrong with that? Now you got leagues that never compete against each other but only against themselves. It's more like Hollywood than professional sports.

First I had to pick my league but I got another idea, which is a common pattern among those of us with original ideas; one leads to another.

I started slow, which is the big advantage of being older; you know how much time you waste by hurrying. I sent a letter to *Kablamma Magazine*. I said, *I can beat your best.* They didn't run it. Thought it was crank mail.

So I sent another: *160 lbs. is all I got, which should be plenty.* They didn't run that one either. So I sent a few more—*Nothing worse than a coward,* and *I have the moves,* and *What's to lose?*—I got their attention. I signed, *The Monk.* So they were primed when I wrote: *I'm down from the mountain where I sat for 30 years.*

I give those 30 years to any wrestler on your roster. I am fluid as water, invisible as light. I am real. I am phantom. I am ready to share my wealth. That's it, no challenge, no threat and no name-calling. I said I'm from Owensville, Indiana. I'm not, but it seems a suitable tribute to the town that produced a world champ who got to the top by a scientific approach to big time wrestling. Verne Dodney invented the giant airplane spin, which iotum may be the jewel in his crown. He only set out to pin the other guy for three slaps. Glory came with the territory.

Not anymore. It's glory, glory, fame and glory everywhere you turn, whatever it takes. Back in the old days the four-cornered circle was a great place to see whom among men—and women and midgets—could transcend the competitive spirit with the spirit of drama. Charging the electrons didn't take so much smoke and mirrors then, when an evening of bouts and nonstop pasta was only two bucks. Of course beer was extra.

I got a P.O. box in Owensville. They wrote back and wanted my phone number. They wanted to talk. I wrote back and said the world is sinking under talk, and a monk down from a mountain feels like warp speed just swapping letters, even through the U.S. Mail. They wrote back and asked if I'd call them, for the fans if nothing else.

Well, I have the physical fitness and I've studied the secret locks that turn a tiny touch to exponential preponderance, once you slip into place easy as a skeeter on your ear at three a.m. More importantly at that stage of the game I have the background in fishing; you never want to take a fish for granted once you get him hooked. You want to play him light and imagine your tackle even lighter. If you're running ten-pound test, imagine two. Let him run, let him jump, let him show his stuff, let him have all he wants, let him play out. You muscle him; you lose him. Well, I had 'em hooked but knew if they laid eyes on a middle-age guy in civvies they'd poo poo the peak physical condition and tell me to go fish. To be honest, I had no plan for this phase. I was amazed they took the bait. Maybe that's why they call it fishing.

They wanted me to come to Boston; they'd pay. They wanted to see me dressed out for a few moves, casual, they said, with Killer Kowalski, who runs a school for up-and-comers in Boston now. Killer Kowalski? He should be ready for mummy tape by now. Nah, I said. Send Killer to the mountain. I'll show him a few non-moves. I don't want to come out, you know, in public before my time. Time? They wanted to know. What? Time?

I went to the archives to get things rolling, because it's easy to forget that a wheel is round, plain and simple. I looked up a few old giants, like Nick Bockwinkle. I found Figure-4 master and also world champ Buddy Rodgers. There's Gentleman Eduard Carpentier, the man who mastered the techniques of others.

A few are gone to greater glory. A few are down for the count. But Rusty Harpoon came out of nowhere—Nowhere, Illinois—to take the crown from Gaffrig Ketchum in '61. He defended twice before Gaffrig took it back, only to lose it the following year to Buddy Rodgers. Rusty lives up in the outskirts of Chicago. At least he was out in the country by the lake, what's left of it, and he'd weathered the years as I hope to myself. He sounded comfortable on the phone and said life wasn't too bad with a few drinks, a fire in the box, some decent groceries in the fridge and a woman he calls one and only. I flew on up.

Rusty was leaning on seventy-five and said he didn't know more than anyone, but then in hardly ten minutes he told me more than ever. He was blind to the wonder of what he did, but Rusty made me feel foolish as a pup who can't make the paper. I was pushing fifty myself but felt like the protégé next to Rusty. He has the ring wisdom.

He laughed at my dialogue with the Universal Wrestling Federation. But he wished he could ditch thirty years and twang the turnbuckles one more time. He looked me over with a squint—Rusty goes two-eighty. You can't carry that weight into your evening years without tickling the ticker, but I told him he looked terrific. He said, "Yeah?" Then he asked me, "Are you out of your ever-loving mind?" That's what's lost these days; Rusty said ever loving. I told him I had a plan.

"You mean a gimmick."

"Sure. A gimmick. You think I want to die in there?"

“I’ve known some who did, or didn’t care anyway.”

“Well, I don’t want to.”

“How you gonna hold down two-hundred fifty pounds of gorilla meat? Hell, you couldn’t pin me in my damn chair. And I’m seventy-five!” He sat up and huffed like a challenge, like this case was closed. He wasn’t telling me to leave but to forget it so we could relax with a beer and a ham sandwich once I shut up about getting in the ring—me at one-sixty pushing fifty? Ha!

I told him I didn’t plan to pin anyone because that wouldn’t work. I looked up about a quarter inch, just enough to move his mind off the huff and puff. He followed me with his eyes, so I reached gently and put my fingers on his wrist, which is thicker than a roll of cheap bologna. Just as his eyebrows twisted and he’s thinking I’m a swisheroo, I told him I’d win by submission. “Submission?” He laughed as I wedged my thumb into the slot inside his forefinger and curled my fingers around his palm and bowed in gratitude, turning his hand gently inward. Yamaoka Tesshu called this technique the sword of no sword. I read the books and practiced for quite a while, maybe not thirty years but twenty anyway. Old Rusty’s eyebrows unraveled quick as a wink. “Oh! Oh! Oh! Hey!” I eased off. He rubbed his hand. “I’m a old man, darn it.”

“Sorry Rusty. I didn’t mean to hurt you. I need to practice some more.” Rusty opened up some, not like he thought I could avoid death in there, but maybe I’d last a minute or two. He agreed that it’s all money now.

“They got this boy now, Tommy something or other, clean looking boy, comes close as I’ve seen to a real wrestler. They ran so many farmers and clowns and Hollywood gimmicks that a clean-cut boy looked different. He was good, too. But the fans are all kids now. They get money from their parents.

"Used to be we could see who was best, didn't matter who won. Sure, it was fixed; sometimes the best guy didn't win, but he'd get the crown sooner or later if he could keep it up. I'm talking physical stamina here, athleticism, style, speed and that. Anyway, they got the kids so worked up now, that Tommy started losing ratings; still the best, but he wasn't new. Get it? What ever happened to heroes?

"So Harv Bartell decides Tommy needs a boost. He's going to get Tommy in the news legit. He says we don't want to kill Tommy, we only want to beat him up. So Tommy, dumb kid, he says, okay, where and when and should he wear his trunks and robe and all. Harv says don't worry about it, I'll set it up. So he hires heavies—eight of them. Oh, Tommy was good, but Harv don't tell them the kid is, you know, like family, and they beat the living daylights out of him. Didn't crack no ribs though. You can't take the falls once your ribs give. That's what got me; ribs. I never told anybody, on account of visual perceptions and that. But I know about ribs. No way in hell a beating like that won't crack no ribs. Anyway, Tommy's all pissed off that he got beat up, put in the hospital and that, and Harv says, 'You know how smart those newspaper guys are?' Tommy says yeah, about as smart as a dog. Harv says, 'There you go, son, if you mean hound dog. You can't shake those news guys, once they take a scent. You'll be back bigger than ever. You'll see.' Calls him son."

I tell Rusty I'm not in it for the money, but you can't be in it at all and not get clobbered or rich in the meantime. Rusty gives me the nod, "Yup."

I tell him how my idea came on one night when I stopped on Channel 19. "These two guys come out. One is a cross between Batman and Tinkerbell and the other looks like a low-budget caveman in a cartoon. These guys could move. They got the air and took some good falls. It's faster than it used to be, and more punches miss the pull. They're taking some shots. Next two guys look like Tiny Tim and Dudley Do-Right, more cartoons. They come out yelling, and one throws a chair and hits a guy in the audience in a cheap suit. Audience guy bleeds about a gallon, rips his suit off down to wrestling trunks and whups up on Tim and Dudley, one, two, three. Next up you got Crocodile Man. Guy looks like Godzilla, and Captain Scott, some palooka from the actors' guild in a Highway Patrol costume. I mean, these guys worked out something for themselves. But it wasn't what it was when *you* were in there going two out of three on speed and agility, comedy and tragedy and the nuance of life as we know it."

Rusty stared and said I hit the nail on the head. He wiped an eye and said it was good to know it wasn't only him who missed the action. He said it's a hell of a thing, old age, with the sentimentality and that. He stared until I brought him around with my idea out of nowhere. "Rusty, I'm going in there. Might not last ten seconds, but I might have a shot. I could use your help."

He shrugged. "A man goes in alone."

"I know that, but the information in your head could make me that much bigger. It's the age of information."

He called over his shoulder, "Oh, Doris! Bring us in here a couple ham sandwiches and that." He turned back and said, "Nothing more I can tell you. You got to stay out of the way. You got to think every punch is going to connect. You have to take some falls and frankly you got no cushion. You'll never pass the audition."

I hung my head. "I know that, Rusty. I think I'd do better with the set up, if you call Harv for me. You don't have to be my manager, just tell him we're friends from way back. You haven't seen me in years—don't tell him how many. Just tell him I might be on to something."

"Why should I do that? I don't know what you're on to. Besides, what do you need me for?"

I shrugged back at him. "Ring wisdom."

Rusty nodded. He liked that. I understood what few of the young ones understand.

Well, to make a long story short, Doris brought in the ham sandwiches and asked if I wanted milk or beer; Rusty takes his with milk and follows with a beer. He went ahead on his first ham sandwich and said, "Mehzhwellgoheh 'n bulk ohn up." So I said milk, like Rusty. We ate, no talking, until Rusty finished his second, sat back and belched. He said my premise was half-baked as the rest of them. "Big deal. The Monk. Little guy in a robe nobody can catch. What're you gonna do? Run?"

"Duh. Dah. Hie," I worked the lumps like a chipmunk.

"You can't duck, dodge and hide for twenty minutes in a eighteen-foot ring. Standard formula requires thirty percent minimum time in clear advantage for each wrestler. Your nifty hand-jive there ain't worth squat once one of these gorillas puts the muscle on you. How you gonna arch out from under a load? With your thumbs? Ha!"

I cleared the debris with milk. "Archie Ellis and Goliath in '65. Archie arched out after two slaps to the mat six times. Goliath went four-fifty."

"You ain't no Archie Ellis."

"No, but neither was Archie Ellis. A man makes a move, another man follows, right?"

"Well, yeah, but it's the pain you got to soak up. That's the problem here as I see it."

"I know, Rusty. How do I get all the way baked?"

"Well, maybe if you had something like, like—I got it. A sickle, like the Grim Reaper. They won't come in on you against a weapon like that."

"No. I don't want to be the Grim Reaper. Might as well have a chair and whip. Or a gun. I want to be simple as an old rag. I know the game. I want to follow the rules, but I want to be different, really different."

"You got no move. No signature move. You can't Figure-4 or Airplane-Spin because you're too damn small. I don't know that you'd make out any better on the basics and that. You know, the tie up. Hammer Lock and Step-Over Toe Hold. Some of them boys is rough; why, they'd make three of you." I reached over and set my hand on his, but—"NAH! you don't." He huffed again, up and out of his chair. Adjusting his stance, dukes up, he said, "Okay, hotshot, let's see what you got."

I stood, looked away, shook my head, stepped up and said, "Rusty. Do me one favor. Open your mind just this much." I showed him a quarter inch in the air, thumb and forefinger. He looked disgusted. I felt his forearm from the bottom and said, "Shake." We shook hands and I ducked under like a do-si-do. He laughed, thinking I figured out how to use small size to advantage.

But he turned gruff and said, "Cute. Now what you got? I'll tell you what you got, boy. You got noth..."

"Yanko nage, Rustysan," I advised, locating the tertiary tendon along the precipital ulna and applying three grams, give or take, just so.

"Ayyyyyiiiii!" he admitted, collapsing in the knees, requiring another gram or two for the electricity, to help him back up. A man his age should avoid impact to the knees. When he was up again I eased off and rubbed the sore spot to hasten relief. He wasn't hurt really and wasn't out of breath, but he huffed again and raised his dukes again. "Try that again. For keeps this time."

He flinched when I barely shook my head. "Rusty. How many times do I have to show you?" I stepped up. He moved back. I sat down. "Please. Rusty. Don't you get it?"

He didn't like it but started to get it. He sat down and watched my second sandwich. I picked it up and started in. He picked up the phone and dialed. I could hear the ring and a little nasal voice going blah blah blah. Rusty said, "Yeah, put him on the line, tell him it's Rusty Gaddis." I got a hot flash. I knew it wasn't really Harpoon. I ate. "Yeah, Harv. Who you got medium heavy, decent speed, knows his pulls and the rules and that?"

Harv Bartell on the other end gave me goosebumps. Harv Bartell! The man behind the dream. Well, Phase I anyway. "No, not me. I got a guy here, old friend of mine. I haven't seen him in years. I don't know how many. I'd like to see him run through it one time." After a series of uh-huhs and okays he said, "They call him the Monk these days." I couldn't have asked for a nicer touch.

But Harv Bartell at the other end squeaked, "Who? The Monkey? We can't do that."

"No. Not the Monkey. The Monk! Like the Grim Reaper but not the Grim Reaper. Different. Simple. Like an old rag. Nah. Nah... Little guy... You know, a few moves, looks quick, like he can soak it up and that. Yeah... Nah... Yeah... Yeah... Nah. Nah. Sure. Okay. Yeah." He hung up. "Says you bugged him with crank letters."

"Yeah. I told you that."

"Says you're a nut."

"Yeah. I guess he didn't have to tell you."

Rusty laughed. "Says one of your letters got into the magazine. Says he wouldn't give you the time of day. He fired the guy who ran the letter, because the fans'll buy anything, but he likes to keep the margins up and frankly, what's to be made on a little guy? Says you get in there and do good, every squirt in the world wants in. Besides that, little guys, old guys; nobody likes to see us take a beating. It's bad for business, bad for the game. Says come on down, he'll take a look, see what you got. He's got a guy."

"When?"

Rusty shrugged. "We can go now."

"I'm stuffed. I go now, I'll get creamed."

Rusty laughed. "Get creamed now or in front of a million hot heads. What's the diff, Monkey?"

"Hey, Rusty. How do we keep them from calling me Monkey?"

"Beat some bad guys."

"I don't have my robe."

"Come on. I know a place. They got everything."

Rusty knew a place with props for any cockamamie idea you got. "Monk's robe?" the guy asked. "No problema. Hood? Sleeves? Full length?"

"Hood, no sleeves, waist length," Rusty said.

"Full length," I corrected. Rusty looked peeved. "I can't grapple anyway, and it makes me look bigger and hides my feet."

"What's wrong with your feet?"

"They tell you which way I'm headed. No offense, Rusty. You missed it."

He looked me over like maybe he ought to smack me a good one to set things straight, but he didn't. We hit a barber shop next, a two-chair place with a candy-cane pole out front. Rusty said, "Monk has a shaved head." We went next for big-time wrestling boots in supple leather, black with black laces and tassels. Rusty wanted some color, so I reminded him he wouldn't see my boots, anyway, and he came unglued. Spinning to put his fist through the wall, he pulled it, spun back and shot me a zinger—"What about when you're up in the air? Feet first?"

He was wrong, not about me and flight but about simplicity. I gave an inch, though, and went along with red tassels over purple and blue laces. He complained that they wouldn't show up like chartreuse and orange.

I explained, "Supplemental colors vibrate off the ropes of your retinas. That's what we want, Rusty; vibration. You'll see."

We didn't talk much on the way in, except when Rusty looked me over and said, "This is crazy. You got no freaking idea what you're getting into."

"Yeah. Well..."

He laughed, "Yeah." We drove. "Good enough way to kill an afternoon I guess."

Harv Bartell made us wait. Rusty hated that. He paced. I hit the half-lotus right there on the bench. An hour passed, maybe two. I didn't mind. I found a point out front and slightly down, which just happened to be the trailhead of the cleavage of the receptionist, which felt like a vortex of the warm and receptive variety. She felt it too, because nature's most dynamic form is the sphere, mother of all circles. The spark between us arced softly across the ether.

She was Holly Hocks and she achieved repose once she got done twitching. She used to be fat but lost a hundred forty pounds with Don Lockwood's 10 EZ Steps to Self-Esteem. These and other iota she disclosed to her headset. Or perhaps I was intended to hear her story. She enticed me into her web. She used to be fat. Now she was thin. She moved lusciously.

In time, Rusty snoozed. Holly batted her lashes, inch-and-a-halfers, and said I was kind of cute. I didn't know if she meant cuddly like a puppy, or if I might qualify for sexual communion. I felt receptive to either one. She blushed generously as a sign, I think, that sexual potential was favored. Then Harv Bartell came out.

"You the monkey? I know who *he* is."

Rusty came around. "I'm the Monk," I said.

"Boy, I'll say," Holly said.

"Hey, Harv. Don't be talking to my boy," Rusty said, rubbing his eyes and shaking hands with Harv Bartell.

Harv chewed a three-dollar cigar, unlit. He pulled the swamp-pulp end out of his mug when he talked, then put it back. "Boy? Looks to me like he's geezer league, Rusty."

"These things take time," I said.

"Hey. I do the talking," Rusty said. "We want on, Harv. It's you or the WWF or the WWC or the WOW. We come here first on account of friendship and all the years and that. You want to see him, we'll go three minutes. He's a hundred sixty soaking wet. But he's got something. Could be hot. Could be a champ."

"Oh, just that simple," Harv said. "Could be a nightmare. You know how many guys are waiting for the line-up? Big guys, guys so cut they got ripples on their ripples. I got a guy waited three years, but did he sulk? No way, bulked up on his bulk, put bulges on his ripples. Veins and mass. Guy was so primed I went ahead and released his book. New York I'm talking! Had 'em lined up three deep around two corners. Ultimate Armageddon I named him." Harv sucked his stump to warm it back up. He savored the tangy bite, then sighed over the inevitability of life and the ring of four corners. " He went one bout. Over and out."

"It's redundant," I said.

"What?"

"Ultimate Armageddon. Armageddon is ultimate by nature. It's like calling someone a stupid dummy. You ever see a smart dummy? What comes after Armageddon? Redundancy reflects poor language skills and no faith. You say it twice when you doubt the power of saying it once. Classic insecurity is a form of fear. If you name a guy

Ultimate Armageddon, you sound fearful. That's all. The guy was a loser going in. He had to lose. Didn't he?"

Rusty gazed. Harv Bartell laughed and chewed. "I think I could use this guy, Rusty, if this was the World Debating Union. As it is, who needs him? I'm busy." He turned and walked. "Thanks for coming down, huh."

"Wait, wait, wait. Harv. I told him to shut up. They don't listen? Harv. Three minutes. He's a pain in the butt. Let's give him some peace of mind. Harv. Three minutes."

Harv Bartell eyeballed me, maybe savoring images of a Flying Slam. "Holly, set it up. Downstairs in ten minutes. Ring six. Bazooka Joe. Three minutes. Ha!"

"Bazooka Joe?" I asked.

"Yeah. He's redundant too," Harv said. "He'll kill you and then beat you up some more."

"A killing followed by a beating would be repetitive and gruesome but not redundant. Bazooka Joe is plagiaristic. He's the cartoon on Bazooka Joe Bubble Gum. Save twenty-five wrappers and get the comic for free."

Harv squared off. "There's no copyright on titles, Mr. Smartpants Monkey."

"Of course not. There's only artistic integrity for the few of us who remember it."

"Downstairs in ten—nine minutes." He walked.

"It's good to meet you, Mr. Bartell. I look forward to a fruitful campaign."

"Yeah, you're fruitful all right," he mumbled out the door.

Rusty rubbed his head. "Geez, give yourself a chance."

"Hey, it's a game."

"The hell. Nobody talks to Harv Bartell like that. Nobody. He doesn't need it and doesn't have to take it."

I shrugged over something conceptual as Holly piped up, "He does too need it. And Bazooka Joe's a stiff. I think you're right." She scrunched her shoulders and leaned in for a nice distraction in the electric second between contemplation and realization:

Three minutes live with a guy named Bazooka Joe.

Like my mind was an open book, Holly said, "Two-fifty and really big muscles but stiff. He can't get out of his own way and doesn't know where to go if he could. He won a few when he played dead and got some guys in the bear hug. The bear hug! That's how smart he is. Hey, little monkey, don't let him get you in the bear hug."

"All right, all right," Rusty intervened.

"Hey. What's wrong with some inside skinny?"

"Any of them get you in the bear hug you're dead. Don't you know that?"

Not necessarily, I thought but stayed mum to the door, where I turned and said, "Hey, shut her down and come on.. Three minutes. What's to worry?" Holly twitched her nose and looked wistful, maybe remembering what was lost.

"I can tell you have self-esteem," she said, "on account of how you..." But the swinging door cut her off with a thwap thwap thwap.

I reminded myself that there is no self and no enemy as Rusty Harpoon and I descended to the future, or the past, or maybe to the eternal moment in between, a solid three minutes worth.

Ring six was off to one side with enough room for a single row of folding chairs so soft they felt gooey. These chairs wouldn't even fold up but crumpled nicely. Harv Bartell pulled a couple real chairs from the main room and called Rusty over and said, "A man goes in alone."

Rusty said that earlier. I'm no stranger to solitude, but I wished Rusty or Holly could work the corner for me. Bazooka Joe looked like a nice enough guy, around twenty-five or twenty-eight. His porcine eyes looked small and amber, beady and possibly evil, but then Halfslab, piglet of my youth, had those eyes. Did she not reside in my heart? Was she not a being like me with hopes and fears? Did she not smile for watermelon and know I would never harm her? Into her eyes I saw the same love, the communion among species. Joe moved simply, forward, reverse, side to side, eager for the trough.

He arrived in character. This was good; life is real, even when it's dress rehearsal. His camouflage fatigues in the Desert-Storm mode fit in the trousers, but were a size too small up top, with no collar or sleeves but with epaulets to hold his crossed bandoleers. He appeared to arrive at Ring 6 directly from the front.

Bazooka Joe was a man of action, a warrior on short notice, one front or the next. He used my barber; I rubbed my pate and grinned. The fleshy folds of his frontal lobe undulated, and he grunted acceptance.

His headband was crooked and his bulk hung flaccidly with uneven sheen, perhaps, I thought, from hurried application of his persona. Musculature stiffens when it fills with blood, and this boy needed a half-hour to fill the massive reservoirs of his neck, biceps, forearms, hands and fingers. I had denied Joe the proper warm up, so his massive bulk was neither pumped with blood nor did his beefy bulges glisten with grease. I had denied myself an advantage here, since the full pump would have rendered him stiff as a robot with marginal swing and pivot. The sheen would have left him spectacularly self-conscious. On short notice he enjoyed full range with humility, both of which I must fear in an opponent. At least he wouldn't be so slick. I couldn't tell if his scar tissue was real or Memorex, but I suspected a combo. I suspected he sought an image: high-mileage, offroad. I respected him in my heart; his mother likely worried for the man/beast she calls little Joey. That's the ticket, respect and sensitivity; Joe was a sentient being with hopes and fears. He laughed and cried for humor and love and thoughts of Mom. I had only to find the opening and go inside gently, gently.

Bazooka Joe looked emotionless, calm as a stone. We shared a reverie. I compared relative girth of his non-neck to that of my thighs. He sneered and let his head swivel on his shoulders. I smiled sweetly, hoping he'd think me insane. I knew he'd seen every stare-down in the book, but he had to be bush-league, a hack, an on-call spar for a nobody out of nowhere.

"Let's go, let's go, let's go. I got a schedule. Ring the bell, Holly."

Holly stepped up from around a corner since Harv saw her anyway. She rang a bell on Ring 5 or Ring 7 or the ring of inconsequence and oblivion. Bazooka Joe stomped in, arms wide, as the cool dank of a Chicago basement put goose bumps on my naked scalp. Taut skin awakened me to the beauty of no beauty.

I wished I'd taken Rusty's advice and got the robe at waist length, for Bazooka Joe was a force of nature. He lumbered like a pachyderm and was easy to dodge or duck under, but leading him took footwork I hadn't practiced in years. I felt fear and a thump in my chest. One tangle in the robe and it would be over, but I put my fear in the vessel of repose. I looked back in time and down from space and played it again, Sam.

Well, anyone knows that a bout begins with the tie up or at least with movement toward the tie up. But who ever saw a bout between a side of beef and a size medium? And who would tie up with a guy known for the bear hug? What? I should step into the jaws of it because that's how it's been done since the Grecos and the Romans? I circled, ducked, dodged and circled, looking, looking. To tell the truth, Bazooka Joe looked hatched from an incubator, like he never had a mother and didn't care, like hope and fear had naught to do with Bazooka Joe.

I admired that too but put admiration in the vessel and reminded myself that every being has an opening or makes an opening or guards a tiny fissure in his soul. This one will show itself, if I could relax, stay alert, aloof and afloat...

"Aw... Whaziss!" Joe grumbled, standing out of his crouch, hands down. "Monkey won't wrassle, Harv!"

I maintained my stance but not like Joe; I find the crouch so adversarial. I feigned a slump in the shoulders, shook my head and exhaled as if I too had a big problem with this Bazooka Joe guy. "By the way," I said, glancing up. "What's your real name?"

Joe looked up, so I closed the distance between us by half and then half again and again half. Joe was puzzled then irritated when fingertips light as mosquito feathers touched his hairy paws of havoc. The next moment was perhaps reminiscent of a dream long gone. Two of his digits were a handful for me but allowed me to lead the rest of him down and around and up in a flutter, to freedom from thought and pain, until he resisted. Poor Joe.

"Aayyyyyiiiiiaaaahhhhh!" Down he went to his knees, his belly and then his chest until his chin banged the mat like a big bass drum, *KABOOM! BAM! BABOOM!* I eased the pressure. Joe scrambled for his turn to provide the hurt, until I showed what a sensitive fellow he really was, with only another ounce of pressure. Poor Joe.

I told him, "Stop Joe. Stop. It's over." I released him, stepped back and bowed. I turn and bowed to Rusty Harpoon. Harv Bartell dropped his stump and gazed. One eyebrow rose, and I faced the bigtime.

Palms up like the Pope, kind of, I invited the minions to partake. Joe accepted on cue, grabbing my wrists from behind in doubtless compensation for his sorry show so far. He stepped into String the Bow, Draw the Arrow.

This is a painful move bound to the unwritten law of circular movement. I couldn't trust Joe's timing but could count on his centripetal relationship to our Mother Earth. The stubborn fellow wouldn't let go, even as I dropped my hips through the trap door, slid back and stood straight as an archer. This, while Joe's foot dangled in thin air where only a moment ago a size medium spine waited like a bowstring for twanging.

In the spirit of stellar bodies we hurled past bows and arrows and barreled across the Milky Way like cosmic motes drifting headlong to neutrality. I disappeared. Bazooka Joe saw the tunnel of clear, white light with deathlike certainty. There was no going back.

Poised in space in the essence of his calling, Joe followed. Rising to the occasion he reached across the heavens just as the first wrestler reached across the Sistine ceiling. What choice does a side of beef have at sub-orbital speed round a planet spinning on an axis? In this particular application, trajectory cleared the top rope. Mushy chairs cushioned Joe's fall.

Harv Bartell was on his feet. "Sonofabitch! You know what those things cost?"

Joe was reduced to slo-mo writhe, no more conscious than he was three minutes and vast experience earlier. He mumbled, "Hey. Wait a minute. Do that again."

"Ah, shut up," Harv barked. "You're wasting my time. Can't even show me what this shrimp's got without falling out of the ring. Geez. Get out of here. Get dressed."

Joe sat up and shook his head like a shaggy dog shaking off the wet. He smiled and frowned for a think-through and showed his hand. It was spades and clubs mostly; I knew Joe. Guys like him throw a few and take a few. They hump it double-time and keep their mouth shut. It's that or bussing tables or shining shoes or hanging out at the track and waiting for a winner. I could see it. So could Rusty and Harv Bartell and Holly Hocks, who I would learn did time with this Bazooka Joe when he was fresh from make-up and showed some promise with his muscles pumped and evenly greased.

She looked down on him. Like old beef marked down for quick sale, Joe sat in a heap.

"Hey, numbnuts," I called. Joe hung his head. The others watched. Harv laughed. "Not him, you. Harv Bartell numbnuts. That's what the Monk's got. You think the fans won't love it?"

Rusty looked convinced. Joe looked anxious. Holly looked puzzled but pleased.

"They'd call me crazy, I shoved a shrimp down their throats. You can pull a heap of crap on the fans, but not that much heap."

"Heap? Get up here, Harv. Let's go a half-minute in the crap heap."

"You had it, Mister. You wanted three minutes. You're into twenty already. I got a schedule."

"You got nothing, Harv. You can't see what I got?" Harv scowled. Rusty commiserated with him. "Yeah, yeah, nobody talks to Harv Bartell blah blah. That's the problem."

Rusty said, "Harv. Give him a prelim. No billing. You know, what they call a test market. Let him work something up with Joe here. The kid took it beautifully. Sure, the chairs get pricey, but it was a nice touch, big guy smashing a whole row like that. Something new, you know, wholesale destruction in one fall. Might work in a folding table and some electrical equipment, you know, with the high voltage and sparks and that."

Harv looked down, stood up and walked away in his own dramatic presentation of the news. I.e., Rusty, Joe, Holly and I were wrong, because nobody could choreograph this dance but Harv Bartell. With that load off his chest he looked back and grumbled, "Set it up, Holly. One fall. Ten minutes. These guys work it out. The monkey gets the win. I want measured reaction." He chewed briefly. "And I don't want to be bothered. Capiche?" He headed out.

I thought he should have called me the Monk instead of the monkey and would have said so but Rusty waved me off with a headshake. Joe shrugged; nobody likes losing to a monkey, but it would only be a single fall, a prelim with no billing and no promotion, a market test. By a fluke in the system that will not yield to mortal pedestrians we would have a chance to demonstrate our skill in fakery. For ten minutes the lights would shine on us, only us.

It would be a comeback for Joe, with a new name, maybe with a mask or more scars or no scars, except for those that won't go away. He pondered potential.

Holly Hocks titillated. I doubted her comprehension of the mystical silences, but she looked receptive to training and seemed aortically warm. I wanted to show her everything. I sensed big-time romance, which would only be another random point on the greater circle, but it could ring with such lovely consequence.

Holly Hocks has the power in the World Wrestling Union. Sure, Harv Bartell calls the shots, but Holly says when and where and how much. She needs Harv's approval on her set-ups, so she waits to the last minute with all the phones ringing to hit Harv up for the go-ahead. What can he say? No? She can give us a no-promo prelim tomorrow or nine months from now. It's her baby. I want it now, because time can show stretch marks worse than a steroid-bulked buffoon in this game.

"Not necessarily," Rusty says. "You want to wait and play the biggest draw." He scans the schedule to see who's up. We settle on a Friday night two weeks out. "Friday's your biggest night for ring action. People all wound up from a whole week with no relief." Besides that, Three Prong Calhoun, a Haystack knock-off without the skill but who packs the house because he goes five-fifty, is top bill with Mozogoomba, the giant African-American in an Italian suit, felt hat, black shirt, yellow tie. Rusty says, "Win or lose in this game, you want the numbers."

The numbers disgust me, but I stay mum, accepting the way of the world we live in. I rub Joe's pate. He looks up and smiles like the pig of my youth. I wonder where she is now. I won't scratch his chin, but I suggest that we begin. "We have work to do," I say.

"Work ain't the half of it," Rusty says. This bout can't go one way, he says. The fans pay for solid beatings all around and he, Rusty Harpoon, has yet to see a small man take what must be given.

"I can take it," I say, hoping I can take it.

Joe says don't worry, and don't get him pissed off, and don't land in a bear hug. "I dunno. I can't do nothing but my very best on that one." I understand his feeling.

Joe is really Joe Ficjs, pronounced fee-case. He got into big-time wrestling with a name everyone can say and some can even spell. Despite his appearance, Bazooka Joe enjoys a lucid understanding of that gossamer interface between true artistry and the decadent world we live in. That is, he perceives a big-time in which win and lose don't matter. Champions come from the action—from sheer, feisty vitality, dirty tricks and heroic escapes. He can take a folding chair on the chin and bang the big bass drum with his skull for a mallet. He loves the give and take and sees a 24-karat opportunity here, if he can get higher and fly farther at the hands of a tiny magician.

He laughs at my Single Wing Windmill as I fling him round the ring. He shoots from the ropes like a stone from a catapult, until I cut his throat from two steps out and drop him like a ton of bricks. The guy has moxie, knee-walking to his corner to putty up a blood bag between his jaw and clavicle. And he says, "Do that again."

This time Joe screams bloody murder and grabs his slit throat. Blood gushes down his chest and splashes his face and me. He topples to the mat, stunned, until he sits up reflectively and says, "It's too soon for the pin, but it's the beginning of the end. Lemme think. Okay. Try this..."

We try a Step Over Toe Hold, but I'm not so young anymore, and he's two hundred fifty pounds. I warn him. "Yeah, yeah, yeah," he says. We forego some old favorites—the Figure-4, Rock-A-Bye Baby and Hurry Sundown, because I can't get around him.

Rusty watches and says, "That's it. You got it. Like you said, submission, and Joe can lay there and bleed to death, you know, twitching and that. I'll set up some stretchers and an ambulance like they have at the football games now. I want to see some big throws and three bounces into the throat thing. It's gonna be unbelievable. A comeback by the Monk. Know what I mean?"

I didn't bargain for a comeback. But life is full of what you never bargained on. We practice the Forehead Smash to the Turnbuckle, the Knee to the Face and the Standard Forearm Smash. Joe pulls them close. I swell below the trachea and suffer his fat ass landing on my face. It hurts, it's disgusting and throws meditative repose out the window.

We review the punishments I will endure plus a few extra, because you never know. All agree that Joe might get pissed off, and we need some place to take it if he does. Joe says we're better off, forearmed. He assures me his fits pass in a minute or so. I assure him that I understand but should be spared further practice. I am not a renewable resource.

Rusty says the denouement should bring the house down with a move a big-time wrestler needs for his debut. "Nobody wants to get famous for slitting throats, but what a way to say hello."

I defer. More importantly, I endure practice with less residual pain—swollen joints and bruises mostly. Soon our rigorous rehearsal leaves us with only butterflies and pain pills. Not so bad, all told.

Holly Hocks compounds my anxiety. She is an object of gratitude, yet I fear her softness. I don't resist but address the situation calmly, according to my training. She is a woman of modern times, far younger than I, and I think she is nearly free of romance-based anxiety. She keeps our dialogue whimsical, just how I like it. "What do you think will become of us?"

I tell her, "People seek another self for refuge, often making potential for two new enemies."

"That's why you don't have a woman," she says. "You talk that trash; pretty soon you believe it."

"I do believe it." She rolls out and hits the showers, reminding me of life's delusion. She returns cheerily and wins my heart, though her skin is sallow and her posture incorrect. But she doesn't care who thinks what about which, and she's willing to let nature take its course. From her flirtatious lilt, her blonde hair and her beauty mark to her passé notion of what a man and woman can do for each other, she defers to my schedule.

Our first bout is by the book. Heavy eyeliner and glittering lids like opening night over cheeks as rosy as mat burns—she hits me with a wild flutter and asks where such a little guy with such big cajones came from. I correct her; I'm not so little. She says that's right, honey; there's nothing too little about you. I think we talk to opposing viewpoints, but I stay mum so we can scratch our collective itch. Later, we go for drinks—only one for me, with training in mind—and dinner. She says I'm classy. I order braised vegetables, which aren't on the menu but can be arranged. She has the surf and turf, hold the onions.

She says she really loves a guy who doesn't have to yak all over the place about who he is or worse, what he's gonna do or worst of all, what a tough life he's had. I agree; two people can share silence as easily as one. But she wonders what we'll talk about sooner or later. She gazes and finally answers herself, "What's the rush? We don't have to worry about that until tomorrow. Do we?"

I agree.

She won't see me the night before the other bout but calls to say she's seen wrestlers come and go, and she thinks I'm onto something. She can't stop thinking about it.

"Thinking about what?"

"You know. The way you do...that thing."

To which thing she refers I am not certain, but then of course I am. I say thanks and wish her sweet dreams. She chirps, "Yeah. Like that." We hang up and fend new butterflies. They swarm around that thing.

It goes famously. A horrific cold snap with freezing rain, record snowfall, slush melt and flash floods have canceled springtime in Chicago. Major arteries ice, causing multi-car/truck pile-ups four days out of five. The one-hour commute becomes three or six. More ice and brownout precipitate runs on gasoline, milk, bread, eggs and beer.

Old people who only last summer survived the heat now face mortal cold. Young people are warned of dirty snow. People in between are warned to change their habits or else.

By Friday night they want out. They want action. They want blood. And if Three Prong and Mozogoomba aren't coming on for twenty minutes, they want it now just the same. Rusty comes back rubbing his hands; hot dogs and beer are through the roof. The night is prime for carnage.

Harv Bartell wears a shiny suit—shiny green, shiny gray, shiny purple blue, depending on your angle—tailored somewhere between Italy and Zoot with some Eagle Eye Fleagle shoulder pads and a cinched waist.

Mozogoomba says, "Hey! Give me that suit!" He one-ups Harv with gold lamé side stripes and the image of a shrunken head on his back in flaming orange. Harv wears a thick wig with billowing waves, like Holly's but with oil and a crest like breaking surf.

He sweeps it gently with is hand. He feels good, carousing with the boys in his forced gravel voice. He encourages the boys to start talking that way as well, because you never know when the KWKK TV Action Cam will slam into a slow news night and show up at the Coliseum. To me he says, "Ah'm gonna tellya somethin'! When I get my hands on... That bum'll learn some respect then!" I wait for meaning or, short of that, for a basic speech pattern, verb and noun, or even marginal coherence. Finally, he says, "So? Whaddya think?"

I shrug. "Happy to be here, Harv. Thank you."

"Nah! You gotta talk right." I'm game, but things might be changing with the Monk. I try a blissful scowl and a low grumble. He slaps me on the back. "That's it. You got it." What a relief.

Joe takes a locker two rows over but eases near and says, "Showtime." Then he froths and fires, Forearm

Smash to the locker, Knee to the Groin (also of the locker), Head Butt and out. He wants first walk-on, says he deserves it, and nobody gets it going like the first guy out. I suspect altruism; challenger first, champion second.

Out in the lights we go to pure instinct and more improv than I'd considered. We have the moves down, but you can't leave a hundred pounds on the table and not compensate somehow. I know what to do and bring the all of all to my center. I breathe deep, stand ramrod straight, relax and relax some more. I trickle like the water between your fingers. Yet I am the rock, around which the river must flow. I smile from the eyes and stride into the future.

I thought Bazooka Joe was in character when we first met in Ring 6. He was not, for he left out the happiness of mayhem and the joy of violence. I laugh at the 20,000 volts of destruction he could send up my spine if I let him. But I won't let him. He shows the fans and me what the fans want. They cheer. They scream. They stomp. They yell for me and against me. They encourage and threaten me. They torment and praise me with catcalls and calls for glory. They call me monkey. They stomp for the Monk.

I turn them into a word and take the word to a vibration. I focus on a point through half-closed eyes then enlarge the point to a space that surrounds Bazooka Joe and fill that space with love. It's fixed, like life, and all we have to do is play it out. As I suspect I'll do in the final moments of life itself, I hurry to remember what I know while I can.

Well, they love us. They love Joe; he's so mean, so ugly, so up in the air and so bloody and twitching and nearly dead. They love me, so small, so quick, so inured to the beating little guys and old guys shouldn't have to take. They howl when I find the thinnest thread of sense and pull myself back up and come back.

I miss a basic pull and thumb him in the eye, but he takes it like a trooper. Howling along with the fans in utter outrage he follows my lead from a gentle lock on his wrist, bouncing off the ropes three times back to the center in a blind, helpless sprawl to have his throat cut. The blood on my hands is proof of its letting. I jump the top rope and grab a folding chair to beat him with, and I don't even know which are the mushy chairs, but I don't care. Joe is my friend, my partner, and we're on, and he can take it.

Great balls of fire I am high.

I win.

In the dressing room Joe agrees. "You hadn'a poked me in a eye, I'd a creamed your spinach. I was getting pissed off, you know."

"Let me see." I check his eye for ocular hematoma but see only minor surface trauma. We ice the area at intervals for twenty minutes, and he feels much better. Holly comes back to see what's keeping me and provides relief for the awkward moment between Joe and me; Bazooka Joe has never before been cared for, not by a friend and foe.

Mozogoomba, the giant African warrior in the Versicelli three-piece with the black shirt and glittering tie and lamé racing stripes and shrunken head scorns us on the way out. Holly advises him, "Go on, ya lug. You're next."

What a woman!

Mozogoomba hovers, his scar tissue throbbing. Hip to proper warm-up, Mozogoomba sweats. It rolls off him, drip drip dripping from his nose and chin. His smile bares fangs filed to points in the custom of his forebears from the bush. He watched our bout from a distance. Now he generates the macabre fantasy undermining our once proud sport. Him threatened by me? I think he is shaken by the 7.1 tremor for a shrimpy white guy. In menacing undertone he says, "Next time you come as Florence Nightingale."

I step up toe to toe and look up. "Mozogoomba. I've always admired you." His face twists. "You are a living legend." I offer my hand. He takes it, squeezing like a vice yet melting under my stoic serenity. I set the pain aside, and he knows: his black ass is mine.

He grins, his grip seeking what I will not reveal. Soon he fades from a thousand pounds per inch to eight hundred, three hundred, fading to the realm of the physically spent. I tell him, "You're the best, Mozo. Possibly the very best of all time." His grin fades too, back to the uncertainty of youth and the naked innocence of the inexperienced. "Just relax," I tell him. "It only hurts if you resist."

He harrumphs and leaves. I'll get that win as well. Joe watches from one eye. Holly asks, "How do you do that?"

"Do what?" I ask back.

And so it comes to pass. From a ten-minute, no-promo prelim to a fully-hyped second billing, we climb the ranks through the Snake, Mongoose, Paul Bunyan, Jack Flamboyant, Gorgeous Jim, Diamond Mike Grady, Natty Bumpo, Bruce Knuckles and up to Mozogoomba.

I win; victory is foregone. He complains but Harv stands firm. Mozo is granted the unspoken championship of African-America. Harv says Mozo's fans will better accept the loss coming from a diminutive Caucasoid, because small stature can be viewed as a perfect extension of smaller everything. Mozo ponders smallness. Harv closes him easily. "Twenty thousand dollar bonus, Mozo. You'll earn it."

Mozo takes the check but can't accept the script as written. But he must accept the script, as we all must. These are the rules we play by. He is scripted to lose by disqualification, so he can save face. He sees value in saving face but wants to change the shape of my face.

I won't detail my bout with Mozogoomba other than its overwhelming show of wills. Mozo will suffer delusions of superiority to his last gasp. He's bigger than big, making the basics nearly impossible for us. He can span my chest with a hand, palm me like a basketball, but then what? What will his fans think if he spearchucks a twig like me? I can't actually see him blush, because I'm airborne, levitated, as it were, but I feel chagrin in his fingertips the instant they boo.

He drops me unceremoniously, and I sense his uncertainty—how can you forearm smash a mosquito?

I flit in and under and gently grasp my favorite digits. He follows reluctantly, heavily with flat feet, lumbering like dead weight. So I give the gift of voltage to help his posture and speed him along to destiny, up and over the top rope, my first overthrow since my debut with Joe.

The difference is: this one is improv. It's a dangerous move I consider mandatory; Mozo so carelessly shows his hand as predestined loser. He leaves me no choice but to save us both and save the game. Don't worry, I spin him once around the world to scan potential targets. I bounce him off the ropes, duck under so he can bounce again, then I follow his Flying Bolo with a sweet embrace—the man is looking for a head to shrink, but I prod him aloft, aiming for that section ringside most populated by timekeepers, judges and administrators. For the Monk knows about authority in the scheme of life. The fans hunger for anarchy. They gorge on hot dogs and discombobulation of the suits with relish.

It's the zenith of my career in the ring. Three moves off the cuff with the giant Mozogoomba. To my regret, he will not forgive me.

But Joe is my friend. He provides inside skinny when he can. I help him with his new character, Pop'n Fresh. My idea, it's unoriginal and lets him smile while inflicting pain. I encourage him to perceive power through silence. He develops nicely as a lump of dough that awaits reshaping.

Rusty comes down now and then to chew the fat and remember when. Holly and I join him and the wife for dinner. We're a match, Holly and I, one fall, no time limit. She really likes me and calls that amazing. I share her feeling, seeing her funny hair-do, bright red claws and push'em up dresses as vestiges of a dying heritage. She dances her step; I dance mine. We entertain each other.

I've never been beaten.

Muddy Brown took the crown from Pile Driver only a month and a half before losing it to Jack Flamboyant. Everyone called Jack a burnout with a dull edge and no air. He got the title because he'd been such a favorite—and Muddy Brown wasn't Championship fodder.

Jack Flam was only adequate as champ. Revenues slipped, so he got scheduled for major whiplash in a five-car pile-up. He staggered from the wreckage with no memory of who he was or where he'd been. He failed to see the future, too, leaving a shoo-in for whoever got the next bout with Jack Flamboyant. That would give Jack a year off in Florida and a new market slot on a comeback.

But Jack couldn't wait a year and didn't trust the empire, so he made his comeback before he really went away. Wearing an inflatable head in white with a happy face painted on, he calls himself Double Jack with Cheese.

We're on for Friday night.

The weather is foul. I've added girth, more like a Buddha than a fat guy, I think. I let the butterflies in for the thrill of it. I may grow a beard or go full-length on the robe again or get some wire-rim glasses or leave my hood up or all of the above. But at the last minute things change.

Mozo gets the shot. The Monk is out.

"I beat Mozo!" I protest.

"So? You can't be World Champion," Harv says.

"I can't be World Champion?"

"That's what I said."

"That's okay," I lie. "I don't want to be champion."

Harv shrugs; he knows the game. "Look at you." I step up with intensity long devoid of subtlety, with a gentle reach for his trapezius. "Hey!" He whips a blackjack from a desk drawer. "You can't be champion. They don't believe that stuff. I don't believe it. Nobody can see it."

"You can feel it."

"So? This sport is visual. There ain't enough of you for a world champion."

"Harv. Less is more."

"Maybe where you come from. I got shrimps coming out of the woodwork since you. They got nothing on you, but this I can't allow; hot and cold running monkeys. You can't be champion, and that's that."

We share a silence. "I'll leave the WWU."

"Whatever you need, kid. Mozo's my next champion. He's earned it, and his fans spend more than yours."

I sit and stare. Harv rambles over money and me and the WWU. "Harv. I don't want to leave the WWU."

"Good."

"Leave the guy who made me what I am today?"

"Stop. Walk if you have to."

"I told you I could beat your best."

"Yeah, yeah, yeah."

"I made a ton o' dough for you on an angle you could never guess. You fought me like a disease."

He leans in. "You look. When I tell you something—"

"Idea! Worth millions. Just listen..." Harv shuts up for the love of his life. He sits back with his this-better-be-good look. Crunching stats and graphing maybes, he listens and thinks. With forehead veins pumping, he nods slowly, and I know: his fat ass is mine.

The shameless pattern of the game is imitation. The Snake (WWU) gives rise to Leather Boa (WWC) and Slithermeister (WWQ). Big deal, each league has a muscle-bound stiff who wears a snake into the ring, all talking like the same dummy. Likewise, Jack Flamboyant, Rick Flair, Jean-Michel Mascara and the new golden boy, Curry Favor, with his horn-rimmed glasses, his threadbare corduroy and his latest novel in hand. He reads purple prose on approach, while climbing into the ring, while being interviewed or pinned. Curry has no skill just as Mozogoomba lacks the *savoir faire* required of a tailored suit. After all, Mozo was only Stan Jefferson, until he got the "idea" from Kuntaguido, who stole it from Don Juanbozulu. Unreality outreaches itself. No idea is left unsullied.

I, the Monk, give rise to the Reaper (WWC) as Rusty suggested. The guy is soft and, unlike me, limp. He won't take his hood off, so he walks into Sunday punches and nearly suffocates on a simple Head Scissors.

The WWQ knock-off is Satan, dull as last year's hash and way too old. They want to out-do us on the old factor. But a wobbler? He can go three minutes because everyone is embarrassed to hit him. Make-up over at WWQ pulls out the stops on a gluteus build-up to contrast his shriveled chest. A set of stumpy horns cuts to the quick on a chilling likeness of the dark prince himself. Both the Reaper and Satan take my bit in a wrong direction, showing silence as a source of evil, as magic darkly directed. These guys don't know what I know. I wonder if they could learn it.

Another WWQ knock-off is good-guy Jesse Christy, who spawns envy from Harv Bartell. Harv bellows, "Aw, come on!" meaning he wishes he thought of it first. I watch

Jesse. He has cajones, coming into the ring dressed identically to Jeff what's-his-name, the actor who played Jesus in *Ben Hur* and died in a car wreck, and many people thought it was a message that you shouldn't play Jesus.

Jesse Christy never saw the movie or doesn't care or really wants his shot. His long hair and beard and tattered robes are incidental to his moves. I suspect Jesse Christy developed himself, and Joe tells me he's fresh off a six-month hiatus after bombing as Killer B. Lee.

A new outfit out of Cleveland, the WWO, has a roster that includes Buddha Boy, which seems disrespectful and unimaginative, so maybe it'll work, but the guy is only fat—can't lead, can't follow.

Scuttlebutt on the vine is that the WWO's first champ, www.InterNick.com the Computer Nerd, came off the drawing boards on the rebound from cancellation as Ayatollah Gomaimit. Fearing fundamental reprisal, he came up with this www.InterNick.com. So now the WWO is stuck with www.InterNick.com and Buddha Boy, as unconvincing, non-compelling and doomed as any duo of fat guys who ever kissed a turnbuckle.

The fact is, I carved the niche with the Slam of No Slam, big air and love-in-the-moment mania; I alone give the fans what they want most: a hero of simple reality. And what do I get? Knocked off out the wazoo. I stay one step ahead by winning and developing, by plowing hours on end into the silence. Then I get dumped.

So I say to Harv Bartell, "I want Jesse Christy." He shrugs; Jesse isn't his to give. "I'll get him myself. You let it happen." I explain the market pie and how it now slices; the fans follow a favorite league, but a crossover will bare the flank of the WWQ, exposing our (WWU) stars to new potential. He looks worried; the door swings both ways. "We're better! They got nothing they didn't copy."

I pick up the phone and ask Holly to get Jessie. I'll wait. She murmurs but doesn't falter, and like he was sitting by the phone, it's Jesse on the line.

I put it to him. He says, "What're you asking me for? You know it's gotta go through Gordy."

"How do you feel about it?" I tense, waiting for the question: Who gets the win?

But Jesse only says, "Hey, if Gordy says go, I says which way and how far and when. You know?"

"Thanks Jesse. We'll be in touch."

Gordy goes along on a sixty-forty in Harv's favor. In exchange for the win for Jesse we get a rematch inside thirty days with a win for me. The rubber match will be sixty days after with the win to be determined by money, or chance if the money can't be settled.

Harv loves it. He hides his excitement better than Mozo but can't stop the wheels from turning. They smoke and grind. So what can he do, give up the dough on the rubber match for another season out of the Monk? I doubt it. Maybe the gate will grow as I hit sixty and seventy, and a new generation of fans will pay more to see old guys and little guys take the beating they deserve. And maybe not.

I figure Harv more likely to sell me down the pike in a heartbeat; he'll go in asking for thirty points over half and settle for ten. No, my time has come.

Let me put it this way: the noise surges past tickle to marginal pain. The noise tells you they want more—more as a concept, more as a way of life, more for all time. They want it all and right now. Then they want more. Throwing in the towel on budget constraint, Harv and Gordy show faith that the gate and pay-per-view might only break even in the first go-round but will go through the roof on the rematch and sear the clouds on the rubber.

I don't see Holly for a week; her idea. Joe comes over to help salvage the silence. He worries that the commotion will dull my edge. As bodyguard, he steps outside to tell the press, "The Monk is in repose." I taught him that word, repose; he thinks it has to do with late payments on cars but goes along. The press runs with it.

Rusty calls for a debriefing. He says I've tapped the mother lode on this one and maybe should consider challenges to the reigning champions of each league. I see Mozo at the gym. He sneers anew, losing his thunder once more on the little white peck.

The media hums coast to coast and round the globe and kicks into warp speed when ABC runs a "color piece" on what is real in the world today. CBS and NBC follow suit with reality coverage on the evening news.

Entertainment Tonight includes advance ticket revenues for the upcoming bout in its weekly tally of artistic success around the country.

ESPN calls it the hype of the century then runs bios on Jesse and me and interviews with a few grade-school teachers and distant cousins who remember what we were really like back then.

CNN begins daily coverage a month out with analysis of each wrestler's potential benefit from aberrant weather and traffic jam. Then comes legal analysis of liability, culpability, believability and of course the burden of proof.

Jesse severely undermines the blitz by stopping on the street for a series of personal questions. He is led from the basics—Will he win?—to the noose of complexity—Why does he call himself Jesse Christy? He says he will win because he knows he will win, because Gordy will not take him into a match like this without knowing he will win—not like it's fixed; no; it's like, like, you know, like you know you will win, or can win. You know?

He says Jesse Christy was Gordy's idea and he laughs; all ideas come from Gordy. As Gordy imagines, so the real world evolves. Jesse closes by downshifting to the mean and macho with a gravel-voiced threat to tear the Monk limb from limb, to pound me a new face and rip my arms from their sockets and stretch my blah, blah, blah.

I wish he wouldn't do that. We're supposed to be different, the Monk and Jesse Christy. But damage is minimal. The segment is tedious; it plays only once, latenight, and is passed over by the wire services. The newsdogs know enough to bury this bone for later, maybe for a night so peaceful the news runs like molasses. But Jesse failed the test of the modern champion, the interview.

I am also hounded in public and asked for response to Jesse's threats. A newsdog jams his mike in my face, so I lead his hand down by the wrist, just enough to make him wince, no whimpers. I half-smile for the camera and say, "Lightning slashes the spring wind." I am also consigned to the midnight vigil and the staring eyes of those whose minds are stuck on simmer. What an image. I make a few morning shows. But then talk of imagery turns to talk of poetry, which is fine in its place, but what about the Monk and the show?

On the night of nights the din of human agony wails anew. Diatribe drowns in decibels of deafening density, sorry for the audio difficulty. Way past tickle and pain, we delve in psycho-audio flashback. Up and back in the non-time of ultimate density we regress to the final moment of the first infinity, Ylam.

Back to the bang that blew the galaxies, systems, stars, planets, asteroids and nation states to their diasporic spin and out to the nether yonder where weeds flutter hot and sultry over the detritus stench of a marsh at low tide, we go.

Oh, I let it all go, pulling my own stops, enjoying the show from the depths and summit of silence.

I grasp the low rope finger by finger and pull myself up. Jesse matches my moves; I lead by following him. We approach and ascend in simultaneous tumult, according to the terms and conditions wherein the party of the first part and the blah, blah, blah.

And here we are, Jesse pumped to take it on the nose and comeback for the win, me with my secret, the one I saved for a noisy day. The announcer gives up, fading to flutters, his lips flapping over *You both know the rules...*

A bell ripples in the fuzzy distance. I step forward. I bow, rise and wait. Jesse approaches. He wants a tie-up, hardly a hundred fifty pounds himself and old enough to make me look chipper. But I step aside and circle. He shoots in, and I sidestep again and send him to the ropes, where he bounces to improv, in case that's what I want. But I sidestep again, and his fling off the ropes loses momentum on the far side. He stops. He smiles. He understands.

We go to character in another simultaneous sidestep. He opens his arms, palms up. I bow.

And it's over.

Somewhere in deep space a pin drops to a floor and clangs like the Liberty Bell. We've won, because two aging stiffs draw a line and stand firm in the second infinity. We go down in history as the men who stole the glory.

We steal the money too; no rematch, no rubber. The lecture circuit pays more than working ever paid, and if I can't hack the travel I can always make a few bucks with a comment or an opinion. And some people are catching on when they ask about my marvelous career in the cornered ring, and I tell them:

Ommmmmmmmmmmmmmmmmmmmmmmmmmmm mmmmmmmmmmmmmmmmmmmmm.

Ommmmmmmmmmmmmmmmmmmmmmmmmmmm mmmmmmmmmm.

Ommmmmmmmmmmmmmmmmmm.

Ommmmmmmmmmmm.

Mmmmmmm.

Lonely Hearts, Changing Worlds

Who wouldn't want to live in Paradise? Balmy weather and skimpy clothing make for playful days and nights. Love and garish flowers waft with riotous scent and expectation. Succulents drip nectar in fulsome effusion and tribute to the goddess of life.

Yet for months I longed for escape from the sweat and dust of this Never Never place. I broke out one morning over strong coffee and a news account of two local men, brothers, who got even with two white men, also brothers. A white brother had achieved sexual liaison with the ex-girlfriend of a local brother, who agonized to critical mass; she was so blonde, so svelte and innocent. The local brothers took the white brothers at gunpoint in a small boat five miles out to sea and shot them and threw them overboard.

They drifted a day and a night, the white brothers. One died. The other held onto him until sharks came, and the surviving brother then let the dead brother go. The surviving white brother was picked up, and the local brothers were directly pinched and arraigned.

They pleaded aggravated homicide, the local brothers. In their cheap suits and clip-on ties they stood humbly, heads bowed before the court. Yet when they looked up, the eyes had it: *I kill you, you white fuck.*

I picked up the phone and made reservations for six and in twelve more calls I recruited five others on a lark. I knew they'd go along. Why not visit Fiji? The violence in the news came up on the phone, but nobody wants to dwell on murderous racism. We wanted only away for more of the fun and beauty we held dear.

Fiji is a vast archipelago with mind-boggling reef. Clear water and soft corals at sixty feet are habitat for fish populations long gone from the sovereign republic we called home. Arrival late one day and a dive early the next got us going. The real world slid further away over lunch in an Indian cafe. Curry and dahl and bitter beer at seventy cents a pint pungently underscored our exotic arrival, and our young waiter beamed at us, delegates from modern times.

Cranking Rod Stewart, Debi Harry and Jimmy Cliff to warp level on his Hi Fi, he strove to please us. An old ceiling fan on tired bearings strobed sunbeams leaking through the roof. The Great Council of High Chiefs looked down from their portrait near the eaves. Humphrey Bogart and Peter Lorre smoked Lucky straights and murmured in the shadows.

Prakash the waiter could not contain himself. "Oh? You are from United States? Have you tried marijuana? What did you feel? How many leaves did you smoke? I have tried it once but what we have here is not very good, so I cannot get drunk. But in America!"

"But we are not from America," I said. "We are from Italy."

Prakash considered Italians. "That is good too!"

He followed his new Italian friends out the door, saying no more lunches today. He went the other way around the square and met us by chance on the far side. "Prakash!" we greeted him.

"Ah! They know my name! They know my name!" He pointed out this familiarity to his friends and asked what kind of fun we might like at night. "You may find much drinking and dance at the Hyatt." He pressed us; would much drinking and dancing strike a fancy? The question failed to rouse us, so he said, "Ah! You are staying at The Lighthouse. You must know my friend, Nita Nancy Vanivalau. I must tell you, she is very beautiful. You will see this. And you must know she is my friend, my very close friend. As you are my friends. I will introduce her to you."

Yes, yes, whatever you say. Of course, yes, maybe later. Goodbye for now. Prakash sensed a blow-off in modern terms. Not to worry; we would soon see.

Nita Nancy Vanivalau came to my cabana that afternoon on special assignment. And yes, she was a striking beauty who moved gracefully with cheer and innocence in asking, "Are you Italian? Prakash tells me that you are Italian."

Gazing upon her I felt only compelled to honesty. "No. We are American. We lied."

"You lied? Good. It is good to lie to Indians. Do many people lie where you come from?"

"Yes. I usually don't. But I can do it. I can lie with integrity if necessary." Her own gaze twisted in perplexity at my strange candor. "Sometimes I practice to stay in shape."

"I just live down the road. That way." She pointed south. She pointed north. "That way is the Hyatt. I will love to go there!" I said yes, we could go there easily. She made the bed and said, "Well, maybe. I might come back. I might. I must change my clothes."

But she didn't come back. I left her a note on my door and joined my friends for too many cocktails. I only toyed with dinner. I declined an outing but returned to my room to read the history of the place in my travel guide and then stare at the window louvers until the louvers on my eyes went shut.

By morning she was a pleasant delusion, displaced by another spectacular dive. She came that night at one in the morning, knocking and whispering urgently, "Hello? It is me, Nita Nancy! Yesterday never comes!"

From a deep sleep I told her to wait. I got up and rinsed my face and mouth and opened the door. She slipped in like a shadow and practically whimpered, "Now we can go? The Hyatt!"

I laughed and said no. "I am sleeping, in bed. You can stay if you like."

"No, no, no. Not here. Never here. No, I must go home now. Good night. Tomorrow will come."

Morning coffee was slow and tranquil, what we'd come for. Then came talk of comings and goings in the night and questions of prudence. Could sexual relations with a third-worlder be wise? After all, uh hum, uh hum.

"Your concern is appreciated but possibly racist," I said. That shut them up; nobody wants to be a racist. "This isn't Africa. The dreaded disease has dramatically lower incidence in the South Pacific. We're farther from the source than we ever were at home." I based my contention on the natural direction of all migrations, to the west. I had no idea if I was right, but they bought it. "Besides, since when has wisdom been a factor in sexual motivation? Besides, I have a rubber. And besides, you haven't seen her." I didn't have a rubber but planned to get one.

A woman in the group named Sheila made no secret about favoring what the men in the group most favored. She sat sternly up, which usually signaled a tongue-lashing over sexism or lookism or manism. But she only concurred with conviction if not pleasantry, "He's right. You didn't see her."

From an envious male came moral turpitude. I sluffed it. I know sour grapes when I hear them. "But how can you do such a thing?" he asked. Sexual imperialism was the accusation, I think.

"She came to my room," I said. "You assume sexual contact. I won't correct you. She came to me. Her teeth are perfect. Her eyes are big and clear. Her shape is exquisite. She smiles like moonlight and moves like soft coral in a gentle current. She came to me. My response was easy. It's natural."

"You're stealing Prakash's girlfriend."

"Yes. That's a problem. But I trust her discretion. And the little soldier insists."

"You're disgusting," said a woman in the group, perhaps because nobody came to her, nor did a visit seem likely. But I hung my head in concession for the good of the group; yes, of course; disgusting was I.

The morning dive was another plunge to perfection at sixty feet. Among the giant fans and tiny fish so brilliant with color, we surged one way and the other, yielding to the inexorable surge as worldly cares melted away.

Nita greeted us at Prakash's restaurant with the beauty and warmth of another implacable force. The women among us stared as if at another lovely wisp in the current. The men ogled. Nita fluttered. Lust and envy, curiosity and desire stirred our placid waters. Nita Nancy shook their hands and settled beside me, touching and hugging, for I was the one. She asked my age.

I was nearly forty then. Young for a man, she said, though she felt much older than a woman of twenty-two in America would feel. Most of her childhood friends were grandmothers, but not her; no, she wanted more of the world before throwing in the towel. And tonight we would go for much drinking and dance. At the Hyatt!

Modern starlets spend fortunes on such a "look" and don't come close to the velvet softness, the ink black skin or fleecy hair. Her sharp nose and high cheeks underscored her deep sockets and bright eyes. As if it weren't enough, then came the lips, thick and succulent to make me swoon with narcosis; nothing made sense like the depths of her. In a real dress her figure was thin and agonizingly shapely. Who does floors with such delicate long hands? How can a nymph rise from a scrub bucket? How can such a spirit seem so needful? Never mind; she desired contact as fervently as Prakash did, and so we would go for drinking and dance, at the Hyatt!

It was her favorite of all places, her very, very most favorite—"Prakash can come too?"

"...Yes. Of course..."

She leaned into me with shameless affection. Caressing me she whispered, "It will be okay. You will see. He is poofta. He will like you. You like boys? Why not? Why don't you try it?" I laughed weakly and shrugged and was surrounded by her arms. Her face pressed mine. "Good. I am glad you don't like boys. I tell him he should like girls. He says he knows. Soon."

Prakash watched from another table, clearing and wiping it clean and grinning ear to ear.

She wore the same dress that night and downed four drinks in a few minutes as if making up for lost time or maybe hurrying to avoid additional waste. She loved the six-dollar tourist drinks with the sliced fruit and preserved cherries and paper parasols and foam on top. Power derived from the simple act of ordering them without a care, and she flowed with pleasure in proximity to Americans who don't even blink at prices, at the Hyatt!

She danced every dance with fervor edging to frenzy. I fancied that her forebears danced with similar glee over prospects of fresh white meat. She led. I asked if she practiced at home, and she said, "Oh, yes!" Darting in close with affection, moving back with indifference she left a scent, unbathed but not unclean. She was third world by chance, and it was a bad chance in her view of things. For me, it was exotic, more than simple amusement, I hoped. She reached for maximum fun for three hours.

On the way out through the lobby we met her friends. Introductions were formal, but acceptance seemed natural. Bright eyes were common here, and they shone with good cheer for Nita Nancy, the girl who wanted more. "He is Italian," she said.

Squeezing into the little rental car for the drive home my hand rested naturally on her thigh. Her legs opened, easing me in for warmth or security or maybe a gentle massage. The six others crammed around us feigned indifference to her squirm, and everyone squealed on the swerves around cows in the road. We headed slowly through town toward the fields where Nita Nancy and Prakash had lived as neighbors since childhood. In a strained singsong laughter Prakash said we could only go so far—beyond would not be possible to penetrate. He and Nita Nancy would hike the last short distance but not to worry; it is okay.

But in the last half-mile she was all over me, fast and rough with a deep, course whisper, "Come on, come on, come on. I want it. I want it. I want it. Let me feel. Let me feel." Gripping my knee she pulled up my shirt then pulled my head to her chest. "I can tell you something, you can really dance!" She thrust her hand down my pants. I said no and fended her off, telling her she was too rough. So she grabbed my dick outside my pants and rubbed it. "I have danced at the Hyatt plenty of times, but all the other men weren't like you. They were shy."

I conceded affability.

She knew what that meant and grabbed again and squeezed. I shoved her away. "Can I take it out? Let me take it out!"

She would not relent, until Prakash broke the deafening silence. "You are a whore. A whore! Stop!"

She calmed to mild fidgets and soon giggles and sweet caresses of my head and face, and we rode silently past the clapboard shacks with sheet metal roofs on the fringe of town near the outback. They got out sadly, as if the coach was suddenly a pumpkin. "Tomorrow. Lunch," I said.

Prakash cried, "Yes? Tomorrow? Lunch? Tomorrow? You will come for lunch? Please!" Prakash, embarrassed, drunk and desperate, staggered where he stood. Nita Nancy slumped beside him, drunk and forlorn. "Say goodnight to your friend. Say goodnight!" She smiled, and the Americans pulled out waving at the dark couple melting into the shadows and their engulfing reality.

A hangover in the morning made a good excuse to miss the day's dive. The real reason was unspoken but the others had seen her now. They wished me well and left. I waited in my bungalow. A knock on the door in mid-morning announced an older maid who came in and said, "So. You go dancing with Nita? How late did you stay? Two-thirty? With Nita? Oh. At the Hyatt? She is working today at the manager's. Just knock on the door."

A jumping spider crouched on the knocker. It jumped when a young girl opened the door. "Is Nita here?"

"Yes! I am here!" My heart swelled with her beauty and spirit. She begged please that I go quickly. We would meet and talk later after the dive and lunch. I slept it off.

Prakash was reflective in his hangover. I told him no, we could not go again tonight for much drinking and dance. Tonight would be a night dive, what we came for. "Ah!" he shrank in fear. "You go into the ocean at night?" He observed his new friends anew, pondering their flirtation with evil.

Nita waited near the car after lunch wearing her much drinking and dance dress. I told her she was the best dancer I ever knew.

She said thank you so much; it was the most wonderful time of her whole life.

I said I too was grateful. She looked down. I said I didn't want it to end there in the back of town.

She asked what I wanted.

I want you, I said. You know that.

She said yes, of course, she knew. She asked if I did that often, you know, with women.

I said no, not so very much.

She said no, not so very much for her either.

I asked if maybe tonight we could be together.

She said yes, maybe, at the Hyatt!

I was to pick her up down the road from the Lighthouse Cabanas because she would be fired if caught socializing with the guests. I told my friends my night dive had been moved to an alternate site. They smiled with scorn or envy and left in another car. I met Nita and said we could go, if she wanted, to the Hyatt! "Yes!" She wore her same dress.

But I honestly preferred her place.

She asked why I would want to go there.

I imagined a hut with a thatch roof and primitive, charming facilities. I told her a man far from home likes being far from home. The Hyatt was not good for me. But the thought of seeing her home pleased me, if I wasn't being too forward.

"No, you are not," she said. "We can go to my house." She looked troubled. "But you must know..." She struggled with the truth. "We cannot go all the way by car. We must walk up the hill. And..." She could not reconcile a modern man in her home.

"And what?"

"Nothing. You will see."

"Yes. I want to see." She lost her spark, her electric spirit changing to manual. Like a hand-driven pump she gave in and went along with the necessary task. I said we would stop for good things to eat, that we would take these things along to her house. She nodded all right and pointed the way to an Indian grocery.

I bought fried fish, fried chicken, sausage, fried vegetables, dahl, fruit, lemonade and beer, bread and tins of fish. I dropped thirty bucks looking for the fine thin line between giving and excess. Her spirit revived with my largesse. She saw a new bond between us.

The glimmer and hope shone faintly past the town lights over the shacks and sheet metal roofs, onto the outback road, past the sorry puddles encircling the scene of last night's farewell. This isn't bad, I told her. This isn't the bush. I shut up when the road submerged entirely under the puddles that soon became one, like a pond. Nita piloted us through, pointing out the shoals and deep trenches. Blackness cloaked the countryside; she raised a hand pointing the way, but it was invisible. I said I couldn't see, and she laughed harder than she'd laughed all day. Pointing to a cane field she said, "Turn here." In ghostly silhouette she glittered from the eyes and teeth.

"Turn where?"

"Anywhere. There's no road. You are far from home. Turn!" I turned into the three-foot cane, ready to fall off the edge of the earth. "Go this way!" She tugged to the left. "Now this way!" She pushed to the right. I looked for her in the dark, wondering what she had in mind. She said, "We must go around the ditch."

"Of course. The ditch. Where is the ditch?"

"Stop! Now this way—no! Go backward..." KERTHUNK! The front axle rested on the ditch edge with the front wheels hanging over as my heart and the little engine pounded baseline to her melodious refrain, "This is the ditch! We must walk from here."

"What about the car?"

"Tomorrow," she said. "We must find help to move it." Commitment gained clarity. So did the meaning of a third-world woman seeking contact with modern times; tomorrow her neighbors would see her new suitor. We could have just as well stayed at the Hyatt! But images of electric lights, linens and room service vanished in two steps with my exotic date. Alone on a night dive with no light and no buddy, I stood still. I sensed the ditch looming invisibly within an inch of my life. It yawned. It groaned. In the fearful abyss I sensed mambas, crocs and, of course, the old chiefs. Yet a soft darkness within the greater darkness wove its lovely fingers in my own. I grasped her hand and followed through the cane across another ditch, closing my eyes and finding no difference between one darkness and another. At the base of a hill we leaned up it toward a dimly lit box that shone like a fading lantern.

In a few steep strides we gained delineation like charcoal on pitch. Starkly stacked cinderblock and a shingle roof looked like a house but not a house. Door and window openings void of doors and windows and a concrete slab floor with no plumbing or electricity suggested a house whose construction abruptly stopped.

What was to be of it was done.

It glimmered faintly as a failing pulse, but she said, "Feema!"

Nita explained that her little sister Feema moved to the city last year to seek her fortune but came back most weekends. It was Saturday already, so Nita thought she wasn't coming. Animate in final ascent through the mud, Nita tittered over good timing and so much food and the feast we would now share with Feema.

The dark and dirty front room seemed unchanged since the concrete was poured. But the kitchen was neat and clean, as were the two bedrooms. Feema sat in the back bedroom, simply sat, awaiting visitation. She looked up calmly at our arrival and said, "Hello."

Nita spread the bounty on plastic doilies on the floor. Feema guzzled lemonade and giggled as Nita filled her in on all the news, leading with her great good friends, especially me, and much drinking and dance, at the Hyatt! Feema could not share the excitement but understood Nita's need.

Nita said the beer was for me and tore open the paper bags where they sat on the floor. Feema set the kerosene lamp in the center. Feasting on the floor like children playing house, we soothed another hunger. Feema was not so famished as Nita Nancy but wanted to know about America and diving and Prakash. What part of America did I come from? Did I see sharks? She giggled; did I know Prakash was poofta? I said I came from far outside the main part of America. Yes, sharks were common, and yes, I knew Prakash.

"Poofta," Nita said. "He likes boys. He likes you."

"He is your friend," I said.

"So? I tell him what he does is evil and dirty and that if he does not stop, he will die a wicked death. He stops sometimes. But now you are here. He wants me to lead you to him."

I laughed; intrigue seemed more accessible in the bush than at the Hyatt. We ate and drank. In the soft light Feema said, "He is very fond of Nita. Don't you think so?"

"Yes. Yes I do," I said. We finished eating and sat back in quiet repose.

"Would you like to lay down?" Feema led with the lamp. Prone on the bed was a position of honor; a man should lie down after eating. She asked if I'd seen a sea cucumber. She saw them in the market but they looked so awful she could not accept them as living creatures. I said yes, they're alive as you and me, and sensitive. They go like this; and I writhed slowly on the bed in my best sea cuke impersonation.

She said, "You know that is very good. Have you seen a sea urchin?" I nodded again, pointing my fingers up and moving them slow as quills. She laughed and said, "I am very tired now. I will go into the other room so that you may be alone in case you will want to become lovers." I loved her too and wished she would stay. I lay in the silence so foreign to a modern man and could hear nature taking its course.

Nita went for her bedtime preparation. From the designated area in back came the sound of pissing in the dirt. She called: if I wanted to piss I should piss now, and the sisters giggled in their tandem squat.

She came back to the room and undressed quietly as a whisper. I rolled over to watch. Down to her threadbare slip she leaned to douse the light. No, I said. I want to see you naked. She blushed, yes, and with a nervous smile let fall the tattered fabric to reveal the shape transcendent of manly pursuit.

Yet from natural beauty she tensed and stood straight as a pointer scenting game. A finger darted to me then to her lips. She pulled her slip back up and waited, and in a moment Prakash entered the cinderblock box with his own kerosene lamp. "What are you doing?" he asked from the front room. She dropped her guard and moved easily again, clearing paper bags and moving clothes. "What are you doing?"

He entered the bedroom.

I said hello, Prakash, but he didn't care who knew his name. He screamed instead, "Fuck you bitch! You are a bitch, and I fuck you! Bitch whore! Whore! Your mother is a whore! And you are a whore! I fuck you! I fuck you in your mouth! I fuck you fuck fuck fuck you in your mouth!"

"Go home poofta."

"I... I... I fuck your asshole and your mouth!" He stormed out yet his spirit lingered, or maybe I only feared his return in the night. I sensed knives. But Feema stood in her doorway beautifully back-lit, giggling and smiling.

"Oh, he is so angry," she said. "He is really angry that you will be lovers and not him." She shimmered with amusement and backed into her room. My heart called out to her.

Nita laughed. "Poofta. He likes boys." She lay down beside me in her threadbare slip. We lay savoring our intimacy and what would come of it. The warm, muggy air barely moved over us, but when I touched her she trembled. She felt fearful.

I hoped it was the act upon us and not I, at the root of her apprehension. Easing her straps off her shoulders I moved gently, touching my cheek to her breasts. Yet rather than a sensual tingling of soft tissue I felt the dire functionality of the third world. Big and firm for suckling babies, these glands were aimed at survival, not amusement. And why would a grown man want to suck them? She squirmed, more from this embarrassing perversion than from stimulation, I think; not even the animals behave like this.

We verged on the realm of procreation, and I understood. I think she fancied a real house with a husband and fried fish with lemonade every night. A new dress now and then wouldn't be bad, and the rigors of daily life could ventilate as necessary, at the Hyatt! Her prince had seen the dim light. He had eaten on the floor and looked upon her pissing in the dirt. Yet he remained ready to slay the void in which she lived. In a simple thrust we might conceive what she hoped could be hers all along.

As a modern prince I was indeed prepared to end her spell with more than a kiss. I wished for a rubber but understood the value of wishing in such a place. I didn't have one, because you can't get them in those places most dying for them. I didn't think we would make a baby, because that's what men lying next to naked women think. Nor was toxic fluid exchange a factor; just feel the life inside this shape. The little soldier seemed confident, so full of the can-do attitude his kind is famous for.

Yet fate as well made its presence known. Yes, it can change with free will, but there I was and would wish it again. For what man of sound mind would rather be elsewhere than where I lay then, in the center of the swirl of the best of life? Would we make a baby? Soul arrive, I thought, if you so choose. You will be lean and spirited and close to the world around you. You will never want for love with such a mother and an aunt. Never for fried fish and lemonade will you hunger or thirst with such a patron. I would not forget them.

With consequence accounted for, I felt free to proceed, beginning with what industrialized men are led to believe is most wanted by all women. I thought she might enjoy a white face between her legs—oh, I am game, never mind marginal hygiene and the mephitic scent of life close to the ground. But she shunned further perversion and made it seem hazardous, like a taunt to nature's intention on specific body parts. I lay there in amused rejection, that such a spirit as Nita Nancy would so quickly reject the world she wanted to experience. As I pondered proper presentation of my request for a blowjob, she interrupted with a firm offer. "You may suck my titties," she allowed.

"Thank you." I complied with clinical composure. This isn't it; I wanted to tell her. But she seemed pleased to please me, so I suckled in apparent satisfaction before she dispensed with further foolishness. I wondered how she could be so inured to touchy-feely but only briefly. She got down to what we came for by reaching once more and pulling the little trooper up by his nose and putting him where he ought to go. A gentle kiss tasted like fried chicken, fish, sausage and lemonade.

And there, far from home, I received the favor a woman bestows on a man in simple terms, which is the gift of yoni, the perfect solution for the nagging problem. In its fundamental essence the squish was like honey on yams after the rigors of hunting, gathering and shelter. She lay still and apprehensive as a brave child receiving inoculation, opening her legs as if revealing her heart. I wanted more, because I'm American. But she did something subtle with another twitch of a sub-equatorial nature, bringing us quickly to another chasm. She led me over with a shared grunt, sharing my relief, I think, in a behavior common to all mammals. Efficiently separating man from seed, she rendered me sleepy in moments. I rolled off as men most often do prior to sleep.

Mosquitoes buzzed through the five-by-five yawn in the wall that overlooked the latrine and far fields. A swarm hovered near us, maybe for the scent of woman and pecker juice. We lay there unable to sleep, until she said wait; she would get the fan. My dulled brain envisioned a gentle breeze in slow oscillation. She returned with a cardboard fan showing Krishna on one side and plain white on the other. Caressing me like a romantic after all, or maybe because tenderness for some women comes after the grunt, she fanned the buzz away.

Her arm gained weight and settled above my head. Breathing slowly, then heavily, she soon snored.

I lay awake another five hours, sensing Prakash, until my bladder swelled with beer and lemonade. Nita slept sweetly beside me, our skins warmly numb where we touched. I moved, but she didn't stir. I savored this rare interlude, but the tired little soldier could not stand down with such urgent pressure from within.

The moon was down and a billion stars lit a vague opening into the hall. I found my way slowly to the next room and searched for a beer bottle. Exceeding a pint seemed a distant worry and a pint away, but such concern was incidental. The trash overflowed with tins and cartons but no bottles. I doubted I would find them in the recycling bin.

The stillness resettled. Easing toward the exterior opening and stepping out, I moved toward the remembered sound of two women pissing. But what difference could it make? I stopped and waited, readied the bloated soldier and let loose the torrent. It would be a minute or two, so I reflected on the rare potential of certain moments, the warm and nubile woman awaiting my return. Reverie ended with a nervous singsong in muffled tones, "Not there! You cannot peepee there! You are bad!"

Not peeing was not a viable option. So I pissed like a Belgian fountain, still as stone. The outlines moved, and from the shadows Prakash stepped up, his eyes darting here and there as if sensing predators, up and down as if measuring prey. "What are you doing? What is it you have done?" He whispered urgently. I hardly needed to tell him I was taking a ferocious piss after making union with his childhood sweetheart. Nor could I go along with his innuendo that I, a man with so much, had invaded this innocent, hospitable world and taken everything from him, a man with so little.

So I only asked back, "What are you doing?"

He turned away. "I want to tell you something." I waited. "Can you..."

"Prakash. Lunch. Tomorrow. You will tell me tomorrow at lunch."

"Yes. Maybe. But..."

I wanted to fold up and walk away to end our untimely discourse, but the end zone remained ninety yards out. "We came to look for you. We had a feast."

"But I am at home!"

"No. A man at home isn't out prowling in the bushes."

"I want to show you something."

"I have no doubt that you do. I want to see what you have to show. I want the recipe for your dahl. I want to tell you about the ocean. I want to drink beer. Tomorrow. Lunch."

He watched me walk back into the house, where I lay another two hours sensing his need.

Sunrise at the cinderblock hovel shared by the Vanivalau sisters seemed brilliant over the stark world it lit. Two women chattered happily as larks over another sunrise, as I watched them side by side, pissing in the dirt. They cleaned themselves and tossed the tissue to the tissue pile. They reviewed prospects for lifting the rental car from the ditch. No one mentioned breakfast or a cafe. Even coffee or tea would require a fire. And we'd eaten only last night.

So we marched down the hill and through the cane to the ditch. Nita and Feema pushed while I heaved, and it was done. The intrepid little rental car started reluctantly and trembled in the chill, morning dew. But it warmed, gaining confidence and purpose.

We watched it, standing in the awkward transition of getting to know each other and saying goodbye. I gave Nita all the money I had on me, thirty dollars or so.

Feema asked what for.

Nita said no, it is okay.

Two days later at home in the official Paradise of the richest nation in the modern world, waking up only minutes away from church, schools and shopping, I watched another sunrise. First light embodied the dancing motes.

Gathering in the dazzle they drifted like stellar orbs, like us, perhaps, lost, perhaps, in need of a gravity around which to circle. A fine sweat rolled down my ribs, underscoring the discomfort, decomposition and torpor of that which so many people fantasize.

The morning reporter said the two local brothers had attracted the services of Jimmy Hockman. They couldn't afford his airfare from LA much less his kind of legal talent, and they made it clear that they were not papolo (black) but a virulently proud mix of Filipino, Chinese, Japanese, Portuguese and don't forget da kine, Hawaiian.

Jimmy Hockman displayed the finest bridgework money can buy on each and every question posed. Grinning like a canary-stuffed Cheshire, he said the operative component of aggravated homicide is the aggravation. He stretched his grin in an amazing demonstration of even greater joy, and he pledged to prove that a heart was in fact irreparably damaged by the shamelessly cruel taunt of its true love. "She told this poor fellow, my client, that he wasn't good enough for her. I will submit these photographs for review of the court."

Tiffany Smits was a ballbreaker and a heartbreaker, especially if you happened to be a leg and breast man like Takao. They posed together, so young, so vital, so much in love. Her twisted torso accentuated her thin waist and huge breasts. He embraced her, his hands resting on an inner thigh and a breast.

I called my friend Sheila, who understood love and beauty. What did she think of me bringing Nita to Hawaii? For a visit. Maybe I expected praise for my generosity bordering on magnanimity.

She counseled cooler jets. Oh, yes, Nita would be on the first flight out. But sending her home could be another matter. "Consider spending a long time with her before you bring her in for a nice weekend. Why not send her a new dress for now and see what happens?"

I picked out a black, slinky number with bright red flowers and sent it priority. In only three weeks I got a thank you that read with the same lilt as her speech. She loved the dress and loved me for sending it. She loved the memories we shared and those we would share in the future. Could I send money?

How much seemed so crude to ask, and another thirty bucks seemed cheap. And what about the precedent I would establish? I felt cheap and sent fifty. I got a longer letter asking when would be good to visit and telling of the beating Prakash sustained in Sigatoga. A broken arm and many cuts and bruises had him laid up worrying how to pay for his medical needs.

I sent three hundred. I got a much longer thank you saying the money got Prakash started on the road to settling his debts, with enough left over for a deposit on a ticket to Hawaii. Don't worry, she said. She would find me with the help of the cab driver.

The murder trial took only a week. The local brothers won when Jimmy Hockman changed venue from Honolulu to Waipio, where he was able to show that an abused heart is a loaded weapon. In this case it went off at the very person who loaded it.

The following week Tiffany and Takao were betrothed. They spoke happily to the nightly news team about a June wedding and the spirit of aloha.

I sent five hundred and said goodbye to Nita Nancy Vanivalau. Don't come here, I said. I have a beautiful wife and three small children, I said. Please take care of Prakash and Feema, I said.

She never wrote back, though I still get Christmas cards from Prakash.

My Teacher Has A Big Red Apple

It was the most amazing thing when I was a boy, that you could hold your tongue between thumb and forefinger—get a good grip on it—and say *My teacher has a big red apple*, and it would come out every time as *My teachuh hath a big wed ath-hole.*

Which was outrageously, often tumultuously funny. We laughed till we cried. Or till we hushed enough for Jeff Smith to attempt: *My father's a sheet splitter, he splits sheets. He's the best sheet splitter that ever split a sheet.*

It wasn't until a few years later that Billy Ayers told us calmly one day, *My father's a fig plucker...*

Twat you say? The novelty of this question amused us for weeks on end. The answer sustained us into summer. *I cunt hear you.*

Then came the story of Tommy Fuckerfaster, who had a yen for the you-know-what and one day got caught slipping the goods to little Janey Brown in the barn. "Oh, Tommy Fuckerfaster!" his mother called.

"I'm going full speed now, Mom!" Tommy replied.

How we laughed, once the shock wave dissipated. When you thought about it, it was bound to happen to a guy named Fuckerfaster. But we laughed just the same. If he had a sister, what would her name be? Doreen?

Does your dick hang low?

Does it wobble to and fro?
Can you tie it in a knot?
Can you tie it in a bow?
Can you throw it over your shoulder like a continental soldier?
Does your dick hang low?

The sheer genius of these rhymes made sense out of our childhood, our years of innocence that could perhaps be viewed as wasted by those of a more delicate cultural backdrop. But we did grow up to take the baton in the wealthiest nation in the history of the world. Did we not?

Asshole, asshole, assoldier went to war.
Fuck you, fuck you, fucuriosity.
To piss, to piss, two pistols by his side.
My cunt, my cunt, my country t'is of thee.

Benny the boilsucker came next, to crown our giddiest fervor and plumb the depths of our depravity. We were boys and loved the ardor with which Benny the boilsucker approached a boil. He roamed the countryside seeking people with boils—big, old boils, swollen with puss. He sucked them at reasonable rates.

A grimace here or a cringe from your audience with *Eeyeeeww!* confirmed proper delivery. Benny was tricky, however, since excessive gore could drive your audience away, especially the nice girls.

Anyway, Benny prospered, sucking boils, until he'd sucked every boil around. First disappointed, then depressed, soon he was starving. Down and out, on his last legs, he begged for one little bitty boil to suck, but there were none, and nobody knew what to do.

Until this guy comes out of this sleazy bar in this crummy little town where Benny had finally collapsed. The guy says, "Look, Mr. Boilsucker. You sucked every boil in town, but we have one more. I never mentioned it before, because it's on the asshole of this big, fat, greasy, stinky, half-dead whore out back in the alley. She has dandruff, too."

Benny whispers, "Hey, I'm dying here. Show me where." So the guy takes Benny out back to the alley and helps him pull the pants off this big fat whore.

Embroidery is optional here on skin blemishes and further symptoms of an unhealthy life, depending on audience reaction.

So they roll her over and get her legs spread, and she's groaning about what a relief it's gonna be, getting rid of that whopper on her asshole; the thing is huge and it's killing her. With a sense of purpose Benny feels better already. He gets in there, sniffing and feeling around with his tongue and finally says, "Hey! I found it."

He's sucking away, and everyone could have lived happily ever after, when the big whore cuts a tremendous fart, and Benny pulls his head out and says, "Oh! Lady! You're disgusting!"

Oh, how we howled.

The boys liked that one far more than the girls did. In fact, Benny endured through high school, often recalled in awful glory with the simple epithet, "Oh! Lady! You're disgusting!" We laughed our asses off at Benny sucking boils in blushing proximity to polite company. We were not polite, unless of course the genteel manner was forced upon us, which made it all the funnier.

We can be scorned in hindsight for the racial overtone Benny's adventure often took; the big fat whore was not of Caucasian descent. I don't think we were racist but only goofy boys at an all-white high school seeking maximum cringe on a dank asshole searching for the last, best boil with our collective tongue. We could have made her a Serbian Croat, an Albanian or Mexican, but those were simpler times, in the early years of television.

At heart we were open-minded and ruled by a sense of fair play. For example, I thought it wrong that Benny McDougal was nicknamed Benny the boilsucker just because his first name was Benny. Benny was unusual to be sure, more comfortable with skipping school than anyone else in our class. His shaggy, greasy hair and naturally unkempt demeanor fit well with his constant good cheer. You couldn't get him down, and you didn't see him depressed, because he enjoyed life, even when the boys called him the boilsucker or yelled down the hall or across the street, "Cheese'm up, Benny!"

This latter handle, cheese'm up, was said to derive from Benny's habit of smearing cream cheese on his dick, so his dog would be happy to lick it off. I found this hard to believe and in fact found nobody who actually witnessed the event, though Benny confided that you have to be careful to spread the cream cheese very thin or else the dog will puke before you're finished, and that was a drag.

Perception changes quickly in youth; I instantly saw Benny as mentally marginal rather than socially abused. He went as quickly from marginal to unacceptable when he asked if I got to fingerfuck Marsha Vanderberg. When I didn't answer, he asked if I would maybe find out if she would let him fingerfuck her. Benny went straight to disgusting, and nobody laughed.

Marsha Vanderberg was not only beautiful but delicate, sweet and kind. She didn't mind talking to me and in fact, I felt, she often enjoyed it. I made her laugh, and in our senior year she said yes, she would go with me to a movie maybe and maybe for something to eat.

I was high; me, in pegged pants and pointy shoes going out with Marsha Vanderberg, a pompom girl, which was practically a cheerleader, and she had the most famous ass at Norton High School. No boils up there. How could you even think such a thing? It was perfectly taut and concise and round. It swung happily and was a conversation piece more common than the weather in some circles. Did I want that imagery, that prospect tarnished by the foul thoughts of Benny McDougal?

No, I did not, and in fact I imagined my date with Marsha Vanderberg to be a turning point in my aesthetic development. She was a girl. She wore dresses and got good grades and had a great figure that included an Olympic-class ass. Today they might call it the Official Ass of the Olympic Games. But I digress.

In the way back bye and bye, I anticipated that we would display manners and intelligence in each other's company. She was perfect—the mere thought of getting into her pants would not even compute; she was so beautiful, so feminine and everything.

She divulged on our date that many of the girls could not believe she was going out with me. She saw my look of surprise and said she didn't mind my reputation, because she'd much rather go out with a smut-mouth than a dullard. "You make me laugh. I love to laugh. I might like it more than anything."

"Smut-mouth? Me?"

"Oh, come on. You yell 'Cheese'm up, Benny' down the hall, and you're always making nasty cracks."

"Nasty cracks?"

"See. You can't help it. I don't care." She smiled like an angel of mercy.

"As long as I make you laugh?"

"Yeah."

"I can't do that on cue. I don't mind if you think I'm funny. But I'm not a smut-mouth. I never yell at Benny. I think it's mean. I think it's mean that you didn't even take the time to see who's yelling and who isn't."

"I'm sorry. But I'm not mean. And it's other stuff, too."

"Yeah? Like what?"

"Oh, you know. Wisecracks. You always put a sexual meaning on things. You make reference to bodily function. You do it all the time."

"And you think it's funny?"

"No. I don't think so. Not conceptually. But I laugh. I must like your delivery."

I had to think that one over. She accepted what the other girls rejected, but only because of my delivery. "Can you give me an example?"

"That's so hard."

"That's what Ruthie said." I regretted my glib wit instantly. Ruthie went to a rival high school. She had abnormally large breasts and was known to let boys feel them—inside her bra!

"See. All I said was nasty cracks and that's so hard, and you made reference to sex and bodily function." We moped. "Okay, and all the girls know it was you who started, 'If it smells like fish, it's a dish.'"

We moped some more. I didn't bother telling her that the fish/dish line was a health tip, because perfumed scent can hide a horrible truth. "You're right. I need help. But you didn't think those things were funny?"

"No. I think you can be funny without that stuff."

"It's not so easy. Can you remember anything I ever

said that was funny that wasn't sexual or smutty?"

She laughed. "No. Well, yes, I can. When you told Miss Morehead she shouldn't take her loneliness out on you just because you're a boy. You said, 'What bothers you happened a long time ago. I'm not one of the guys who were mean to you.'"

"That wasn't funny."

"No. I agree. But it was poignant. It made me smile inside. She's such a horny old bitch."

"Poignant?"

"Yeah. You can be incisive. You could be great."

Well, incisiveness and greatness notwithstanding, and leaving poignancy for digestion later, I was satisfied that evening to savor what I took to be profound compliments. Marsha Vanderberg let me kiss her with equal profundity; she thrust her tongue down my throat and seemed receptive to a breast feel, what we loosely called outside second. She delineated her limits by clamping her arms to her torso in defense against inside second, or what we crudely called bare nip. Bare nip was presumably wild for both parties, but nice girls waited until the fourth date, or at least the second date in deference to reputation. A date then with a movie or bowling and something to eat could run ten bucks, which wasn't chump change. A few dates needed to stack up to represent investment, which was and perhaps still is precursor to commitment.

I got there and everywhere else a boy dreams about. Marsha Vanderberg and I engaged as well in the exotic behaviors some marriages require. Yet with age comes understanding that requirements are short term with no guarantees on the long term. Suffice to say we're still friends, Marsha and I. She got half of everything plus the house and sixty percent of everything on the horizon. She sent a greeting card when I turned fifty asking if all my hair was gone yet and filling me in on her family and the anticipated promotion for Steve, her second husband. He makes less than my former payments, but at least now she's in love.

She gave me something rare as well, which was insight where I least expected it. She made me blush for years by simply reminding me all those years ago, of my cruel jibe at Miss Morehead. Oh, clever youth; what I wouldn't give to go back and hang my head and say, "Yes, Ma'm," to that lonely woman.

Miss Morehead wrongly accused me of neglecting my homework or botching an easy exam or saying something that someone else had blurted out. She condemned me aloud before my peers to a life of casual failure. She profiled me as a loser that day in class. But rather than eat her serving of crow, I was bound by teen machismo to pierce her heart and twist the knife.

Miss Morehead was thirty-one, which was old in those days and older yet if you were homely, shapeless, nervous and spuriously cheerful. White blouses buttoned to the neck didn't help, nor did cardigan sweaters with brooches, usually a virgin pin or a rhinestone peacock. Her glasses dangled on a cord on her paltry bosom while she wrote frantically on the blackboard, diagramming deductive reasoning in her oblique way. She and plane geometry were required. Her personal exposure on the social plane was limited to a daily dosage of teen spirit.

I skewered her and left her for dead. She didn't cry in class. She stepped out to the hall for that. Marsha smiled inside, showing what ticked even then beneath her bare nip.

If I was eighteen and Miss Morehead was thirty-one,

she'd now be, let's see, three, carry the one—sixty-three. Not so old. I determined to call her up. I wouldn't apologize per se; she most likely forgot my offense, and if she didn't, I hardly wanted to reopen old wounds. No, I would simply tell her she was right. No, she wasn't right. She was a bitch. I would tell her...

Let's see. I would express gratitude for her...her insight and poignancy in plane geometry. Oh, hell, I would simply call her and say hello, I've been thinking about you and wanted to call you and say hello. Goodbye. But that won't happen. She'll carry her end of it in her spuriously cheerful way.

She was listed, S. Morehead. "Hello," she said.

"Miss Morehead?"

"Yes. Who is this?"

I spared her the embarrassment of not remembering a former student by following my name with the year and the subject. She said, "Yes. I remember."

"I just called to say hello."

"Why?"

"I don't know."

"You must have some idea. I doubt it has anything to do with geometry."

"No. Just a call." We waited for purpose. "Do you remember Marsha Vanderberg?"

"Yes. A feisty little girl who wore very tight skirts."

"Yes. That's her. We were married."

"Congratulations. Are you satisfied?"

"Yes. I am. We're divorced."

"You always were a smart boy. Isn't that too bad?"

"Not really. Things play out, you know."

"So I've heard. How did you play out?"

"Still playing I suppose." I waited for the obvious

question, 'What do you do now?' We shared instead a bracing silence that spanned the years with white noise. I had nothing to say and regretted calling. I could hear the stone coldness at her end, her wall of joyful indifference towering over all else.

"You called to apologize, didn't you?"

"Yes. I did. I didn't know if you'd remember."

"I remembered. One boy in thirty years made me cry. You left a lasting impression."

"I'm sorry."

"It's about time. But, actually, you shouldn't be."

"Yes, I should. I don't know if it's any consolation, but I was so young. I didn't know how mean I could be and, well, now I know. It hurts me now, maybe as much as it hurt anyone."

"Oh, I doubt that."

"Please, Miss Morehead. I apologize."

"That works conveniently for you, doesn't it?"

"I don't know how convenient it is. This call isn't convenient. But I do want to say I'm sorry and let you know that in my humble opinion you were a good geometry teacher. That's all. If you can't accept my apology, well, then, I'm sorry for that, too."

"I'll bet you are, just as you've always been sorry for the old maids and wallflowers."

"I haven't been sorry for nearly that much. I had no idea you sustained such bitterness."

"Why shouldn't I remain bitter? Tell me something. Are you a lawyer?"

"No, I am not a lawyer. And bitterness can eat you up inside. I think I was mean, but I'm not beyond the pale of forgiveness." I resisted recalling *her* meanness.

"Beyond the pale? What? Don't tell me. You were an

English major. You teach."

"No. I dropped out."

"I should have guessed."

"Yes. You always had me pegged for failure."

"Did you fail?"

"No. You gave me a D."

"Mm. Didn't want you back. That's why."

"Thanks for that, anyway."

"Do you remember what you said to me?"

"Not exactly. But it was mean."

"You said I shouldn't take my loneliness out on you."

"Yes. I remember."

"Do you remember what else?"

"That I wasn't one of the boys who were mean to you."

"Yes. But you were. Weren't you?"

"Yes. I was. In the act of denying guilt I was guilty as charged. You never spelled out your accusation. I sensed it from your brevity, your tension and body language. You disliked me because of my guilt. I was guilty of meanness before I ever committed the crime against you. I *was* one of the boys who were mean to you. I think I still am. I think we're stuck, Miss Morehead. You and me. Well, it's been interesting. I'll talk to you again sometime, maybe in another, what, thirty-two years?"

"Ha. Very clever. We'll both be dead. No, I don't think you should wait that long."

"I'm fit. I'll only be eighty-two."

"Are you in town?"

"Not far away."

"Come see me. Take me to dinner. Buy me a flower."

"You gave me a D."

"I'll change it. I want to see what you've become. I want to review your behavior. Do you remember saying to me, 'If you see Kay, tell her I want to talk to her?' I always thought you strange, but I wondered for the longest time, who's Kay. Then I got it. F-u-c-k. Ha! You paged Mike Hunt on the P.A. and, worst of all, tormented poor Benny McDougal with that awful nickname."

"I didn't. You wrongly accuse me again."

"I thought you'd grown out of denial."

"But not out of the truth. I never called Benny the boilsucker. Besides, you didn't know the whole story on that one."

"Tell me. Not now. At eight. With a rose, just one."

"I...uh..."

"I remember when you died your hair orange. Ahead of your time, I suppose, and you wore those tight green pants and pointy black shoes. You were so thin, my God, I actually worried that you never ate. And you were gifted; you could have excelled in calculus, trig, physics, anything. I remember Marsha Vanderberg all right. Couldn't take her eyes off you. I'm not surprised that..."

Miss Morehead wasn't surprised that life passed in a blink these last thirty-two years. Marsha seemed remote and long ago as the building long since rubble that once housed events we would remember forever.

Yet surprise was the note of the day, for Miss Morehead sounded like she'd sat by the phone for my call. I didn't fully comprehend her oblique motivation but agreed to swing by at eight. I sensed fantasy unfulfilled, perhaps the common bond of teenage boys and older women. She was disturbingly insistent, and seemed, in a word, game for an evening of grand reunion.

I went in a jacket, no tie, and had the car washed. At a grocery store check-out I bought six roses, the three-dollar-per-half-dozen variety with no smell. I picked up a decent bottle of wine as well, to loosen things up before dinner, or maybe to balance the rigors of three decades gone in a blink, to assuage the lingering difficulty between us.

I sat in front of her house toying with the idea of uncorking the wine for a stiff slug in the street. I keep a wine key in the door pocket for such emergencies. And she could hardly think worse of me for arriving with a sampled bottle. Still, certain aesthetic development comes automatically with the years, and opening the wine in the car seemed a chore with marginal return. I slipped the corkscrew into my pocket to assure quick opening inside, in case she was a teetotaler or never drank wine or moved too slowly. Still, I wished I'd had a few beers, for the courage they could provide, and so I wouldn't look so thirsty. As I calculated the distance to the nearest quick shop, her front light went on. So I gathered my wine and roses and headed out and up and in, wondering what mysterious force in life compels us to pursue that which we know, deep down inside, cannot result in any positive return or renewed interest or gain on any level.

Miss Morehead opened the door like an impresario. Interior lighting was muted but focused on the message of the decades. Comprehension required a moment or two—not so much to see the obvious, which was a woman whose face was smooth as stretched silk. She bore the unreal, unwrinkled flawlessness of too many lifts, leaving her neck, cheeks, eyes and forehead with sculpted curvature. She touched her cheek and drew her fingers down to her neck as if demonstrating her connection to reality. She smiled. Her teeth were perfect, her lips enhanced. I suspected collagen, though she wasn't as far gone as the modern starlets who look bee stung into a permanent pout.

I wondered what surgical procedure had come along for perfect hands, but needed no wondering on her breast implants. I suspected cellulite reduction and saddlebag removal beneath her skimpy dress as well.

I smiled with honest politeness. "I wouldn't have recognized you," I said.

She laughed. "Good. I'd feel terrible if you did."

"I mean I would have, but not right away. I mean, the nose and cheeks are still you, but something is different. I mean, the chin and..."

"Honey, the chin is new, but I don't need another diagram. Why don't you come in?"

The obvious questions of when did you do this and what are you doing now and why did you do this and why did you call were preempted by her honest hospitality. We'd learned a few things over the years, Miss Morehead and I, and though the evening seemed as rife with hallucination as evenings of drug experimentation long ago, it seemed as well a rare and poignant opportunity to go where few men go. "Thank you," I said when she opened wider and stepped aside.

She had a corkscrew, sparing me the embarrassment of a thirsty man caught high and dry. In fact, a decent red resuscitated nicely on her living room buffet. This was not the same house she lived in back then but a certain upgrade of recent years. I didn't press the issue of other upgrades, although I think she waited to see if I would.

She seemed cured of spurious good cheer, maybe from the time she'd spent as a voluptuous woman. She was sixty-three but only showing fifty-five or so. I was curious but then I understood the power of a casual remark. Just as Marsha had hit home with a simple statement that stuck with me for thirty years, so had I remained in Miss Morehead's company.

I gave her the flowers. I thought of hugging her but then thought not, because she might think me sexual, but then thought yes, because a woman who spends thousands on surgical enhancement wants the sexual, but then thought no; what?

Miss Morehead and me?

Get outa here!

Maybe I swayed fore and aft between the yes and the no.

She smiled and said, "It's okay."

I moved into the hug. I hoped all was forgiven. I suspected it was not, for she failed to arch her back and thus remove her crotch from contact with my own. Nor did she seem reluctant to sway side to side, generating slight friction in the region now obtrusively between us. "It is good to see you," she said. I couldn't help but think of it as outside second *and* outside third concurrently. I didn't want to appear repulsed by pulling away too quickly, so I only tested for resistance. She held firm. "You know, I've wanted to tell you something for years."

I relaxed, because I was no longer young enough to fear what a woman might tell me. I smiled. "Why didn't you call?"

She touched my lips with a finger. She moved subtly below the waist. "I did this for you."

"No, you didn't. You did this because of me. Or maybe you did this with me in mind. But you couldn't have done it for me."

"Do you like it?"

"You. Look. Marvelous."

To her credit, she took me seriously. She broke away and poured the wine in proper stemware, though she improperly went to the brim. We shared a more comfortable silence then with a few hearty sips to buffer what the years had warped.

Or maybe the years had removed the warp. Who cared? We had a buzz. I felt good about this surreal contact with my past. She seemed somehow willing to get laid or somehow balance a debt or compensate a wrong or a right or something. We drank more to help us along with our chosen reunion.

"Tell me something," she smiled.

"All right," I said, realizing that this exchange was as pleasant as geometry should have been.

"What's the oldest woman you ever had sex with?"

I was startled in spite of her prior innuendo but was more scared of further damaging what I so obviously damaged years ago. So I stayed calm, reflectively feeling my chin, and I said, "Well, she was thirty-nine."

Miss Morehead looked puzzled but not troubled; she knew there was a catch.

"I was twenty-two. So she's sixty-seven."

She smiled as if justified.

I wanted clarity between us. "If she's alive. That was in New York right at the beginning of AIDS, before anyone wore rubbers, and I think she was promiscuous. She may be dead."

"Why do you think she was promiscuous? Because she had sex with you?"

"Not exactly. She was sucking me off inside thirty minutes." Miss Morehead displayed admirable composure of her own, despite a shift in her seat. I did not want a back scratch with Miss Morehead, so I addressed her like one of the boys. "But the main thing was, she told me she was hanging out with her friends, these gay guys, who were trying to teach her how to open her throat. She wanted to practice." I shrugged. "I was twenty-two."

"How did she do?"

"Oh, I think she was a natural."

"Were you married then?"

I smiled. I nodded.

She drank. She poured. I drank. She topped me off. We caught up with ourselves. I doubt she was any hungrier than I was, at least not for dinner. I took it a step further. "Did your life change with your new appearance?"

"Well, yes, in a way, but no. I suddenly had men interested in me, which was wonderful at first because I... I..." she blushed profusely, even into the space-age patina of her face. "I never had experience with that sort of thing. I didn't...have a man, until I was forty."

"How did he do?"

She laughed. "He left."

"You mean he didn't stay the night? Or you were with him for awhile and then he left."

"I mean it doesn't matter. One left in ten minutes. One stayed the night and left. One stayed two and a half years and left."

We seemed plagued by a sudden deluge of reality with nowhere to go. "Well. That makes three."

"Eight altogether. Not so many. The last was four years ago. I'm safe."

My turn to stutter. "Miss Morehead. Safety is hardly an issue here. Besides, I think gestation on the dreaded disease is seven years."

"He was married and hopeless. I was his first fling in seventeen years. He was safe, so I'm safe. Besides, safety is always an issue between a man and woman."

I drank and re-poured, time for a new bottle. She opened it and poured. "I'm not trying to get you drunk."

"Oh, but you are."

"Getting you drunk? Or trying?"

I would have asked what difference it would make. I would have made a joke about changing my grade from a D to a B. I would have feared her challenge to make it an A. I would have asked about the budget and timing on her many lifts, extractions, injections, spreads and separations. I would have politely reminded her that our shared objective was dinner, and I would have asked if she were hungry.

But I was too buzzed.

She turned the light lower still. I think she practiced this light show on her own, seeking optimal luminescence for maximum return on her many years, her thousands of dollars and her heartfelt effort.

Like a magician she brushed the front of her dress with her hand, and it fell open.

Like a hopeless male, I looked. And I knew: all was forgiven. This was not true love with its unconditional condition but love gone awry, love salvaged, conditional and brief. That's not to call it unworthy but rather to say it would be closer to friendship. That was my belief.

That was my hope. She succeeded in her constraint until we were prone, where she verily hurried me along, hurried me in, and she bore her eyes into mine as if this was the moment thirty years had led to. I wasn't entirely comfortable, nor could I help wondering what the boys would say, if they could only see me now.

She compounded my discomfort by whispering in hot short blasts that she loved me from the first day and always would but don't worry, because she knew I could not return the feeling but every now and then if I wouldn't mind, I could return the favor. Because she knew now what the boys and men wanted all along, and this was better than a blow-up doll. Wasn't it?

I smiled and drove her gently home, dreading what I would sense tomorrow.

But I had to give her credit, rolling me over and easing herself off the couch. She said that was fun. I hadn't considered fun in a few hours. She said the bedroom was better, but we'd save it for another time. She went for a damp wash cloth and cleaned me gently as a nurse. She slipped my shirt on and wore it like a co-ed, pouring more wine and lighting a cigarette.

And she said, "Oh! I forgot." She swept away to the kitchen and came back with an apple neatly cored and sliced on a cutting board. She offered it.

I took a slice. "What did you forget?"

She shrugged. "It's corny. But I never got one. Not once in all those years, and I always wanted to share an apple with my prize student."

"I was never your prize student."

"Mm. No. But you are now. I mean, for awhile. Aren't you?"

"Miss Morehead," I said. "If one side of a right triangle is equal to half the average of the hypotenuse and the other side, then what's the circumference of a tree?"

"Mm," she said. "You've been a very good boy today. I really didn't expect it."

I took another slice. "You must have had an idea."

The Plan

Men stare.

Women see.

So too, the young people gaze shamelessly at the spectacle we become.

I'm eighty, which isn't nearly so old when you get here. Nor is natural rhythm an oddity, if you could cut the rug at sixteen, thirty and sixty. Yet they stare as if two statues came to life for a slow one round the floor.

Youth loves attention like this, and an octogenarian should achieve indifference to foolish curiosity. Yet I'm sensitive. I suspect a morbid scrutiny, a necrophilic appetite and, I suppose, a simple sentiment as well; they're amazed that bodies so slumped and worn can rise up and carry on like this. Maybe they suffer sweet denial that they too may one day dance for youthful gawkers.

The women often say *It's so sweet.*

I hear them. I see them, even as I lock my gaze on that of Evelyn. Dear, sweet Evelyn, fifteen months my junior, forty-two years my wife. I think she too must see and hear them. But I doubt she thinks like me. She's much nicer, always has been. I think she cherishes the moment rather than assess it for social meaning. She's a moment-cherisher for one thing. And we move like water in a deep stream for another.

She used to tell me she loved me in times like this. She still lets me know of her love with the sparkle in her eye, to which the upward curl of my mouth reciprocates. I love her, too. We understand the meaning of the end and what we'll take with us. She says she hopes she goes first, though she could fill her time as she always has, staying happy by staying busy, and she fears no solitude; yet she suspects an old person alone has very little fun.

But then, she asks, who would take care of you, if I went first?

You have a point, I tell her.

And you can go to the dog pound, I tell her. Get a dog. Or a cat. Now there's some decent company who'll love you till you gasp your last.

I know I plan to get a little pussy if she goes first. This last I don't tell her. She wouldn't mind. Hell, I think she wouldn't mind now. It would take the pressure off. Not that I pressure anyone, but I do believe certain bodily function survives other bodily function, and the certain and the other vary from one individual to the next.

I can't dance like I used to, but I still find the old fluidity. I step on no toes and meander round the bends with no hard turns, no turbulence or undercurrent. I get over my head from time to time if the young ones pay too much attention, but who can blame an old man for a stumble?

I can't do the other like I used to either, but I find the fluids and swerve and bend and flow and hump like a jackrabbit—well, an old jack, but still. Evelyn just lies there. Sometimes she calls me amazing. Sometimes she laughs. Sometimes she gets tired, but she never says no. She's old school; a man and a woman should take care of each other in all things. That's the deal they call marriage.

You get to be eighty and you think old is ninety or a hundred. You think a hundred ten is more like it, but you know in the thinking you could drop dead anytime, dancing, screwing, eating your damn prunes.

I'll tell you what I like: We're waltzing the light fantastic with our eyes locked soft as a gnat's landing, and Jimmy La Coeur and the Starlighters are putting out "Des Jours et Nuits" sweet as yams and honey. The young ones are staring, digesting reality and death and sweetness and love and the end of all things, no mo no how no way.

They used to watch me and Renée with greater curiosity near the high part of the pitch of the thing, to see what I was saving up my sleeve by way of turns and spins and what have you.

Now they watch to see how an old two-stepper plays it out when the music stops, nothing left in the world or on the dance floor but him and his equally ancient main squeeze. I don't have a problem there; I give her a squeeze and a kiss on the lips like we used to do—goddamn the decrepitude and thieving miserable life stealing out of you like you got nothing to say about the whole damn thing. No; I give them what they want to see but never expect to see it.

Then I stroll over, maybe bent in the back some and dragging a game leg some and shuffling the foot at the end of the bum wheel some—but this is the part I like. I pick another filly for another dance, easy as you please, just to show what a gamecock can do. And them sitting on their cans, stretching nothing but their necks.

I think of this new one as Renée.

Well, hell, it's not Renée. I don't know if Renée's still alive, haven't spoken to her in thirty years, since we both remarried, and she bought into a fellow who couldn't rub two nickels together and had four children already from two other women. I told her what for. She said he had a good heart. I didn't ask if she thought mine was made of cow pies or what, didn't have to.

I can catch a drift. And she could pierce your heart that way, just splay it down the middle soft as razor blades and stand there like she was looking both ways before crossing while you bled to death. That's why we split up. Had nothing in common, Renée and me. Wasted twelve years finding it out.

Oh, I say nothing in common, and nothing is what I mean. Back then people didn't go pouring that sewage in your ear about how the sexy part was terrific, but you just couldn't get along. I was drawn to Renée hopeless as a young buck was ever drawn to a salt lick. Knew her since I was fifteen. She was twelve and even then had a way of drawing the boys in with her squared shoulders and the way her hair swept up off her forehead and back down over her shoulders. Don't ask me what it was, because all I could ever tell you in the years I asked myself the same thing was that it made no sense at all but boiled down to chemistry, which is what they call it now when they can't figure it out sensibly. Didn't make any more sense to a boy of twenty-two, which is how long it took me to bed her down. Didn't have a thing in common then either, except I was making good dough down at the car lot by then. She loved that all right, and I knew she was weak for any man who could pave her way with a few dollars, so maybe I was weak too. Maybe she grew out of her penny-ante whimsical nature, but I doubt it. I never could see what her next fellow had going for him, he was so broke and couldn't have been much more of a stud stallion than I was, except maybe she felt what I'd felt with her.

Who knows when it'll hit you or who with or why?

We fooled around some as teenagers but never once did it buck-naked lying down. I was getting my fair share anywhere I wanted it then, and I think of that time as the glory days—even had a theory that any man could have any woman he wanted with some patience and a few jokes and decent manners. I had a wild idea on the queen of England one time; that's how pussy crazy a boy can get. But it all went south on Renée, because it was different with her, not really different once you factor the holes and rhythms and time between, but I thought that's why they called it love. I promised to honor and support if not obey her. Obey her, hell; she was loony.

But pretty as a cameo, she kept me coming on. I don't believe she ever loved hitting the hay like I did. She'd get hot and hard-breathing but then she'd close her eyes and go inside herself like I was hardly there, leastways hardly more than your ultra-deluxe electrical ramrod with the automatic squirter that wouldn't go off until you were darn good and ready. Oh, I was good in my prime.

Gynette Porchier might get as pumped up as Renée used to get. I don't know that she does or did, or if she ever thought about it. I'm just saying she has a way of squaring her shoulders, reminds me of Renée every time I see her. Makes me smile. I feel certain Gynette sees my good humor as a personal interest and returns my curiosity with a playful smile of her own. She's a sweet woman, maybe a few years younger but not much. Evelyn sees us carry on but doesn't mind, as if the women surviving this many decades need to look after each other as well as their men, like our wagons are circled, what's left of them, and it's share and share alike to get us through the siege.

Evelyn didn't even care when the President of the United States of America got caught with his pecker in the puddin'. She only sighed with sympathy for the wife, who must have known what was going on and now faced the grim reality of ventilating her man's pressures with no help from the outside at all. No, she said, it was wrong of all those congressmen and senators to stick their noses where they didn't belong, where a man and his wife got a little relief from the burden nature imposes on some men.

Not that I ever fooled around with Gynette. I did not. We only flirt. Nor would I ever tell her she reminds me of my first wife, because relief takes different forms in men and women, and I suspect Gynette might be relieved that a man can still look at her and think those thoughts. I don't begrudge her that small relief, but I'm not yet ready to meet her for lunch, maybe because I have too many recollections of that youthful, learning time with Renée.

I remember the day I turned one of the sharp corners that come at you in life, the day I proposed the plan that would solve the problem between Renée and me, which was that of sexual desire. She allowed me her favor right around twice a week, maybe three times now and then but only once, often as not. No matter how you count it, it's not enough for a man of my means and can't begin to reach the itch, much less scratch it for a man sixty years younger. So I told her with all sincerity that I had a plan by which we could close the sexual gap between us, which is what I perceived our paltry frequency to be. I proposed that once an hour—that's by the clock, sixty minutes—we would hit the hay buck-naked and do the do. Didn't have to include the perversities unless she wanted them, or some of them. Didn't have to take any more time than a few easy slides, because I could spill the mustard easy as I could hold it for the well done. In this way, given time for recovery, renewed appetite and longing of no more than fifty-seven, fifty-eight minutes, we could cure the beast in no time, few weeks most likely, few months on the outside. For beastly is what she perceived my sexual appetite to be. By gorging it till it...till it fell over dead or passed out and stayed out, we could achieve peace in the family. I was willing to work through this if she was.

Well, I know for a fact that millions of women all over the world would count a proposal like that among the luckiest of happenstance. Not Renée. Nor did she utter a single syllable by way of consideration, dialogue or refutation. She just stood there, her beautiful brow squeezed tighter than a turnip ready to bleed, staring in amazement at the loss of what precious little sense remained between us. She breathed short, but not like she did at the summit; it was more like the awkward resignation of a woman suddenly realizing what her life has come to.

Then she walked away.

It was a week and a half before we got up next to each other buck-naked again, more than a month before we dabbled in the perversities. Things dwindled from there.

They say a man married once will most likely marry again. I don't know. I did, but only after years of the single life. I don't think you ever warm to the flames in middle age like you do in youth. Then again, you can't understand the simmer and savor when you're only a pup. So it all works out. I do believe I felt the chemistry with Evelyn, and moreover a love I never felt before. I know she takes care of me.

But what I really like is the second go, when I park Evelyn on a chair and slide sideways on over to Gynette. I give her that look I used to give Renée to no avail, but Gynette never knew Renée or that I had a first wife.

She thinks that look is the first of a potential series of items that could grow rock solid between us. I don't discourage it, because a woman likes to feel wanted, and another woman appreciates the help. Maybe one day Gynette and I will meet for lunch and love each other with the same love we'll not let die for Evelyn, though she passed before us. I anticipate that with enjoyment, if I survive my wife. If not, I anticipate a more thorough solution to my problems.

But what I really like in the meantime is three beats to the measure, Gynette and me locked eye to eye soft as a lifetime of love between us, waltzing down the parquet to Jimmy and the bunch doing "Les Coeurs Perdue" maybe a little up-tempo. And all those young ones staring, the bucks grinning because the old coot's still a cockhound, the women looking startled or disappointed or maybe a little bit curious.

Oh, don't you worry; Evelyn won't sit alone for long.